SPIES

and

Prejudice

SPIES
AND *Prejudice*

TALIA VANCE

EGMONT
USA
NEW YORK

EGMONT

We bring stories to life

First published by Egmont USA, 2013
443 Park Avenue South, Suite 806
New York, NY 10016

Library of Congress Cataloging-in-Publication Data

Vance, Talia.
Spies and prejudice / Talia Vance.
p. cm.
Summary: Berry Fields's life working for her dad's investigation firm and searching
for clues to her mother's death unravels when gorgeous Tanner arrives in town and
changes everything.
ISBN 978-1-60684-260-7 (hardcover) — ISBN 978-1-60684-304-8 (electronic book)
[1. Private investigators—Fiction. 2. High schools—Fiction. 3. Schools—Fiction.
4. Mothers—Fiction. 5. Mystery and detective stories.] I. Title.
PZ7.V39853Spi 2013
[Fic]—dc23
2012024478

Printed in the United States of America

FOR DAD, THE WORLD'S GREATEST PRIVATE
INVESTIGATOR, AND A DAMN FINE FATHER:
THE TRUTH NEVER LIES.

———————————————

Chapter 1

The only thing worse than a guy who cheats on his girlfriend? A guy who cheats on his girlfriend and doesn't flaunt it enough for me to capture any proof on film. Mary Chris and I have been sitting in Sconehenge for two hours, waiting for this guy to do something skeezy. So far all I've got is a picture of his date looking insanely bored while he drones on about the horrific levels of pesticides in fruit.

Mary Chris glances over her shoulder to where the mark stuffs another fry in his mouth. "Is that his second basket of garlic fries? There's no way she's going to kiss him now."

Mary Chris has never had the patience for stakeouts. She's only here to field test the spy-cam she built for extra credit in her mechanical science class. The camera is embedded in the lens of a pair of fake eyeglasses that are so big, I'm sure I look like I'm channeling a fifties movie star. Still, the giant tortoiseshell frames camouflage the controls perfectly. I've got to hand it to Mare, this works infinitely better than anything on spystuff.com.

I turn toward the booth where the mark runs a greasy hand

through his hair. I tap my finger on the frame of the glasses to zoom in. I get a perfect shot of him talking with his mouth open, complete with a chunk of parsley on his front teeth. His girlfriend should dump him even if he's not cheating.

"You don't have to stay. The camera works great."

"Nice try, Berry." Mary Chris blesses me with an angelic smile. She's pretty without trying, and while she never uses it purposefully, I can't help smiling back. "But there's no way I'm leaving now. Things just got interesting."

"He is kind of a train wreck."

Mare isn't watching the mark. I follow her gaze to where two guys trail the hostess to a table in the back below one of the fake rock sculptures. The restaurant theme is supposed to evoke Stonehenge, but the rocks look more like a Disneyfied Mayan ruin.

I glance back down at the history book in front of me and attempt to read the same sentence I've already read at least sixty-seven times.

Mary Chris taps my arm. "Don't you think the blond one is kind of cute?"

I look over my shoulder to where the two boys sit, accidentally making eye contact with the dark-haired guy's ice-blue stare. He's too good-looking to be called cute. Everything about him is sharp, from his strong jaw to his prominent cheekbones. His face is cut like he was sculpted that way, in hard, jagged lines. Even his hair is razored, hanging in points around his face.

I know the type. In twenty years, I'll be snapping pictures of him so his first wife can maximize her divorce settlement before he moves on to his trophy wife. For now, he probably dates a cheerleader while trolling the halls of his high school for underclassmen willing to make out and keep their mouths shut about it.

It's not that every guy messes around, but I've been working for my dad's private investigation company long enough to notice a few things. When a guy looks like that, his ego won't let him say no to the throngs of girls throwing themselves at him forever.

"He looks sweet." Mary Chris smiles into her diet soda.

"Sweet is not the word that comes to mind." *Lock up your daughters* comes to mind.

"The blond one?"

"We're here to catch a cheater, not check out guys." I glance at the mark. His mouth is moving, but I can't make out a word he's saying. I pull my receiver out of my messenger bag. The receiver looks like an iPod, but works like a pocket amplifier, picking up sounds and magnifying them through the earpiece. In theory. About half the time all I get is muffled garbage or an annoying clamor of several conversations at once. It's what I get for buying spy gadgets on the Internet.

Mary Chris grins at me while I put the earbuds in. "Your mark has no shot. Look at the way he's shoveling in those garlic fries. We might as well have some fun."

"I don't get paid to have fun. I get paid for proof." I keep my eyes deliberately focused on the mark as I tuck the receiver in my pocket. I flip on the volume control, but the voice I pick up is not the mark's.

"The girl in the beige jacket? With the blonde ponytail and glasses?" The low voice reverberates through the earbuds, traveling down my spine and settling in the pit of my stomach with a soft hum. "Pretending to read a history book?"

I freeze, my hand still buried in the pocket of my beige hoodie. I keep my eyes pinned to the history book in front of me, forcing myself not to turn around and look at the boys behind me.

"Dude, she's pretty," another more normal voice says.

"She's alright," the bass thrums again. "But nothing amazing."

Years of training fly out the window. I crane my neck to look at them. The guy with dark hair raises his brow smugly when he catches me looking, and I spin back to face Mary Chris.

"What?" Mare mouths. She knows not to talk when I have this amplifier on.

I shake my head. So what if some idiot thinks I'm pretty or not. There are more important things to worry about at the moment. Like finally catching this cheater in the act. I turn to the mark's table in time to see him brush the girl's arm as he reaches for the ketchup. I snap the picture too late, missing the shot.

I never miss the shot.

Mary Chris doesn't even try to hide the fact that she's looking over my shoulder to the guys' table. She lifts her arm and waves her fingers.

"Did you just wave at them?"

Mary Chris just violated the number one rule of investigations: never, ever draw attention to yourself.

Mary Chris shrugs. "He waved first."

The smooth voice comes through the receiver to my ears. "What are you doing?" Thrum, thrum, thrum. I curse my gut for reacting to the tone of his voice.

"Dude," the other guy stretches the one-syllable word in nearly a whisper. "She waved back. I think she likes me."

"Fine," the smooth voice responds. "You take the hot one. I'll take the friend. She might be tolerable if she loses those ridiculous glasses."

I rip the earbuds out of my ears before I have to listen to another word. I have half a mind to walk over and dump what's left of my Diet Coke in Mr. Nothing Amazing's lap. Lucky for him, I'm on a stakeout.

Mary Chris watches me slam the receiver back into my messenger bag. "Is everything okay?"

I take a breath. "I've been tailing this mark for two weeks, and I still haven't gotten a picture I can use. Dad's going to pull me off the case if I don't get something soon." It's a lie. Dad knows I have a better chance of catching this guy than he does. I'm his secret weapon when it comes to covert surveillance. Teenagers are practically invisible to adults.

I shift my focus back on the mark. The girl's hand rests lightly on his arm. He leans forward and says something into her neck. Now we're talking. I click the frame of my glasses and get the shot. Finally, a step in the right direction.

Until Mr. Nothing Amazing steps right in front of me. "Hello." His hands rest in his pockets, his head cocked slightly to the side. A Doberman masquerading as a retriever.

"Sorry?"

He completely blocks my view of the mark. Apparently, it's not enough for him to insult me. He's got to ruin my surveillance too.

"Do you go to McHenry?" He gestures to the history book that's still open in front of me.

"I might." I concentrate hard on my book, hoping he'll take the hint and leave.

He doesn't.

"Cool," he says, forcing me to look back up at him. "I'm Tanner." He points to the table where the blond guy still sits. "That's my brother, Ryan."

Ryan nods and flashes us a goofy smile. Mary Chris waves at him again.

Okay. These guys look nothing alike. Ryan is softer all around. Wavy blond hair brushes his shoulders and round eyeglasses rest low on the bridge of his nose. He looks like a cross between a surfer and an accountant.

Amateurs. Ryan should've been the one to make the first move.

"Brothers?" I finally meet Tanner's eyes, calling him out on the obvious lie.

"Stepbrothers."

Ryan walks up with a friendly smile. "Hey."

"Hi." Mary Chris motions for Ryan to take the seat next to her.

Seriously? I lift my chin toward the mark's table, hoping Mary Chris will get the hint. I am trying to work here. I have to crane my neck to the side to even get a glimpse of the mark over Tanner's shoulder.

Tanner takes the seat across from Ryan. Next to me.

"Presumptuous much?"

"Are we keeping you from something?" Tanner glances at the textbook that's been open to the same page for the last forty-five minutes. Not that he could possibly know that. He probably just expects me to drop everything the minute he opens his mouth. When I don't answer his question, he forges ahead. "We thought it'd be cool if we knew someone our first day at McHenry."

These guys are going to our high school? Good luck to them. They'd be better off knowing a posse of bodyguards to keep all the swooning girls away.

Mare jumps in. "I'm Mary Chris Moss." She's not kidding. She was born on Christmas Eve and her parents have a wicked sense of humor. Our crazy names are what brought us together the first day of kindergarten. Mare has embraced it, wearing her name as proudly as the cupcake-decorating badge she won in junior scouts when we were seven.

"Cool name." Ryan grins back at her and they launch into a private conversation like they've known each other forever.

Tanner assumes my silence is an invitation to keep talking. "We just moved down from Orange County." He says it like that's a good thing. "Irvine."

Tanner sits at an angle so his broad shoulders totally block my view of the mark. I twist a little to look around him. The mark still munches on fries, but the girl's hand rests on his free arm.

I should be getting some pictures.

Tanner leans toward me, searching my face until I look at him again. When I do, his eyes brighten and his lips curve into a smile.

My breath catches in my throat.

Okay, no. My stomach did not just flip itself inside out and sideways. I've seen countless men look at a girl in just the way that Tanner looks at me now. Right before they run off with their secretary, the grocery store clerk, or some random girl they meet on a bus. It's nothing to get worked up over. Almost automatically, I finger the frame of my tortoiseshell glasses and snap a picture.

I struggle to regain my focus, looking resolutely over Tanner's shoulder to where the mark and the girl giggle. The mark probably told her his one joke about a horse going into a bar. Then again, maybe not. She actually laughs.

Tanner tries again. "Is everything okay? You seem distracted."

I look straight into Tanner's eyes. "I was fine before you came over here, and I'll be fine after you leave." A little harsh maybe, but it's an absolute and unequivocal truth.

Tanner inhales. I can practically see the gears turning in his head. A girl is supposed to bow in his presence. Especially one who is nothing amazing.

"Let's try this again," he says. "I'm Tanner Halston." He holds out his hand.

I stare at it. A handshake? Really?

He starts to pull back, convinced I'm going to leave him hanging. He's right to think that. I totally mean to. But before I realize what I'm doing, I reach out and take his hand. His grip is solid and confident. I bet parents love him. If the little flutter in my chest is any indication, not just parents.

"I'm Berry," I say, deliberately withholding my full name.

He flashes that smile again. "I'm Berry pleased to meet you."

Drop dead good-looking?

Check.

Squee-inducing grin?

Check.

Razor-sharp wit?

Not even close.

I finally smile.

Mary Chris laughs from across the table. "Can you believe Ryan knows binary?"

Mare's ability to make instant friends is legendary. She's never turned away a person in need, starting with me. Looks like Mare's foster friendship program just picked up a new project. I can only hope the stepbrother isn't part of the package.

Over Tanner's shoulder, the mark stands up and lays a twenty on the table.

I've got to get out to the parking lot to see how this date ends. "I need to go."

Mary Chris notices the mark leaving with the girl. "Oh right. You had that thing."

I stand up in a hurry, sending my history book careening to the floor.

Tanner stands up to retrieve the book, but he doesn't move out of my way. "I was hoping we could hang out."

I glare at him, willing him to move. "Yeah, not happening." Out of the corner of my eye I see the mark heading outside.

Tanner holds the book out to me, his eyes clouded with something that looks like disappointment. I'm sure I imagine it. I take the book and shove it in my messenger bag. I brush past him, ignoring the tingling heat where my shoulder hits his chest on the way by.

Ryan's voice carries across the restaurant as I push through the front door. "Dude! You totally struck out!"

The statement is nowhere near as true as it should be.

Chapter 2

Within a few minutes, my stakeout is back on track. The mark walks the girl to a green VW Bug and holds the door open for her. The girl twirls a strand of her hair but makes no move to get inside.

Here we go. I savor the surge of adrenaline that comes whenever I'm close to getting the evidence I need.

The mark trails a finger along her elbow to her hand.

Bingo.

I know the exact moment when he moves in for a kiss. He leans forward in excruciatingly slow increments, testing the waters. She stretches up to him, garlic breath and all. I snap away, capturing their kiss in pictures that more than make up for the two weeks I've spent trailing this guy. After a few more shots, I've got everything I need. I push the heavy eyeglass frames against my nose and lean against the planter.

I could go back into Sconehenge for Mary Chris, but that would mean more time with Tanner Halston. Not a chance that's happening. May as well get home and upload the photos.

A man nearly trips over my feet as he rushes past the planter. I glare up at him, ready to tell him to watch where he's going, but stop myself when I see who it is: Mary Chris's dad. It's not like he's a bad guy or anything, but I instinctively keep my mouth shut. There are some laws of nature you just know. You don't go poking lions with sticks.

Michael Moss looks past me, searching the parking lot for something in the distance. He doesn't seem to notice me. I don't know whether it's these glasses or the fact that Mr. Moss seems to have a singular focus, like he's looking for someone in particular. He waves and picks up his pace, leaving me staring at the streak of white in the back of his black hair.

I don't make a conscious decision to follow. I just do. It's more habit than anything else. Mary Chris's dad being here is all wrong. Mr. Moss spends most Sunday afternoons at Valle Vista Country Club. He is not the kind of person to eat at tacky theme restaurants, and I'm pretty sure he's never shopped at the mall.

A leggy brunette gets out of a black sedan and waves at Mr. Moss. Her hair is cut in a blunt line that hits at her shoulders. She's dressed in a black pencil skirt and a gray flower-print blouse that says she's not here for the garlic fries either.

My stomach sinks. He's meeting a woman.

I don't want to see this. I like Mare's mom. I love Mary Chris.

But it's not like I can look away either.

Mr. Moss puts his hand on the roof of the car and leans toward the woman, blocking my view. I have to dart around an SUV to get a good vantage point. I can't hear what's being said, but I can tell Mr. Moss is talking quickly by the way his lips move in tight bursts.

The brunette doesn't look enamored. She looks deadly serious. On closer inspection, she's older than she first appeared, maybe ten years older than Mr. Moss. Flecks of gray dot her hair and tight lines frame her eyes. She folds her arms across her stomach, clutching a manila folder.

I slip a few cars closer, ducking behind a minivan. Mr. Moss speaks in a hushed whisper. "You're sure this is all of it? They didn't get anything else?"

"Of course I'm sure." The woman purses her lips. "I don't know why you didn't destroy the files years ago."

Mr. Moss runs a hand through his thick mane of hair. "Maybe I trusted your people to keep them safe."

The woman wrinkles her forehead. "We've taken every precaution." She waves the folder in front of him. "My advice? Get rid of everything. They won't stop trying now that they know you still have it."

Have what? I inch closer, trying to get a closer look at the folder in the woman's hands. There's nothing identifiable on the outside. No writing. No labels.

"It's your job to see they don't get near it." Mr. Moss's voice is more emphatic.

"We've already put a team in place."

Mr. Moss nods. "Good."

The woman hands him the folder. He opens it, revealing the top half of the first page.

My hand flies to the frame of my glasses and I click off several shots as Moss skims the paper inside. He nods his head and then snaps the folder closed. "We can't afford to have any more leaks. Not now."

TALIA VANCE

•

12

The woman's face looks pinched. "Understood."

Mr. Moss tucks the folder under his arm and walks away without another word. Just as he reaches his silver Mercedes, he glances over his shoulder. I duck back behind the minivan, holding my breath. After a few seconds, I peek around the corner. Mr. Moss is sliding into his car.

Okay. He didn't see me. Which is good because no one likes being spied on. Especially not people with secrets.

Not that it's ever stopped me.

Chapter 3

I drive into our neighborhood of detached condos. Every house is painted exactly the same salmon pink and dominated by a two-car garage in front. Perfect cover. With two bedrooms and two baths, our house is just big enough for Dad and me, not quite big enough for Little Lulu, our Saint Bernard.

Lulu stands on the other side of the door as I enter from the garage, her tail thumping against the wall. I push the door against her massive body and wedge sideways, sucking in my breath. It's a good thing I passed on the fries today, since the door only opens about six inches. Lulu licks my arm as I press my way inside, leaving a trail of slobber along the sleeve of my jacket.

The alarm chirps in warning. With only thirty seconds before the full-scale blaring starts, I push past Lulu and enter numbers into the keypad. The beeps grow louder and more frequent. I enter the code again, northbynorthwest, no periods. As I hit pound, the noise stops and a flashing green light comes on. I sigh and sag against the wall. Lulu licks my arm again.

"Hi girl." I pat her on the head as I make my way to the computer in the living room. Lulu lies across my feet with a sigh that sounds more like a snort.

I upload the files from the memory card in the frame of the glasses, clicking through the pictures of the mark and his date at Sconehenge. The photos from inside the restaurant are even worse than I thought, but it hardly matters, since the shots from the parking lot will tell the whole story.

I freeze when I get to the picture of Tanner.

My breath catches. Again.

I can't remember the last time a guy smiled at me like that. Maybe never. Most of the guys at McHenry know better than to even think of flirting with me. At least not since the spin-the-bottle incident in eighth grade involving Collin Waterson and a bottle of pepper spray.

Looking at the picture of Tanner now, I almost wish I went back inside the restaurant. Until I remember Tanner's obnoxious pronouncement that I'm not amazing enough for him. I have to sit on my hands to keep from throwing something at the screen. Only when I'm sure I won't take my anger out on the monitor do I allow my fingers the freedom to hover over the delete button, ready to erase Tanner's perfect face and banish him from my life forever.

Something stops me. It's not like I save the picture to Favorites, or make it a screen saver or anything like that. Maybe I'll print it out and use it for a dartboard. I could edit in a twirly mustache.

I smile to myself as I click forward to the shots I got in the parking lot of the mark and his date. They're perfect. Even without the establishing shots of them at the restaurant, the mark is readily identifiable in the photos. And the girl he is kissing is most definitely not his girlfriend. Case closed.

I check out the last few shots I took of Mr. Moss. I zoom in on the best shot of Mr. Moss holding the open manila folder. The folder is turned at an angle, so the top of the page inside is clearly visible.

I zoom in closer. It's some type of letterhead. The pixels are fuzzy, but the name across the top of the page is almost legible. The page is upside down, so I rotate the photo until I can just make out the letters.

There's a high-pitched squeak that could only have come from my own mouth. Lulu whines softly and lifts her head.

No way.

I read the name again, just to be sure.

It's not possible.

Caroline M. Fields, PhD.

My mother.

I have no idea why Mr. Moss would have a piece of paper with her name on it. She was a psychologist. As far as I know, she had nothing to do with Mr. Moss. Besides, Mr. Moss has no reason in the world to keep my mother a secret.

She's been dead for eight years.

Chapter 4

The sound of the garage door opening has Lulu jumping to her feet and running for the door. She stands in the hall, tail thumping madly against the wall. I take one last look at my mother's name on the screen before I close the program out and shut down the monitor. I stuff the memory card in the front pocket of my jeans.

Dad squeezes past Lulu and makes his way down the hall to the room that serves as our combination office and living room. "How'd it go today?"

I force a smile I don't feel. "We got him."

"That's my girl." Dad looks over my shoulder at the dark screen. "Can I see?"

My heart races as I flip on the monitor. What if I didn't shut it down right? I can't let my dad see the picture of Mom's letterhead. He's been doing so well, even without the antidepressants.

The only picture that flashes on the screen is our desktop background, a photo of Lulu as a pup, chewing on a rope toy as big as her head. Now, that toy would be a choking hazard.

I let myself breathe as I click open the case file.

"Nice!" Dad admires the photographs. "How'd you get in so close?"

"I didn't. I field-tested a new camera for Mary Chris." I pick the glasses off the desk and hand them to my dad, grateful to have something to talk about besides the pictures I got today.

"Unbelievable." Dad tries on the glasses and plays with the buttons on the frame. "Mary Chris is a genius."

"Don't get too excited. She's already promised them to me."

Dad takes the glasses off and hands them back. "You can use them again on a new job for Shauna Waterson. She invited us to dinner on Thursday. I'll let her fill you in on the details then."

"Please don't tell me you expect me to go to dinner at the Watersons."

"Shauna refers us a lot of business. Is it too much to ask for you to fake your way through a two-hour meal?"

Way, way too much.

"Two words. Collin. Pepper spray." Technically it's three, but my point is made.

Dad reaches down to pet Lulu. "If I recall, Collin got the sharp end of that stick."

He wouldn't say that if he knew that my desire to avoid Collin Waterson has less to do with his attempt to kiss me with tongue in eighth grade and more to do with his current tendency to turn every conversation into a crude proposition. I try another tack. "I'm buried right now. I'm helping Mary Chris with her mechanical science project." I hold up the glasses.

"The same project that worked perfectly in the field today?" Dad is not buying it. "Shauna specifically asked for you to come."

I hate being beholden to anyone, but as a divorce attorney, Shauna Waterson does feed us a steady stream of business. Turns out there's nothing like uncovering a dirty little secret to gain an edge in a custody battle.

"It's not like I'm the face of Fields Investigations." It's been less than two years since Dad even trusted me to handle my own stakeouts. And it's not like Dad parades me in front of his clients. Most don't care how we get our information. Just that we get it.

Dad sighs and sits on the couch. Dots of pale skin peek through the thinning brown hair at the top of his head. "I wouldn't ask if I didn't think it was important." He wipes his brow, avoiding eye contact. "You know I never meant for you to get this involved in my business. You need to spend more time with kids your own age. Enjoy high school."

"You say that like it's remotely possible."

"Maybe if you gave it a chance." He stares across the room to the kitchen. "I just want you to be happy."

"Then don't make me go to the Watersons."

Dad smiles at me like he always does, a pity smile meant to comfort or encourage me. I'm never sure which. "You can't a hold a grudge forever. I'm sure Collin is looking forward to seeing you."

"That is not a selling point."

"Six thirty Thursday." End of discussion, as far as Dad is concerned. Before I can protest again, he deftly changes the subject. "So tell me about the pictures you shot today."

I finger the memory card in my pocket. I know he's talking about the photos of the mark, but I can't stop thinking about the picture of Mr. Moss with my mother's letterhead. I can't tell Dad about the letter in the folder.

I won't.

"It was no big deal," I finally say. "The guy was bound to slip up sooner or later. They always do."

Dad smiles again, a real smile. It catches me off guard.

"Great. This job was for one of Shauna's clients. You can bring Shauna up to speed on Thursday."

Argument over. Dad: 672. Berry: 3. Not that I'm keeping score.

Lulu, the product of one of my three victories, lies back down across my feet.

"I'm close to a breakthrough too," Dad says. "On the school board case."

"No way." At least Dad doesn't ask any more questions about my pictures or launch into a pep talk on how I should be hanging out with, or worse, dating boys like Collin Waterson. So far that's one of the other arguments in my favor. Dad's convinced it's just a matter of time before he wins that one too.

"Way." Dad heads into the kitchen. "Should we order a pizza?"

I let out a breath as soon as Dad is out of the room. Mom's letterhead could be nothing.

It's probably nothing.

I make a run for my bedroom while Dad calls Martucci's. By the time I toss the little memory card into a drawer and flip on the television to a *Cops and Lawyers* marathon, I'm nearly convinced.

It's definitely nothing.

Chapter 5

When I get to school on Monday morning, Mary Chris is in our usual spot, a low wall on the southeastern corner of the quad. She leans back on her palms, long blonde hair blowing in the breeze, her face raised to the sun. Most people never get past her face. They assume that Mare is exactly as she appears, sunshine and light personified. It isn't too far from the truth, but a person doesn't make it through eleven years as my best friend without collecting a few battle scars along the way.

She checks her watch. "Morning stakeout?"

I shake my head. I'm usually rushing to get to my first class before the second bell, but today I'm here early. I wanted to get out of the house without talking to my dad. I may be good at uncovering secrets, but I'm not used to having my own. But I can't tell Mare about seeing her dad with my mother's letterhead either. It's not exactly the kind of thing you can mention in casual conversation.

So, do you think something was going on between your dad and my mom?

Is that what I think? No.

No way.

"Don't tell me you're hoping for some quality time with the McHenry student body?" Mary Chris smiles in the direction of the growing crowd gathered on the quad.

"Please, no."

"They're not so bad." Mary Chris has a massive blind spot when it comes to people's faults. The more pathetic and alone someone is, the more likely Mare is to take them under her wing. It explains why we've been friends for so long.

Mare pushes a lock of hair behind her ears. "Plus, Jason's bringing lattes to celebrate his role in the musical production of *Hamlet*."

"I didn't know there was a musical version."

"There is now. Some sophomore wrote the music."

"Tell me we won't have to go to every performance." Not that I can ever say no to Jason. I'll probably end up at the dress rehearsals too.

Most of Mare's strays hang around for a couple of months or so, until they find a more permanent home. While Jason could've moved on to the drama crowd full-time years ago, for some reason, he stuck.

Mare sits up. "Aren't you going to ask me about the guys from the coffee shop?"

"Should I?"

Mare looks out at the quad with a satisfied smile. "Ryan might've asked to hang out with us today."

"Please let it be just Ryan." Surely his stepbrother has found a groupie by now.

"What do you have against Tanner? He doesn't seem so bad."

"Trust me, he is."

I catch a flash of Jason's highlights out of the corner of my eye. He walks as fast as he can without running, balancing a cardboard tray of coffee in his hands. He somehow manages to keep the coffee from splashing on his purple skinny jeans and fitted button-down. "You guys!" He's slightly out of breath. "Have you seen them?"

Mare reads the chicken scratch on the coffee cups, searching for her extra-shot mocha. "Who?" But she's smiling again, like she knows exactly who Jason is talking about. Sounds like the stepbrothers from Irvine have graced McHenry with their exalted presence.

Jason sets the remaining two drinks down on the wall next to Mary Chris. "Only two of the hottest guys to ever set foot on the campus in the history of McHenry."

Bingo.

Jason's eyes travel out across the quad. "You guys," he says again, as his eyes come to rest on someone in the distance.

It's impossible to miss Tanner, standing in the center of the grass at the top of the knoll, on display for the entire student body. His hands rest casually in pockets of jeans that are faded to just the right degree. A light-blue golf shirt hugs close enough to show off the fact that he's ripped, loose enough to look like it isn't intentional. The ice king cometh.

If my heart rate kicks up a notch, I'm sure it's just the anticipation of watching the feeding frenzy that's already starting to stir on the quad.

Kennedy Patton and her entourage, which consists entirely of girls named after dead American presidents, move in. Reagan, Madison, and Taylor form a semicircle around Tanner, an impenetrable wall of miniskirts and high heels. Tanner nods, but still scans the crowd over their heads while they chatter.

Next to me, Jason audibly sighs. "Did you see the one with dark hair?"

Like there's an eye in the place that isn't gawking at Tanner. The quad buzzes with energy. Even the guys seem impressed.

Mary Chris hops off the wall to get a better look. "Wait until you see his brother." She points to where Ryan stands just behind Tanner, looking slightly lost.

My gaze gravitates back to Tanner. I know the second he sees me. His eyes stay fixed on me as he lifts his chin in greeting. When I don't respond right away, he lifts his hand over Kennedy's shoulder and waves.

No, no, no, no, no.

Before I can look away, he shouts across the quad. "Berry!"

Three hundred heads turn in my direction. The Dead Presidents' jaws fall to their chests in unison. It must be a cheerleader thing.

Tanner marches past them without a backward glance. His brother Ryan falls alongside, grinning at Mary Chris. They walk straight toward our little wall.

Mary Chris bounces on her heels as she takes a sip of her mocha.

Jason starts to hyperventilate.

It cannot be a good sign that I am on the same page with Jason Yakamoto. I try to slow down my breathing. As a rule, I avoid the spotlight. Especially on this particular stage. There's no room for public displays when you spend your life documenting other people's private drama.

Tanner stops a few feet in front of me, seemingly oblivious to the hush that's fallen over the quad. "Hey," he says. "I was hoping we'd see you." His low voice thrums.

"Hey." I stuff my hands in the pockets of my hoodie. Whatever I did to deserve this karma sundae, I take it back.

He pushes a strand of razored hair away from his face. "You're not wearing your glasses."

"Can't get anything by you, can I?"

Jason looks from me to Tanner. "How do you know Strawberry?"

Tanner's smile is smug. "Your name is Strawberry?"

"Jason is the only one allowed to call me that." My mother was a Beatles fanatic, even though John Lennon died when she was eight. She gave me the name Strawberry Fields and then died when I was eight. It's a legacy I've been trying to live down ever since.

"You must be Jason." Tanner shakes Jason's hand and introduces Ryan.

Mary Chris points to the piece of paper in Ryan's hand. "Is that your schedule?"

Ryan hands her the paper. "Tell me we have some classes together."

Tanner starts to roll his eyes before he catches himself, silently but effectively communicating his feelings about any budding relationship between his brother and Mary Chris.

"You have some sort of problem?" I ask.

"Problem?"

I lean my head toward the wall where Mary Chris and Jason are giving Ryan a rundown on the teachers on his schedule. "Is there something wrong with my friend?"

"You caught that?" He doesn't even bother denying it. He could at least pretend he's not such a jerk.

"You aren't exactly subtle."

Tanner shuffles his feet, his hands pushed back in his pockets. "It's not your friend, okay?" He glances toward Mary Chris. "She seems nice."

"Your brother?"

He shrugs. I'm not going to get an explanation. Not that I want one. As far as I'm concerned the sooner that Tanner finds some other poor girl to entertain with his complete lack of manners and unearned snobbery the better.

I cross my arms in front of my chest, hoping he'll get the hint that he's not wanted. "Why are you here?"

"I told you. We moved here from Orange County."

"That's not what I meant." I scan the crowd gathered on the quad. Several people have the decency to look away and pretend that they haven't been staring at us the whole time. Most don't bother. Kennedy Patton looks like she's about to have a meltdown. It's a waste of her energy. She can take him. Please.

"You and Mary Chris are the only people we know here." Tanner kicks a blade of grass with his sneaker. He doesn't even believe the stuff that's coming out of his mouth.

I stare until his eyes come back up to mine. "You don't know me."

I think I see the beginnings of a smile cross his lips. He steps closer.

"You're right." His low voice drops to nearly a whisper. "Maybe I want to."

"You'll get over it." I step back and turn my attention on Ryan. "So you're a junior too?"

"We both are."

Tanner's presence is like virtual chum. Kennedy Patton and the rest of the Dead Presidents circle our group once before marching up to Tanner, teeth bared in pasted-on smiles.

Kennedy grabs his left arm, wedging herself into the little space between me and him, even though there is barely room. Just one of the advantages of being a size zero. "A bunch of us are going to get some frozen yogurt off campus at lunch."

There is no mystery to Kennedy's popularity. She isn't particularly rich. She isn't particularly bright. She isn't even particularly nice. What she has going for her is that she is particularly and singularly beautiful. Her life is mapped out accordingly. Date hottest guy in school, make others' lives miserable, marry rich, possibly famous man. Repeat.

I ask Ryan a question about his schedule while Kennedy launches into an intellectual discussion on the merits of granola as a yogurt topping. As near as I can tell, Tanner doesn't participate. He just stands there and bleeds vanity. I try to focus on Ryan's recitation of his class schedule, even though I don't hear a single thing.

Then the Dead Presidents are gone and Tanner slips closer to me.

Jason watches the Dead Presidents walk away. "What were they doing over here?"

I reach for my latte, still sitting in the cardboard container on the wall. "Hitting on his royal hotness, what else?"

Tanner's voice is low and warm next to my ear. "You know I can hear you, right? I'm standing right here."

I clutch the latte to my chest, creating a makeshift shield. "So you are. What's the matter? Yogurt not your thing?"

"Something like that." He starts to smile. "You think I'm hot?"

"You think you're hot. There's a difference." I spin away, heading in the opposite direction even though it's nowhere remotely near my first class. At least I don't have to see his smile.

Chapter 6

The rest of my morning passes in an unending barrage of not-so-sly glances and hushed whispers. I do my best to ignore it. Tanner hasn't shown up in any of my classes. By the time lunch rolls around, I can almost pretend he's not here.

I'm nearly to our spot on the wall, when I see Ryan and Tanner chatting up Jason. There's no known universe where Jason will side with me when it comes to kicking the eye candy to the curb. And from the way Mary Chris hit it off with Ryan, I'm pretty sure that I'm going to be outvoted on this one.

I turn down a row of lockers and slip into a crowd of seniors headed for the parking lot. I turn left at the library and send Mare a quick text. "Have some work to do. Will catch up after school."

I duck into the library, where at least I'll have free Wi-Fi. That's what I tell myself anyway. The truth hovers in the thin space between consciousness and denial, waiting to leap up and bite me in the back.

I don't stop at any of the empty tables in the main room. Instead, I head through a small corridor and take a deep breath. The random squeak of my sneakers on the linoleum is the only noise, a sound that seems to echo despite the narrow walls.

I stop at the tiny periodical room at the end of the hall. Old newspapers and magazines are great places to find information on a mark's past, especially if you're researching people with pre-Internet lives. But I'm not here to look up someone's loser husband. I'm here to read about her. The woman formerly known as Mom.

I should let it go.

Whatever the letter in Mr. Moss's folder says, it can't change anything. The ending will always be the same.

A short, square woman with black hair cropped close to her scalp sits behind the high desk. She's not much of a talker, which works well for both of us. I rattle off two dates. She doesn't even need to write them down. She probably knows them by heart.

She reaches under the desk and wordlessly hands me a CD. I say thanks, but her expression stays blank. Part of me can't help wondering if she knows why I always ask to see the same two days of the *San Diego Union* from eight years ago. She probably thinks it's for a school project. Worst case, she knows what's on the disk and thinks I've got some weird obsession with my mother's death. So what? It's kind of true.

I find a desk in the farthest corner, popping the CD into the drive of an ancient computer. Dust clings to the monitor. Thick particles hang in the air, coating my lungs as my breath comes faster.

I know what's coming and that somehow makes it worse. I click on May 15. The day after. The front page flashes on-screen. I skip right past it. What I'm looking for is on page B-2 of the Metro section.

There are two pictures. The first is a professional photograph of my mom wearing a dark business suit. The second is of a car being pulled from the San Diego harbor on a giant hook.

The woman in the picture has long brown hair and a slightly crooked smile. She looks exactly like I remember, but I can't tell if it's because she really looked like this or because all I have now are the pictures. It's as though all my memories are two-dimensional.

The second picture is the one that makes my stomach fold in on itself, crushing my insides until I want to double over. I spent every morning of the second grade crawling into the backseat of that white sports car, setting my purple backpack in the small seat next to me. I can still recall the smell of the gray leather, always stronger when it was warm. I know exactly how my neighborhood looks through the small triangular back window, bigger and prettier than it really is.

In the picture, the little car is suspended by giant wires, water pouring from its doors. The front right corner is smashed, the windshield cracked. I wipe my cheek with my palm and mentally focus. I feel like I can't breathe, which only makes me guilty, because of course I can. It was the car that drowned. Taking my mother with it.

I read the article once, then slow down and read it again. She was driving back from a lunch meeting at the Hotel Del with some soda magnate that she was helping with field tests on a new energy drink. A woman saw the car accelerate into the turn, but then never even try to make it, launching itself at full speed at the guardrail. The right front wheel hit the corner of the steel rail, flipping it at an angle, right over the guardrail and into the bay below. The car was recovered. A body was not. The end.

I write down the witness's name even though I memorized it years ago. Heather Marrone. Writing her name down at least makes me feel like I'm doing something. The paper calls the whole thing an accident, and I read the article a few more times as if doing so will make it true. An accident means she didn't leave me on purpose.

I finally flip ahead to a date three days later, to the write-up announcing my mom's funeral service, which basically consisted of three hours of fending off sympathetic stares from my parents' friends and relatives. I've seen the same expression a million times since, from teachers, neighbors, even my dad. The memorial was the first time people treated me like I was the one who plunged off the Coronado Bridge.

I suck in a breath. Still here. Still breathing.

So Mr. Moss has a piece of paper with my mom's name on it. It doesn't matter. It's not like she wrote it yesterday. Have I learned nothing from my dad's business? The truth is a dangerous thing. No one really wants their worst fears confirmed. They just think they do.

She didn't do it on purpose. It says right in the newspaper. *Accident.*

The air is impossibly thicker. I can't stay here any longer without choking on it.

I take the CD out of the computer and return it to the woman at the counter as quickly as I can. I race down the hall.

I am going to let this go. I have to. Dad always says we already know the truth. We know it in our hearts. That should be enough.

It should be.

As I press down the hall, I nearly collide with a guy coming the other way. He puts his hands out to catch me before I crash headlong into his chest.

"Watch it," he says, grabbing my arms to push me away. The annoyance that flashes in his eyes disappears in a heartbeat. "On second thought, you can run into me anytime." He is close enough that I smell his breath, a blast of peppermint Altoids.

"You can let go now." I give him the stare that has chased away a hundred boys.

He doesn't move. "I could."

I back up, breaking the contact. He wears a long-sleeved tee that says "Dog Is Truth" and black swim trunks. His brown hair holds a hint of red that's probably more pronounced in better light. He's cute in a nonthreatening way that would be perfect for the Disney Channel. I recognize him immediately, since he caused a stir of his own when he started at McHenry at the beginning of the year. Drew Mattingly, a senior who keeps to himself despite the best efforts of McHenry's finest.

He laughs, crossing his arms across his chest.

"Did I miss something?"

"It's just that I came here to be alone, and I'm suddenly very glad that I'm not."

"You came here on purpose?" The hallway is dark and narrow. This is not the kind of place people come to hang out.

"That's the beauty of this place. No one thinks to come here."

"Except I'm here."

"Beautiful girls are always welcome in my world." He smiles again.

Save it for someone who hasn't figured out the algebraic equation for adultery: good looks plus false charm equals betrayal. "Has that line ever worked?"

He puts his hand over his heart. "You wound me."

"You'll recover."

He grins easily. "Maybe."

"Trust me, if I wanted to hurt you, I could." Six years of judo did not go to waste. "What are you doing here anyway?"

"I have a standing date with a small study room down the hall."

Okay, Drew doesn't look like the type that hangs out in libraries, period. He's got a tan that suggests he spends a lot of time outdoors and his arms have definition that only comes from lots of physical activity. Why don't I know more about him? "I haven't seen you around much."

"Maybe it's because I've been hiding in the library so I can use the free Wi-Fi to connect with my friends at home."

Okay, that's kind of pathetic. And just the slightest bit endearing. The rumor is that Drew moved here from San Jose over the summer, and I'm guessing he still considers San Jose home. "You don't have friends here yet?"

He shrugs. "What's the point? I've got enough credits to graduate in December anyway. It was bad enough saying good-bye to one set of friends when we moved down here. I'm Andrew Mattingly by the way. I go by Drew."

I understand him completely. Good-byes bite. But only if you let yourself get too close. I smile before I can think to stop myself. "I know who you are. I'm Berry."

"I know who you are."

"You do?"

He shakes his head, like I've just said something stupid. "Pretty girl with an attitude and a reputation for beating guys up? You might be the one person in this school I don't mind meeting."

My face gets warm. "For the record, I haven't beat anyone up since the sixth grade, and that was only because Mark Holberg hit on my best friend." I don't mention the fact that I got kicked out of my dojo as a result. I never understood that one. What was the point of teaching someone how to take out a knee if you weren't actually allowed to do it?

"Did you really mace some guy at a party?"

"Does no one have a life at this school? That was three years ago."

He laughs. "Don't worry. I think it's hot."

My cheeks burn with a combination of embarrassment and something I'm afraid to put my finger on. "You have some issues, don't you?"

"I'm the one with issues?"

I laugh with him. As distractions go, Drew Mattingly is hitting it out of the park.

Chapter 7

Jason doesn't wait for me to sit down at our lab table during fifth hour. "Where were you at lunch?"

"Had some research to do in the library." I take a breath, hoping that he won't ask what I was looking into. I don't want to lie to my friend, but I can't tell him the truth either. He would tell Mary Chris and then they'd try to get me to do something lame like talk to a counselor, or worse, my dad.

"Today? Are you insane? Tanner and Ryan hung out with us the whole time." He raises an eyebrow at me. "Tanner said you guys met yesterday. Is there something you want to tell me, Strawberry?"

For the first time, I'm grateful for the diversion Tanner provides. "It's nothing. I met him at Sconehenge yesterday, while I was tailing a mark."

"And when were you planning to tell me that a Greek god is crushing on you?" Jason waggles his eyebrows.

Of one thing I'm certain. Mr. Nothing Amazing is not crushing on me. "It's not like that."

"So spill."

"I talked to him for about five minutes. He almost blew my whole surveillance."

"Can you spell denial?"

"Please."

"I always figured when you finally caved, you'd go for some quiet intellectual. I should've known you'd take it to the other extreme."

I hold up my hand in the universal sign to stop. "I don't even like him. He's a complete egomaniac."

Jason tosses a bleached blond strand of hair away from his face with an exaggerated flip. "You say that like it matters."

"It does. Next you're going to tell me that I should be dating Collin."

"Why not? I like him."

"You like Collin Waterson?"

Jason shrugs. "He's cute."

"Huh." Collin is too obnoxious to be considered remotely cute. "What do you know about Drew Mattingly?"

Jason raises his eyebrows. "Seriously?"

"What?"

"I don't know. He's kind of weird. He doesn't really talk to anyone."

"He might've talked to me."

Jason's mouth drops open. "Wow, girl, when you decide to get in the game, you don't mess around." He narrows his eyes playfully. "Or do you?"

I punch him lightly in the shoulder. "No!"

"Your loss."

Before I can respond, Mr. Browning stands in the front of the class and launches into a lecture on bonded pairs.

"Pay attention," Jason whispers. "It's all about chemistry."

By the time school is over, I'm completely drained. I've managed to avoid Tanner Halston, but the more I think about it, the less I think he's even worth the effort. Why should I care if my friends want to hang out with him? It doesn't mean I have to like him. I've put up with worse. Like the time Mary Chris took in Tamberly Lydon after she got kicked off the cheerleading squad. Tamberly ended every sentence with the words "you know?" and made it her personal mission to get me to bring more pink into my wardrobe.

I throw the last of my books into my locker and head in the general direction of the quad. I've barely made it two steps when Collin Waterson sidles up next to me.

"Rumor has it we're breaking bread on Thursday." Long strands of brown hair nearly cover Collin's eyes. "Have you been thinking about it?"

"If you mean, have I been dreading it, then yes."

Collin laughs, leaning closer. "Come on, Berry, you know you're hoping that we'll get a chance for some alone time."

"Yeah, no, I'm kind of over your *Star Wars* action figure collection." The irony is not lost on me. I maced Collin Waterson in the eighth grade and managed to scare off every boy in school *but* him.

"No worries. We could just make out."

He's lucky his mom sends us so much work, because I'm tempted to break him into so many pieces there'll be nothing left to find. "Could you be any grosser?"

He grins. "Yes. All you had to do was ask."

No wonder Collin is the only person at McHenry with less of a dating life than me. "You should go." Before I hurt you. "I'm not in the mood for this right now."

He steps closer. "That's only because you haven't kissed me yet."

Before I can respond, Tanner's low bass rolls down my spine. "She said you should go." He steps up beside me. Like he knows me. Like we're friends.

Collin's gaze flicks to Tanner, and back at me. He opens his mouth to say something and then closes it. "See you Thursday," he finally says, before he walks away.

I barely wait for Collin to get out of earshot before I turn on Tanner. The anger that had been brewing on the surface spills over in a rush. "What was that supposed to be?"

"It looked like he was bothering you."

"He's Collin Waterson. He can't help bothering people. It's in his DNA. You didn't have to go all Cro-Magnon. I had it under control."

"That was going Cro-Magnon? I didn't do anything."

"Please. You might as well wave a club around and drag me off by my hair."

Tanner's face gets darker. "I was just trying to help."

I get that. I do. But the rational side of me is powerless against the emotions that burn hot and want to scald Tanner Halston. "I don't need your help, and I certainly don't want it."

He holds his hands up. "Okay. I'm sorry." He looks more confused than ever. How hard is this to figure out? I'm not interested.

He's probably never had a girl tell him no before. He's used to girls falling in a puddle at his feet just for gracing them with his gorgeous presence. Especially girls who are nothing amazing.

"What? You expect me to be impressed because you chased away the guy I've been chasing away on my own for eleven years?"

He looks almost hurt, which makes me feel almost bad for him.

I sigh. "Alright. Most girls probably would be impressed. But you shouldn't waste your time. I'm not most girls."

He stands up straighter, his eyes getting darker. "That might be the understatement of the century."

I almost smile, but I catch myself just in time. "That I'm not most girls?"

He turns his back on me. "That I shouldn't waste my time."

Chapter 8

I let myself in through the side door at Mary Chris's house. I've been coming and going this way for so long that Mr. Moss barely looks up from the mochaccino he's mixing in the kitchen.

He nods toward the back of the house. "They're in the family room."

I hesitate, frozen in place.

Let it go.

Mr. Moss looks so much different than he did in the parking lot yesterday. So relaxed. More like himself. I open my mouth to say something and close it again.

Let. It. Go.

I take a step toward the family room, then stop. "Did I see you outside Sconehenge yesterday?" The unspoken question hangs in the air. *Did I see you with a letter from my mom?*

Mr. Moss looks up from his coffee. "I don't think so." His voice is perfectly measured, but his eyes watch me with new intensity as he takes a sip of his drink.

"Oh. I thought I saw you." I did. I meet his gaze, daring him to deny it.

He sets down the drink slowly, but a bit sloshes on the counter anyway. "Then you should've said hello." His smile is dark.

There's an awkward silence before I duck my head and hurry out of the kitchen. Round one to Mr. Moss.

I can already hear Jason warbling away on Mare's Rockstar Hero game, while someone bangs on the drum set. Not Mary Chris, since she invariably plays the guitar controller.

Sure enough, Ryan rocks his head in time to the music as he pounds on the drums. Mary Chris only half watches the screen as she plays the guitar expertly, most of her attention focused on Ryan. She shouts a "hey," which barely registers over Jason's wail. He sings an octave higher than is necessary.

Tanner sits on the far end of the large leather couch, his forearms resting on his thighs and his shoulders hunched forward. He doesn't even try to conceal his boredom. He glances up at me and immediately looks away.

It's nothing more than I deserve, but it irritates me anyway. I consider turning back around and heading right back outside to my car. But Mary Chris is my friend. I belong here. If anyone should think twice about hanging out, it's him. I sit down next to him, deliberately invading his space. "Not playing?"

He shakes his head. "Not my thing."

"I get it. Sitting on the couch by yourself is far more entertaining."

He tilts his head, and the sharp lines of his face seem impossibly softer. His lips curve into a slow smile. "Last time I checked, I wasn't alone."

I choke on a breath, standing up and turning my back on him. "Check again."

I walk over to the minibar and fish out a Diet Coke. Okay, so Tanner Halston's smile might be more than a little dangerous. It's like he has this secret weapon that he only brings out when I'm least prepared for it. Even then, it shouldn't have any effect on me.

I feel Tanner watching me from across the room. When I look up, he looks back down at the floor quickly.

The song ends and the wailing and thumping finally stop.

"Dude," Ryan says as he sets down the drumsticks and heads over to a small loveseat. He uses the word like the Hawaiian "aloha," hello, good-bye, and fifteen other meanings rolled into one. "You missed Mary Chris's perfect score on 'Twisted Sunshine.'"

Mary Chris grins and sits too close to Ryan. They already look like a couple with their matching blond hair and happy smiles.

Jason practically falls onto the same couch as Tanner, but on the far end. "You guys want to go to Dragon Holes? They have unlimited rounds for five bucks on Mondays."

Ryan grins. "Tell me that is some kind of medieval doughnut shop."

"Close," Jason says. "Arthurian mini-golf."

Normally, I'd be up for it, but everything is different with Tanner and Ryan here, like we've all been thrown off balance. Or maybe it's just me.

Tanner folds his hands across his lap. "I don't really do mini-golf."

SPIES *and* PREJUDICE

•

Of course he doesn't. It would clash with his twin goals of being better than everyone else and sucking the life out of fun. "Let me guess. Not your thing?"

He narrows his eyes. "Something like that."

Jason bounces on the cushion. "I know! Let's play the question game. It will be a great way to get to know each other." Jason winks at me.

I stick my tongue out at him.

"Cool," Ryan says. "How do you play?"

Jason turns on his high drama singsong voice. "It's like Truth or Dare, but without the dare. Each person gets to ask a question of the person on their right, and then that person has to answer."

"So how do you win?" Tanner asks. At least he's looking at Jason now. I owe Jason one.

Jason giggles like Tanner's said something funny. "You don't. It's just a fun way to get to know your friends."

Where does Jason get this stuff? Probably one of those things they teach at Shakespeare camp.

"Doesn't sound like much of a game." Tanner says it under his breath, but loud enough for everyone to hear.

Jason's face falls.

Okay, as games go, this is pretty lame, but Tanner doesn't need to be so mean about it.

"I'll go first," Ryan says, turning to Mary Chris. "What's your favorite type of music?"

"Old-school boy bands." Sadly, Mary Chris is telling the truth. It's something I've been forced to endure since the first grade.

Ryan flops back against the couch, his hands clutching his heart. "You're killing me!"

Mary Chris hits him playfully on the arm. "My turn." She leans forward. "Jason, if you could play any role in history, what would it be?"

Jason concentrates. "That's really hard." He starts counting on her fingers. "I think I can narrow it down to three."

"Just one."

"Maria," he finally says. "*Sound of Music*, not *West Side Story*. I don't think I could pull off the whole Latina thing."

I almost roll my eyes, but stop myself when I catch Tanner openly doing so.

Jason turns to Tanner. "Describe your perfect girlfriend." Jason can't hide the spark of mischief in his eyes. He's probably hoping Tanner will say that his perfect girlfriend is a guy. Better yet, a blond Asian whose dream role is Maria von Trapp.

Tanner looks momentarily uncomfortable, and for a second I think maybe Jason's ploy might actually be working. He stares down at the carpet and then back up at me. Oh no. I move more firmly behind the minibar.

"She's the most beautiful girl in any room," he starts. "She can talk to anyone, from foreign dignitaries to construction workers. She's great at sports and loves adventure. She has traveled the world and speaks at least three languages."

I should be relieved. Any ambiguity in Tanner's feelings about me can be firmly categorized on the side of "in no way interested." I will never be the most beautiful girl in a room as long as I hang out with Mary Chris. And while I'm sure I can carry a conversation with a construction worker, dignitaries—did he seriously say dignitaries?—are way out of my league. I am not an athlete in the traditional sense, although I can beat the daylights out of most people thanks to years of judo. Finally, I'm strictly a one-language girl. Two, if you count a proficiency in pig Latin developed in the sixth grade. As far as Tanner is concerned, I in no way classify as girlfriend material.

I shouldn't be bothered by this fact. I mean it's not like I expected him to describe a pretty-from-the-right-angle blonde with a penchant for spying on people in their weakest moments. Still. The guy has no chance of meeting a girl like that.

"And she loves me completely and without question," Tanner continues, slamming the door on the possibility of even a random make out session. Not that I'm thinking of making out with Tanner Halston.

Jason practically faints.

Tanner smiles at Jason. "And she's way more *West Side Story* than *The Sound of Music*."

Jason's jaw drops. "Really? You don't think singing nuns are hot?"

Everyone laughs, but not me. Do they not see through him? Tanner wasn't trying to be funny. I doubt he knows how. How can Jason just let Tanner walk all over him like that?

I walk around the minibar and sit down on the floor, even though there's a spot next to Tanner on the couch. "You don't seriously think a girl like that exists?" I ask.

"That's two questions," Tanner says.

"It's a rhetorical question. Get real. You'll never find a girl like that. Sounds like a convenient excuse to never be happy with anyone."

Tanner scowls.

That should be enough, but I can't let it go. "And even if you could find this brilliant supermodel who loves you in spite of your many faults, what then? I'm willing to bet that you'd be bored out of your mind within six weeks. That's the trouble with getting what you want, isn't it?"

Everyone stares at me. Even Mary Chris.

Tanner leans forward, setting his elbows on his thighs. "You're entitled to your opinion, Berry. But it's my turn to ask a question." His voice is dead serious, but a spark of something else flashes in his eyes. "So why don't you describe your perfect boyfriend?"

I freeze.

"You do like boys?"

Okay, the guy is destined to wind up with a Diet Coke in his lap. He's lucky that he's sitting on Mrs. Moss's Italian leather couch, and hasn't opted for one of the vinyl beanbags on the floor.

"Fine." I paste on an insincere smile.

He raises his eyebrows when I don't say anything right away.

I take a breath. "My perfect boyfriend is kind, even to people he might not agree with or even like. He doesn't look down on people just because they don't look like they walked off the pages of a fashion magazine. He makes me feel like I am the most beautiful person in any room, even if I'm not. He trusts me to make my own decisions and doesn't try to tell me what to do."

"Is that all?" Tanner watches me with an intensity that makes me feel like an ant under a magnifying glass. My skin starts to smolder.

"No." I don't back away from his gaze. I meet it head-on. "He will not, under any circumstances, expect me to fall in love with him."

"You don't believe in love?"

"That's two questions." I take a sip of my Diet Coke and turn to Ryan. "What's the biggest lie that Tanner's ever told?"

Ryan's face goes whiter than it already is. His eyes dart nervously to Tanner and back again. I almost feel bad for the guy, but I don't come to his rescue. I want to know the answer.

Ryan laughs and looks right at Tanner with a gleam in his eyes, before he turns his grin at me. "That you're not amazing."

Chapter 9

After two days of watching Mary Chris flirt with Ryan while Tanner stares moodily out at the quad, I've had all I can take. Tanner's attitude is contagious.

On Thursday, I head straight for the library when the lunch bell rings. I find Drew Mattingly in a small study room just past the periodicals.

He looks up from his laptop. "I'd just about given up on you."

"You should give up on me anyway." It's nothing less than the truth. Still, I should consider flirting with him a little. He seems harmless and the skills could come in handy in the field.

"No shot then?"

"I don't do the whole guy thing." God. I have no game. At all.

Drew sits up straighter. "And you think telling me you like girls is going to make me *less* interested?"

"No girls either."

He raises an eyebrow. "Intriguing."

I laugh. "It's nothing weird. I just don't really date. At least I haven't." I basically admit to being pathetic. Flirtation is not a book on my shelf.

Drew sets a brown paper bag on the table and pulls out a sandwich. "That's easy enough to change." He takes out a small plastic container of pudding. "Join me for lunch?"

I set my backpack on the table. "I brought my own."

"Still counts."

I sit down across from Drew. "It's not a date, okay?"

"What is it then?"

"Um, lunch?"

Drew nods. "Lunch. Hmmm. I like it. Has a nice ring to it."

I laugh. "Stop."

We eat in silence for a little while, but it's not awkward. It's kind of nice.

"So what are you running from, Berry Fields?"

The question catches me off guard. "What do you mean?"

"I mean I'm an okay guy and all, but if this isn't a date, I can't figure out why you'd want to come eat your lunch in the bowels of the library. I know what I'm running from. What about you?"

"You first."

"I already told you. I'm running from high school. And people who go to high school. I just want to finish so I can get out of here and go back home." He stares at me expectantly.

I'm hiding from so many things. Tanner and the way he makes me feel like a stranger in my own skin. Mr. Moss and whatever connection he had to my mother. All the doubts about my mom that won't stay buried. I go with evasion. "Maybe I like it here."

Drew looks around the tiny room with its gray walls and lack of windows. "Even I don't like it here. It's the lesser of two evils." Drew waits for me to say something.

I open my mouth and shut it again. I don't want to air my dirty laundry, but I'm surprised at how much I want to talk to someone.

"I can keep a secret." Drew looks around the small room. "Who am I going to tell?"

I need to talk to someone about the letter. So I do.

I tell him everything. About seeing Mr. Moss with a piece of paper with my mother's letterhead on it. About coming here to review the article about her death for the hundredth time. About how much I need for her death to be an accident no matter what the official police report says. About how I can't talk to my friends about it because they think I'm over it, and I want them to keep thinking that. About how I can't talk to my father because I want to believe in my mom as much as he does. I talk and talk and talk.

There's a reason it's easier to talk to strangers than people you love. Strangers don't come with preformed expectations about who you are. Strangers don't hold you to a higher standard than you deserve. Strangers won't be hurt by anything you say.

Neither one of us touches our food.

Drew waits until I'm finished. "You must think I'm a whiny little baby."

"What? No. Why would I think that?"

"Here I am complaining about missing my friends. And you lost your mother."

"Eight years ago." I can live with that. There's not really any other option. It's how she died that eats at me in the middle of the night. It's not ever really knowing if she left me on purpose. "I just need to let it go. That's all."

"Really? So you don't want to know why your friend's father has a letter with your mother's name on it? Don't you at least want to know what it says?"

Of course I do. But I shouldn't. I should trust her. She wouldn't have an affair with Mr. Moss. She wouldn't leave us on purpose. She didn't kill herself. She loved Dad. She loved me. I know it.

I know it.

I shake my head. "Whatever is in that letter, I'm sure it had nothing to do with her death. It's just a letter."

"What if it's a suicide note?"

My mouth goes dry. I try to swallow, but I can't do anything but suck in the thick library air. "A what?"

Drew looks stricken. "I'm sorry. I shouldn't have said that. I'm sure you're right. I'm sure that letter has nothing to do with anything."

"It's okay. You're right. What if it is—" I can't bring myself to say it, like a little kid, I'm afraid that voicing my worst fear will make it come true.

"You have to find out." Drew says it so matter-of-factly, as if investigating my mother's death is as simple as following a college professor and snapping a few pictures.

But if I go down this path, I'll have to stop pretending I don't have doubts about her. No matter what the truth turns out to be, there's no going back from that.

"I'll help you," Drew says, as if it's already been decided. He finally takes a bite of his sandwich.

If I do this, I have to do it alone. I'm certainly not going to bring in some guy I've met twice in the hidden corridors of the library. But he waits for me to answer, and I can't stop the word that slips from my mouth. "Maybe."

It's the same thing my dad always says when he's on the verge of caving. I try not to think about how close I am to giving in to the urge to follow the trail of bread crumbs laid out in front of me.

It's even harder not to think about where they might lead.

Chapter 10

By the time Dad gets home, I've changed clothes three times for dinner with the Watersons. I settle on a baggy sweater with a mock turtleneck and pair of jeans that's a size too big. There's a line of dog drool on the sweater, but I douse it with water and call it good.

Shauna Waterson isn't the only lawyer who refers Dad work, but there's no question that she's important to our business. Shauna was one of Dad's first clients. She's referred him business ever since Dad caught her ex-husband running around with a paralegal. She had the last laugh, divorcing the sleazeball, taking the house, and nabbing all their clients for her own private practice. The only compromise she made was joint custody of their son, Collin. Considering what a mess Collin turned out to be, that was probably a strategic decision.

Dad smooths his hair in the rearview mirror as we pull into the Watersons' driveway. I catch a whiff of Obsession for Men. I know the scent well. It's the preferred brand of middle-aged men on the prowl. "Are you wearing cologne?"

He looks out the front of the car, his face flushed. "You caught that?"

I nearly choke on the smell. No way.

Dad and Shauna Waterson?

Dad and anyone?

No way.

"Seriously? Shauna Waterson?"

Dad can't look at me. He looks out the window instead. "I wasn't sure how to tell you. I don't even know if it's something I should talk about with my teenage daughter."

This can't be happening. I mean, it's been eight years and I'm sure my dad could use some kind of—personal life. But Shauna Waterson? "How long have you been seeing her?"

"Not long." He finally faces me. "I like her, Berry. I like her a lot."

My stomach twists and tangles into a tight knot, and a tear forms in the corner of my eye anyway. I force myself to smile. "That's great."

He watches me and I pray for the tear to stay put. "You're sure?"

I nod and look away. "Yeah. I mean, she seems nice." It's true. She does seem nice, even if she does remind me of artificial sweetener, dressed in pink and too sweet to be real. I wipe my cheek as Dad turns off the car and steps outside.

The Watersons' house is big, with expensive-looking furniture and modern paintings on the walls. A little white dog trails at Shauna's feet, some kind of designer-poo with a red collar and painted toenails to match.

Shauna hugs my dad and then plants a kiss on my cheek. Her hair smells like violets and dandruff shampoo. I've never thought much of her beyond the fact that she gives us a steady stream of work and has hair teased high enough to house a small family of owls, but now I notice the way she smiles at me, like I'm a stray kitten in need of a home. "Oh, Berry, I hope you won't think it's presumptuous of me, but I would love to take you on a shopping spree."

"Hey." I give her a closed-mouth smile and ignore her invitation to bond over shoes.

Shauna's smile falters a bit. Everything about her looks unnaturally plump—her lips, her curves. "I would love for us to do girl things."

I take in the plunging neckline of her blouse and the false eyelashes that rim her eyes and thank the universe that I have been spared doing girl things for as long as I have. I almost wish I'd left the dog drool on my sweater. "I don't really do girl things."

Shauna blinks so hard one of her ultra-long lashes sticks to a glob of mascara on her lower lash like a Venus flytrap. Her lid flutters in a useless attempt to free itself.

My dad puts his hand on my shoulder in warning. "Berry."

Collin walks in, looking almost cute with his hair washed and combed. He's wearing one of his football jerseys even though it's not a game day, which would totally work with the Dead Presidents or one of their minions, but just makes me roll my eyes. His jersey still looks brand-new even though it's halfway through football season, meaning he's on the B roster, a nonsensical group of players who never have any real hope of playing, made possible by McHenry's inclusion mandate.

"Hey," Collin says, oblivious to the tension.

Shauna turns away and tries to separate her lashes with her fingers. When she looks back as us, her left eye is open, but her face looks oddly off center. The spidery lash peeks out from between her fingers. "Excuse me," she says as she bolts from the room.

Dad gives me the look that says I better behave. I know he's right. It's not Shauna's fault. She's trying. But that's what's so awful. I don't want her to try. I've gotten by just fine without a mother, and I certainly don't need Shauna Waterson to take me under her wing. As near as I can tell, my dad's been on a few dates. It doesn't have to involve me. At all.

Collin glances at my sweater, making me glad all over again for the extra layer of armor. "You want to play some video games until dinner's ready?"

"No." The last thing I want is to go anywhere unsupervised with Collin Waterson. I might really hurt him.

Dad squeezes my shoulder. "Go on, Berry. Have some fun."

"Yeah, Berry," Collin grins. "Have some fun."

Dad watches me expectantly. I've already lost this battle. "Fine."

I'm relieved when Collin leads me to a game room that's next to the kitchen. At least we're out in the open. Despite the fact that we're here for dinner, there is no activity in the kitchen. I start racking the balls on a pool table, since I never wanted to play video games to begin with. "Did you know my dad was dating your mom?"

He shrugs. "I figured it was something like that. How hot would it be if they got married?"

"What?"

"We could still go out. It's not like we'll really be related."

"Did you really have to go there? 'Cause I think I might hurl." I line up the cue ball and prepare to take a shot.

"Coach says I can try out for running back next year."

More with football? I'm probably supposed to start sighing and getting all mooney-eyed. "That's great. It'll give you something productive to do with your time." I hit the cue ball and watch as a few of the balls roll away.

"Kennedy Patton invited me to her party. Are you going?" Poor Collin. He's trying to have a normal conversation and failing miserably.

"No. Why would I want to hang out with a bunch of people whose idea of fun consists of dancing awkwardly to lame music and making out with people who will pretend you don't exist on Monday morning?"

"Don't knock it til you've tried it." He walks over to the table and lines up a shot. "I could get you in. Your friends too."

It's not like anyone needs an invitation to Kennedy's annual While the Parents Are Away house party. She's usually preoccupied within the first hour and pretty much anyone is welcome after that. Still, Kennedy has never forgiven me for the time in the third grade when I caught her kissing fifth-grade boys behind the Porta-Potty. As if it was my fault. It doesn't matter, since I've never forgiven her for telling me my mother's death had been ruled a suicide. As if it was her fault. We've reached a tentative peace only made possible by the damage we could inflict on each other if we were outright enemies. We're the high school equivalent of a nuclear standoff, neither willing to launch the first strike.

"I'm not going to Kennedy's house party."

Collin shrugs, "Your loss."

Shauna Waterson flows into the room, her eyelash repaired and the little dog at her heels. "Dinner's ready." Her smile is tentative. She looks surprised when I smile back, but I'm determined to try to get through this without any significant casualties.

Dinner consists of takeout Chinese food served right out of the little cartons. Shauna and Dad sit next to each other on one side of the table, and Collin and I sit on the other side. Collin's thigh inches closer to mine as Dad relays his story about following the school superintendent accused of harassment on his lunch date earlier in the day.

I concentrate on my moo goo gai pan and keep as far away from Collin as I can manage, sitting on the far edge of my chair.

Shauna bats her lashes at my father and giggles too loudly when he tells her how the couple disappeared into the back of a minivan for thirty minutes. Dad grins and pats her hand.

The knot in my stomach is still there, but I can't help wanting to see him smile like that more often. This is good for him.

Dad took Mom's death really hard. For the first year, he almost never came out of his room. The only thing that got him going again was work. He did a few freelance investigations and then a few more, finally making it official with Fields Investigations.

At first, I went along on some of Dad's stakeouts by necessity. It's not like we could afford a sitter. We spent a lot of time hanging out in the car, watching old movies. I loved the excitement of waiting for something to happen. Mostly I loved having my dad back.

Shauna flashes her too-white teeth in my direction. "Steven tells me you were the one who got the shots of Lambert this weekend."

I smile and nod. "That was me." I wait for the lecture about how a girl my age shouldn't be doing such dangerous work, but it doesn't come.

"They're very good."

"Thanks."

Shauna reaches across the table, placing her hand on my arm. She means it to be comforting, but it's terrifying. "I've got a new job for you. It's a big case for us." The way she says "us" is even scarier.

"Berry's the best." Dad says, genuinely proud of the work I do.

Dad realized early on that adults generally ignore kids, which made it almost too easy for me to get in close. It's only gotten easier as I've gotten older. Most adults won't even make eye contact with a teenager.

Shauna smiles and finally takes her hand away. I have to force myself not to wipe my arm.

"You really like her?" I ask when we're back in the car.

Dad looks at me with a mix of disappointment and pleading. "Give her a chance, okay?"

I nod, but I'm already sure that Shauna Waterson and I are not going to be headed to the mall anytime soon.

Chapter 11

D ad is already gone when I wake up on Friday. The door to his room is open just wide enough for a Saint Bernard to wander in and out, which is actually pretty wide.

I hear Lulu's soft snores coming from inside. I slip through the opening. Lulu is stretched out on the bed, her head buried under a pile of pillows. She doesn't even open an eye as I walk to the closet.

It's been years since I've been in here. My stomach clenches when I see Mom's side of the closet filled with men's clothing, golf magazines, and Dad's extensive sneaker collection. The neat row of dresses and business suits that went untouched for so long is gone. When did Dad get rid of her things? There's no sign of her now, not even an empty space where her things had been.

My heart skips a beat. Shouldn't there be an empty space? Something that shows she was really here? That she's missed? It seems wrong somehow. Like she's been erased.

I keep thinking about what Drew said at lunch yesterday. Could there have been a note? She would have wanted to say good-bye, wouldn't she? I shake my head hard, as if I can clear it of the dark thoughts that have already started to take root and spread.

I won't find anything here.

I don't stop to think before I drive the short distance to the mini-storage unit. Dad uses it to store old work documents and all the junk that we should've thrown away long ago, but can't bear to part with.

Our unit is full of cardboard boxes, stacked with barely enough space to walk between. It looks exactly like it always does, with rows and rows of closed-case files and the occasional box of my school projects or judo trophies. I know just where to look. The boxes from Mom's old office are in the back right corner. They're sealed with duct tape and a thick layer of dust.

I take the top box and set it on the floor, staring. I don't know how long I stand there. My left foot falls asleep, forcing me forward with sharp jabs of pins and needles. I pull a box cutter out of my messenger bag and set the blade along the crease in the center of the tape. I just need to know there's nothing here and then I can stop looking.

I push the blade along the silver seal of the box. Is this what Pandora felt like? She couldn't know she would set a plague loose on the world, but perhaps she knew that there would be no going back.

Once the tape is cut, it takes a few minutes more before I open the flaps. Some old framed photos of my parents are on top of a soccer trophy, a paperweight in the shape of a soccer ball, and some fancy pens. I breathe a little easier, even with the dust that's stirred into the air. Mom tried to get me to play soccer once when I was five or six, but I hated it, and she let me drop it after the first game. She didn't even blink when I asked her to sign me up for judo a week later.

The second box is full of empty patient folders from her private practice, the actual notes having been shredded or passed on to new therapists shortly after her death. The rows of empty folders seem pointless, and I wonder what made my father think they might be important.

The third and final box is full of actual work papers. I dig through a pile of research notes for an article she was writing on the psychology of addiction and a few drafts of the article itself. There's nothing to find here. I already know it in my gut, but my dad has trained me better than to abandon an investigation until every last page has been turned.

Is that what this is? An investigation?

I have a new understanding of the women who hire my dad, women whose relationships are already so damaged that they're willing to pay money for the proof of it. I won't believe that she left me until I see something concrete, but I can't trust her either. Will I be surprised when I'm finally confronted with the truth? The ones who cling to false hope always are.

I want to have faith in her. I've tried. But the police declared her death a suicide for a reason. It's not like I can just ignore it.

Once, when I was ten, I asked my dad about it. I made a batch of brownies from a box and sat him down in the living room with a glass of milk. As he bit into a brownie, I just came out and asked him to confirm what Kennedy Patton had told me the year before.

"Do you think she really killed herself?"

I watched as Dad tried to swallow the brownie and took a large chug of milk like it was stuck in his throat. When he finally looked at me, his eyes were filled with tears. "Of course not. Who told you that?"

I shrugged. It didn't matter who. Kennedy was a bully, and I could write off ninety-nine percent of what came out of her mouth. Not this. It spoke directly to the black hole in my chest where my heart used to be. It gave a name to the fear that started with the sympathetic faces at the funeral and grew in the year my father became a ghost who hid behind a bedroom door. What if it was my fault? What if I did something to make her leave?

Dad wiped his eyes on the sleeve of his shirt and folded his hands in his lap. He didn't look at me when he spoke. "Your mom would never leave us."

I wanted to believe him. More than anything.

When he finally looked up from his lap, his cheeks were wet. "She loved you. Don't ever doubt it."

He meant to make me feel better, but it's impossible to see your father cry and not be terrified. Worse, the idea that she could love me and still leave was somehow scarier than the idea that she didn't love me enough to begin with.

The one person with all the answers is dead. The rest of us are expected to believe whatever we need to believe to go on. But what if we can't? What then? I operate on proof, not faith.

I'm nearly done going through the third box. I've already missed my first-hour history class, and if I don't hurry, I'll miss art too.

The letterhead near the bottom of the pile stands out from the black-and-white pages. I recognize the box lettering before I even read the words: *Moss Enterprises.*

I pull the letter out and scan it quickly. A job offer.

My mom was working for Mr. Moss? Mom was asked to take part in a psychological study involving a new energy drink called Juiced. Two months before she died.

The paper shakes in my hand.

It's nothing. I knew she was working for some soda magnate when she died. So it was Mr. Moss. And it would explain why Mr. Moss has a document with Mom's letterhead. Not an affair. Something to do with work. It makes perfect sense. So this whole thing with Moss is about some job my mom did eight years ago? Is that all?

I sigh and lean back against a row of boxes, closing my eyes. What did I really expect to find? A suicide note? A document detailing a brake failure or other proof it was an accident? I flip through the last stack of papers, now more certain than ever that the key to my mother's death died with her.

I stop when I get to a yellowed piece of paper with plain Courier font. There's no letterhead announcing its origin. Not even a signature at the bottom.

Just three short sentences that leap off the page and into my throat, choking me.

```
The lives you think you're saving
    aren't worth your own.
Tell no one.
Stop before it's too late.
```

Chapter 12

By the time I get to school, fourth hour is over and lunch has already started. I have two pings from Mary Chris and twelve from Jason. I send them a quick note that I'm working on a case and make my way to the little study room in the library.

Drew is already there. He flashes me a friendly smile. "Second date?"

I don't answer. I'm way past small talk. "Did you mean what you said yesterday?"

Drew watches me warily. "About running away from high school?"

"About helping me. To find out what happened to my mom?" I don't know what I'm doing anymore, but I'm pretty sure that I don't want to face this alone.

"Absolutely. Are you okay?"

I nod, but I cross my arms around my stomach to quell the vicious butterflies that are trying to beat their way out from the inside.

Drew stands and walks to me, sliding his arm around my shoulders like we've been friends forever. "You want to get lunch somewhere else?"

I nod again, not bothering to remove his hand or push him away.

As we step out of the library together, more than a few people stare. It's easy to ignore them until I see Tanner. He stands at an open locker, but his head is turned at a ninety-degree angle as he watches me with those ice-blue eyes. I see the moment he notices Drew, his eyes narrowing to slits.

I want to march over to him and ask what his problem is. We are nothing to each other, just two people forced to endure each other's company while my best friend crushes on his brother. I stare back, and as our eyes meet, it's like I can feel the daggers poking at my chest, threatening to cut me open.

Drew's arm tightens around my shoulder. I look away from Tanner, letting Drew carry me along to the parking lot. We are safely inside Drew's red hatchback before I can breathe.

"Where are we going?"

"You know the Sand 'N' Sea?" It's one of only three restaurants within a mile of school. "I'm told it's the best chicken salad in Valle Vista."

Likely the only chicken salad in Valle Vista. It's not like we have an abundance of restaurants beyond the typical fast-food chains.

We drive even though the restaurant is just a few blocks away. Despite its name, the Sand 'N' Sea is nowhere near the beach. The only ocean ambience here is a small flock of seagulls hopping from table to floor in search of scraps.

"So, is this our second date?" Drew asks as we settle into one of the wrought iron tables with our chicken salads.

"It's not a date."

"Let's see, I asked you to go somewhere to eat. You came. We're sitting here together. I'd say that's a date."

"It's not."

Drew leans across the table. "Second lunch then?"

I smile. "Second lunch."

"Done. So are you going to tell me what happened, or am I going to have to drag it out of you?"

I'm not sure I'm ready to tell anyone about the note, let alone a guy I just met a few days ago, but if I'm really going to do this, it might help to at least have someone to talk to. Someone who doesn't judge me.

I show him the letter. "This was in my mother's things."

He scans it. "Whoa."

"Do you think it means anything?"

"Do you?"

"I don't know. It sounds like someone wanted her dead."

Drew looks worried. "Sounds dangerous."

Okay, it's too much to ask someone I barely know. I shouldn't involve him. "It's not what you signed up for when you offered to help." It's one thing to help me find out if my mother committed suicide or not. A possible murder is something else altogether. "I'll understand if you say no."

"It's not me I'm worried about. Are you sure you want to look into this?"

"I've never been more sure. What if someone killed my mother?" I stare at my untouched salad. "Is it weird that part of me wants it to be true?"

"I don't think so. It's natural to want someone to blame for her death."

"That's it exactly." I hate the part of me that blames her for leaving. The part that blames me. I need someone to hate. Someone to punish.

"Where do we start?"

He's really going to do this? Now that he says it so easily, I hesitate. "You don't have to do this. It's stupid."

"It's not. If it were my mom, I'd want to know." Drew watches me. "I get it. You need to do this on your own. And I'm just some guy you met in the library. It's okay. I'll back off. But if you need a sounding board, or whatever, you know where to find me."

Hearing my concern out loud makes it sound silly and immature. He is just some guy I met, but I've already told him more about my mother than I've told anyone, even Mary Chris. I take a breath. "We need to know what she was doing before she died. I saw a letter asking her to work on a project for Moss Enterprises. I'm sure it's tied to the letter Mr. Moss has."

Drew nods, taking it all in. "Can you get us into the Moss house?"

"Wow. It sounds so sleazy when you put it that way. Mary Chris is my best friend. I'm there almost every day."

"So that's a yes." He tosses a crust of bread to the ground, creating an instant riot as every seagull within fifteen feet converges. "Invite me next time."

"Like tonight?"

"Okay." He grins. "Third date at Mary Chris's house."

I toss a potato chip at his face, but he deflects it with a well-timed wrist block.

"Nice move."

"Oh, there's more where that came from."

"Good to know. Potato chip defense is a dying art."

"It's a work in progress. Got taken out by a pretzel last week."

I laugh, grateful to Drew for distracting me, even if it is just for a few seconds. "You're sure you want to come tonight? Mare will probably have a few people over. You might have to actually meet some people."

Drew's face gets serious. "As long as I don't have to talk to them or, you know, be nice."

I throw another chip at him. This one hits him right between the eyes.

Chapter 13

Jason corners me at my locker as soon as we get back from lunch. "You had lunch with Drew Mattingly? I can't believe you didn't tweet live updates. Tell me everything."

"Drew is helping me with something. We're friends. That's it."

Jason throws his hands up in a move that looks like a cross between jazz hands and some kind of seizure. "Ahhh! Friends don't stare at friends' backs as they walk away. Not unless they're helping you pick out an outfit."

"I didn't stare at him."

Jason shakes his head. "Duh, I wasn't talking about you."

"Drew was not staring at me either."

"Totally was. What's he helping you with anyway?"

I stare at the inside of my locker, letting my eyes settle on the triangle of dirt in the back corner. I can't keep the truth from Jason forever. He'll drag it out of me sooner or later anyway. "You promise not to say anything? Not even to Mary Chris?"

"Him? You're going out with Drew Mattingly?"

"No! Is that all you ever think about? I told you, we're just friends."

"Friends who check each other out as they walk away."

"Stop."

Jason finally settles down, holding his hand over his heart. "Okay. I won't say anything. I promise."

"Drew's going to help me find out if my mom was murdered."

"What?" Jason looks as thrown as I feel. "Your mom might've been murdered?"

I nod. "I think so. I found a death threat in with her things."

"Whoa."

"That seems to be the general consensus." The bell rings, and people rush by us, but Jason and I stand frozen.

"What are you gonna do?" Jason asks.

"I think Mary Chris's dad has a document that might give us more information. I'm going to look for it tonight. Will you cover for me?"

"If Mr. Moss has something, why don't you just ask Mary Chris for it?"

"I don't know. I feel weird about it. I can't ask Mare to spy on her own father."

"But you can spy on your best friend's father?" Jason looks skeptical.

"Something like that." It's not like I want to involve Mary Chris's family. I just want to know the truth. I need closure.

Jason looks over my shoulder and grins. "Your other boyfriend's here."

"What?" I spin around. Tanner leans against a row of lockers across the hall, his arms crossed, watching me. Waiting. I turn my back on him.

Jason winks. "That's my cue to leave."

"Don't."

"It's for your own good." Jason walks away before I can say anything to stop him.

I should follow. Take evasive action. But why? I have no reason to run from Tanner Halston.

I take my time closing my locker, doing my best to ignore the pounding in my chest. I spin the combination lock a few times more than is necessary. I don't need to look to know that Tanner closes the distance between us. I just know.

When I finally turn around, he is right there. I stand up straighter, in a futile effort to feel less small. I have to look up to make eye contact.

"Where were you today?" he asks.

"Hi to you too."

Tanner blinks. "I'm sorry?"

"The proper greeting is 'hi.' You could also go with 'hey,' 'what's up,' or 'how's it going.' You should at least say hello before you give someone the third degree."

"Is that what I'm doing?"

"Isn't it?"

Tanner leans a shoulder on the locker next to mine. "Maybe."

He smiles and I'm not ready for it. My hands shake against my thighs. "Did it ever occur to you that it's none of your business where I was, or who I was with?" I emphasize that last part, a not so subtle reminder that I was with Drew today.

Tanner's smile is gone in an instant. His eyes search my face like he's looking for a way to get inside my head. I concentrate on keeping him out.

"I guess not," he finally says. Then he puts his hands in the pockets of his perfectly faded jeans and walks away.

I watch him until he disappears around a corner. I sag back against my locker and close my eyes until my pulse evens out to normal levels. What was that? I don't get nervous. It's a professional hazard. I should be able to handle a smile from a good-looking boy. Correction. An arrogant jerk.

Swooning at guys is Dead Presidents' territory. Not mine.

By the time I get home, Lulu's already managed to convince Dad to take her for a walk. Dad grabs the jowl towel as he walks in the door and wipes the lines of drool from her chin. He skips the small talk. "Berry, you think you'll be okay if I head up to Palm Springs for a few days next weekend?"

"I'm sure I'll survive." The fact is, Dad is gone a lot at night. Cheating husbands tend to like the cover of darkness. "Big case?"

His cheeks redden. "Actually, it's a personal trip."

I try to ignore the knot that forms in my chest and constricts. "Shauna?"

He wipes at Lulu's chin without looking up. "She has a condo on a golf course. And I could use a few days away."

I manage to stop myself from telling him to stay home, that I need him after all. That someone might have threatened Mom and I'm not sure what to do about it. "Are you sure about this?" I say instead, giving him an out.

"I am. I know it seems sudden. It was a surprise to me too."

It does seem fast, despite the eight years leading up to it. Because of it. "It's fine, Dad. It's about time you went out and had some fun." My brain believes this statement completely. It's just going to take a while to convince my heart.

"I could say the same thing about you. It wouldn't kill you to get out more. And not for work."

"I hang out with my friends."

"Building spy gear at Mary Chris's house doesn't count."

"We're going to Homecoming next weekend." It's not even a lie. Mary Chris is making me go in exchange for the new portable scanner she's building for me.

Dad smiles so big, that I'm actually glad it's not a lie. "You'll need a dress, right? Shauna wants to take you shopping Saturday."

"Please don't make me go." It's one thing for Dad to date her. It doesn't have to involve me. The less I know the better.

"You'll go. It'll be fun." Dad gives me the look that says there will be no further argument on this.

A direct attack isn't going to work. "So I was in the storage unit today." I let the sentence hang in the air, waiting to see if Dad takes the bait.

"Saturday," he says, not letting me distract him.

"I found this box of Mom's work papers."

I finally have him. Dad looks worried. "Why would you want to look through those?" He tries to keep his voice even, but it raises at the end.

Does he know? He doesn't look me in the eye even though I'm

staring at him. He has to have seen the threat. He packed the boxes. "Did you know that Mom received a death threat before she died?"

Dad's face goes from worried to angry in about two seconds. "What are you talking about?"

"It was in her papers. There was a note."

Dad's hands are shaking. His fingers tremble as he covers his mouth with his hand. Oh no. Did he not know? What am I doing to him? I take it back. I'll go shopping with Shauna Waterson. I'll let her buy me a ridiculous dress and I will smile and laugh and pretend I'm the kind of girl who loves being stuffed into a tube of taffeta.

When he drops his hand all I see is fury in his eyes. "You went through her things? You should have asked me. Her work was confidential."

"I know. But I found—"

"Stop. Right now."

I close my mouth.

Dad walks past me into the kitchen. I stand frozen in the living room. Afraid to move. Afraid to breathe.

He comes back with a bottle of water and takes a sip. "I don't know what you think you're doing, Berry, but you have to promise me you will let this go."

"What? But what if something bad happened to her?" What if this was not her fault? Not mine.

He shakes his head. "It was an accident. It had nothing to do with that note."

That note. He did know. "You don't know that."

Something flashes behind his eyes. In a second I'm taken back to that horrible year when I didn't have a mother or a father. The pain is back on his face, only this time, I'm the one who's putting it there. This is coming out all wrong.

He blinks. When he looks at me again, there's a wall in place. "You think I haven't turned over every stone? There's nothing to find, Berry. You have to promise me that you will not try to chase this down."

"But what if it's true? It can't be a coincidence that someone threatened her and then she's dead? What if the person who killed her is still out there?"

Dad looks like I've punched him the gut. He actually winces. "It's a dead end. I've checked it out. The police checked it out."

The police? "The same police who decided she killed herself? You don't believe that? You never believed that. How can you trust them on this?"

Dad's face is bright red.

A new panic floods me. "You don't believe she killed herself." As if saying it will make it true. "You told me you didn't."

Dad doesn't answer. Water splashes from the lip of the plastic bottle in his hand.

"Tell me."

He turns his back on me. "You have to let this go, Berry."

I don't miss that he doesn't reassure me. All these years I've felt guilty for never fully believing that she didn't leave us on purpose. All these years I thought I was the only one who didn't have faith.

Chapter 14

Mary Chris doesn't say anything about my puffy eyes as I sit on her bed. Oscar, her Himalayan cat, comes off the windowsill and lies across my lap, purring even before I scratch under his chin.

I'm still shaken by the fight with my dad, but I keep it to myself. Mare has already done her penance for being my friend. She stayed with me in the weeks after my mother's death when I didn't know how to do anything but cry. She stayed with me during the months afterward even though I sleepwalked through school and forgot the meaning of the word "fun." She never even mentioned the fact that I went from Barbies to grocery lists to covert surveillance in the span of a year. That's the thing about Mare, her love is unconditional.

Not that I deserve it.

Tonight, I'm going to sneak into her father's office and look for the letter from my mom. I need to know what exactly my mom was doing for Moss Enterprises, and why Mare's dad was concerned about the letter getting out. Someone threatened my mom, and despite what my dad said, I can't let it go.

I ask Mary Chris about the scanner she's building for me. "Can you make it look like a cell phone?"

"Probably. Why?"

"In case I get caught."

Her eyes get thoughtful. "Since when are you worried about getting caught? Whatever you're up to can't be good. Is it legal?"

"Obviously." I grin.

She laughs. "Fine. What else?"

Oh, right. I'm planning to sneak into your father's home office tonight and find out what he had to do with my dead mother. I bite my lower lip. Not until I know exactly what Mr. Moss has to do with anything. Maybe we can laugh about it later, but for now, I need to do this on my own. "That's it. How soon can you have it?"

"A week maybe?"

"Works for me." After eight years, a week is unlikely to make much of a difference.

Mare pulls the technical drawings for the glasses-cam from her desk drawer. "It's all done. I've been talking to my dad about getting a patent." She stops and sets the documents on her desk. "Are you going to tell me what's bothering you?"

I shake my head. "I got into an argument with my dad."

Her forehead crinkles. "About work?"

"Yeah." Sort of. "He wants to take me off a case."

"Which one?"

"It's a new one."

Mare is silent for a minute. The quiet magnifies the sounds of Oscar's purrs, and I wait for Mare to figure out that I'm not ready to talk about this one. She will. She always knows when to let me be.

She flips open a laptop on her desk. "I hope you don't mind I invited the guys over to watch a movie tonight."

I don't have to ask who the guys are. Instead, I use the opening to bring up the subject of Drew. "Is it okay if I invite someone too?"

"Jason's already coming."

"Not Jason. Drew Mattingly."

Mare's mouth falls open, but she snaps it shut. "Drew Mattingly. Huh."

"He's a friend."

"What about Tanner?"

"What about him?"

"I don't know. I thought maybe you guys would go out or something."

"Jason said the same thing. Did you guys go completely insane and forget to tell me?"

Mare laughs. "Yeah. About that charismatic voice in my head that keeps telling me to date, and, you know, have a social life."

I toss a pillow from the bed to her desk. "In case you haven't noticed, Tanner's kind of stuck up."

"You should give him a break. Ryan says Tanner's been home-schooled all his life. McHenry is his first real school experience. It's a big adjustment."

"Really?" How did I not already know this? Oh yeah. I don't want anything to do with him.

"Try to be nice to him, okay?" It's what Mare always says about whatever stray she's brought under her wing.

I try.

I bite my tongue when Tanner glares at Drew the entire time I'm introducing him. I even smile when Tanner suggests that everyone watch some lame action movie with zero plot and a lot of pointless car wrecks. At least we won't have to talk to each other.

I make sure that Drew is sitting next to me as we settle in for the movie. I'm going to sneak off to go to the bathroom, and Drew is supposed to ping me if anyone leaves the room.

Jason sits on my other side. I owe him one. With Mary Chris and Ryan taking occupancy of the love seat, Tanner has no choice but to take one of the beanbags on the floor.

Mary Chris turns down the lights to make it seem more like a real movie theater. Mr. Moss spared no expense on the giant flat screen and surround sound, so the effect is pretty close. Better, since we can relax on the couch and talk as loud as we want.

As the movie starts, Tanner sprawls on the beanbag. He stretches his legs out in front of him and puts his hand behind his head for support, completely at ease in the dark. His chest rises and falls in time with his breathing. He laughs at something on the screen. His laugh is unguarded, completely transforming him. I don't think I've ever heard him laugh before.

I want to hear it again.

"What do you think?" Drew whispers in my ear. "About ten more minutes?"

"Huh?" I forgot about Drew. And the plan. What is wrong with me? "Yeah. Perfect."

I spend the next nine minutes watching the minutes tick down, trying to focus on the task at hand. I try not to notice when Tanner shifts to his side, keeping my eyes fixed on my watch. One minute left. Tanner's laugh rolls up and down my spine. His laugh. No one else's.

I leap to my feet when the ten minutes are up.

"Are you okay?" Jason asks.

"Yeah." A total lie.

Jason nods, and Drew pats me reassuringly on the leg. I step around Tanner and fly down the hallway in the direction of the bathroom. I round a corner and stop to catch my breath.

Okay, so Tanner has a sense of humor. A lame one if this movie is any indication.

I need to focus. I set the phone to vibrate and tuck it in my back pocket.

Mr. Moss's office is at the end of the hall. Mr. and Mrs. Moss should still be in the living room drinking mochaccinos and watching a baseball game. I have at least an hour before the game ends. I only need a few minutes.

I move quickly, ducking into the darkness and closing the door about halfway. Enough to give me some cover, but not enough that I can't claim I wandered in by mistake. I wait for my eyes to adjust to the dark and move over to a credenza on the far wall. Mr. Moss has a lot of papers scattered about, but it's easy to skim when I know what I'm looking for. My mother's letterhead.

I work my way through two stacks of paper and am starting a third when my phone starts to vibrate.

Not now.

I reach back and shut it off. Whoever Drew saw get up is probably just going to the bathroom anyway.

I keep flipping through the stack of papers but stop when I hear footsteps coming down the hall.

I look around for hiding places in case I need one in a hurry.

I set the papers back on the credenza and move over to the large wooden desk. I can duck underneath it if I need to.

I don't get the chance.

Tanner's large frame fills the space between the door and the hall-way. "What are you doing in here?"

Tanner doesn't bother turning on the light as he enters the room. He just crosses the dark and strides toward me like he's going to escort me right back outside.

I shouldn't have to answer to him, but something about his purposeful walk tells me I better. I try to laugh, but it comes out sounding like a squeak. "You caught me."

"Caught you what?" Even in the dark, I can feel his icy stare.

I try to think. "Waiting for someone."

He steps closer. "Who? That Drew guy?" He says Drew's name like it's a bad word.

I try to back up, but the solid mahogany desk stops my progress. "Maybe."

"How long have you even known him?"

The judgmental tone in his voice gives me the strength I need to stand up to him. I push against the desk and close the rest of the distance between us. "What difference does it make? He's my friend. Which is more than I can say about you."

Tanner doesn't back up. If anything he leans closer, so that the heat radiating off his chest warms my skin. "Why did he want to meet you here?" His voice is almost a whisper. I feel it more than I hear it.

I look up at him, suddenly very aware that we're alone. In the dark. "Why do you think?"

"You don't know anything about him."

"You're absolutely right. I mean, he's so friendly and fun to be around. I don't know what I was thinking."

"Berry, I'm serious."

I bark out a laugh. "This from the guy who just followed me like some kind of crazy stalker. And so what if Drew is a total freak? Maybe that's what I go for."

"It's not." The knowing look in his eyes is enough to make me want to puke. The guy's ego doesn't know when to quit.

"Obviously, or I would've gone for you when I had the chance."

He sighs, and I thrill at the fact that I've finally gotten a reaction from him.

Then he steps forward so that I have no choice but to back up against the desk to avoid colliding with his chest. He puts his hands on the desk, so I'm trapped between them, his face just inches from mine. "I'm not sure what I've done to make you so angry." His breath floats along my neck as he talks. "I've tried to be your friend." His perfect lips move closer to mine. "I've tried to leave you alone."

I melt, my insides dissolving into a warm gooey mass. I'm pulled along on an invisible string, stretching toward him. His lips part and I hear his soft intake of breath.

"I'm on your side." The low thrum of his voice fills me completely. His fingertips dance along the side of my cheek, a whisper on my skin.

I lean away from him, focusing on keeping my voice even. "You're not."

He drops his hand and stands up straight, leaving me hanging by a thread that unravels faster than I can gather it. There's a chill where his body heat had been. Even the air rebels at the absence of him.

He runs a hand along the back of his neck. "Fine. Do what you want. Just promise you'll be careful. I don't trust that guy."

The door to the office opens all the way and Mr. Moss's voice carries across the room. "Is someone in here?"

I launch myself at Tanner, throwing my arms around his neck and pulling him the rest of the way to me.

Chapter 15

I crush my lips against Tanner's. He tenses at first, but it takes less than a second for his arms to come around my waist and pull me all the way against him. His chest is even more solid than it looks. He parts his lips, and before I even realize what's happening, our tongues tangle in a jumble of fire and liquid that has me pressing toward him, wanting to be closer.

The light comes on and we leap apart as quickly as we came together. I have to remind my thundering heart that none of it is real. It's all for Moss's benefit.

Mr. Moss takes one look at the two of us and shakes his head. "I expected better from you."

I cover my mouth with my hand. My lips are bruised. I don't have to pretend to be embarrassed. "Sorry." But Mr. Moss doesn't look at me. He's watching Tanner.

Tanner glances at me before he steps forward. "I should be the one apologizing."

Mr. Moss does not look like the concerned father of my best

friend. He looks angry. Dangerous. "This will not happen under my roof, got it?" His voice is reassuring, but his eyes look wild. He holds the door open.

We both nod and stare at the ground.

"And no one is allowed in my office. You know that, Berry."

I nod again. "Right." Did I know that? Mary Chris and I never really played in here, but I always thought it was because there were so many other cool places to hang out, not because there was any rule against coming in here.

Mr. Moss waits for us to walk out into the hallway. He shuts and locks the office door behind him, scuttling my search.

Tanner waits for Mr. Moss to get out of sight. "Are you going to tell me what that was about?"

"What? A girl's not allowed to kiss a guy? Welcome to the twenty-first century. Girls aren't afraid to ask for what they want anymore."

"You didn't ask." He studies my face for a few seconds before he shakes his head. "You don't want me."

Tell that to the part of me that is still reeling from the feel of his mouth over mine. The part that wants to fling myself into his arms. Again. Heat rises in my cheeks. "Call it an experiment."

"What?"

I put on a fake smile that I hope resembles one I've seen Kennedy use a thousand times. "I wanted to know what it would be like to kiss you. You know, see if the great Tanner Halston lived up to all the hype."

"Mr. Moss was already on his way in."

"So it was my last chance. And I took it."

"And?"

I twist a strand of hair around my finger. "And now I know." I wish I didn't. I don't want to know that kissing Tanner Halston is the kind of thing that can make you forget that your best friend's father is *already* in the room. I don't want to know that kissing Tanner Halston can make you forget that you don't even like him. I certainly don't want to know that kissing Tanner Halson can make you forget why it even matters.

I step around him and walk back to the family room. I don't know how I know that he watches me, but I feel his gaze on my back.

I settle in between Jason and Drew.

Drew looks at me sideways and mouths, "How'd it go?"

I shake my head. It's all I can manage. I try to focus on the movie, and for a few minutes the blur of explosions and bad dialogue is enough to take my mind off of Tanner. The reprieve is too short. The second that Tanner walks in the room every nerve in my body stands at full attention, remembering.

Tanner lies back against the beanbag chair, but he doesn't look as relaxed as he did earlier. He doesn't laugh again either. Is he remembering too?

I run my fingers across my lips, but the bruised feeling is gone. The moment is already disappearing. I should be grateful. In time, that kiss will be just another two-dimensional shadow, like the faded images of my mother.

Some people don't even remember their first kiss after enough time passes. I hope I turn out to be one of those people.

When the movie finally ends, Drew walks me out to my car. I give him a brief summary of my failed search of Mr. Moss's office, although I leave out the part where I literally throw myself at Tanner Halston.

Drew looks thoughtful. "Can you pick locks?"

Yes, but that's not exactly something I want to brag about. "I'm an investigator, not a thief."

"That's not exactly a no."

Busted. "You'd be surprised what you can learn on Wikipedia."

"So we'll try again." Drew kicks the pavement with his toe. "I have an idea. There's a catch though."

"You mean besides breaking and entering?"

"When you put it that way, my idea doesn't sound so bad."

"What?"

"Let me be your date for Homecoming. Mary Chris was talking about having everyone over after the dance. Her parents will be out, and we'll have a perfect opportunity to sneak into the office. If we go together, people will assume that we just want to be alone."

"Are you asking me to Homecoming?"

"That depends. You're not going to beat me up or anything?"

"I wasn't. But I might now."

Drew ducks behind my car. "So this is going to sound weird, but I can't actually take you to the dance. I'll have to meet you there later. I can get there by ten or so."

"Wait. You're asking me to a dance that you're not actually going to? This might be the lamest Homecoming invitation in the history of McHenry."

"Sorry. My grandmother's coming to visit and I promised I'd be at the dinner. It didn't seem like such a big deal a week ago."

I should know better. Drew is just trying to help me. "I get it. It's not like it's a real date anyway."

Drew swallows. "It could be."

I look at the ground, anywhere but at Drew. "If you were actually taking me to the dance. Which you're not."

Drew lifts my chin, forcing me to look at him. "Is that a yes?"

"To a question you never asked, for a date you're not going to attend?"

"But it's a yes, right?"

I can't help laughing. "Yes."

Drew's hand stays on my chin. The seconds click by in slow motion before he drops his hand and puts it in his pocket.

I can't decide whether to be disappointed or relieved.

Chapter 16

The dog park is quiet for a Saturday morning. Lulu barks at a chocolate Lab, trying to distract him from the ball he chases.

I turn my attention to the baseball field next door. The game has been under way for forty minutes, but my mark still sits on the bench in the dugout, spitting sunflower seeds on the dirt.

I finger the video camera that hangs around my neck. Come on, guy. Give me something. The mark has been off work for a shoulder injury since last March. His employer is paying us to find out if he's really as injured as he claims. I thought for sure I'd get something when he signed back up for his old softball league, but so far all he does is sit on the bench, pop seeds in his mouth, and spit out shells.

One of his teammates hits a home run and the mark stands up to cheer with his buddies. Number ten slaps him on the back, and he flinches. Maybe the guy really is hurting. It happens.

Lulu gets bored with chasing the Lab and ambles over to me. She leans against my leg for a pat, her tongue hanging out. "You want to go sit down for a while?"

Lulu just pants, which I take as a yes.

I walk her over to a tree-lined lawn on the western side of the baseball field. Lulu lies on the grass and flops her head down. I sit in the grass and wait for the game to end, so I can at least verify that the guy never plays.

I don't know what diverts my attention to the fountain at the center of the park. There's no noise, no unusual movement. I scan the people walking nearby, but I don't see him. That's my first clue that I'm looking for Tanner. I recognize the prickles on the back of my neck. It's the same thing I felt last night when he walked back into the family room. Some primitive instinct barking out a warning. I should run far away.

Lulu lets out a snuffle that's a cross between a snore and a sigh. I pat her absently, but I can't shake the nervous energy that urges me forward. He's here. I know it. I stand up, waking Lulu from her thirty-second nap. She sits up and yawns, watching the leash in my hand with sleepy eyes.

"Sorry, Lu. Looks like we're going for a walk."

Lulu has one speed when she's not trying to throw retrievers off their game. It's more of a meander than a walk. It takes us twenty minutes to circle the park once. I'm just about to give up when I see him.

Tanner leans back against a large eucalyptus tree with his arms folded across his chest. Ryan stands beside him, staring at the ground. Neither one of them looks happy.

I don't know whether to be glad that I'm not completely insane, or upset that Tanner might actually be stalking me. I guide Lulu through the trees, trying to get closer without being seen. Staying out of sight when you're walking with a one-hundred-and-fifty-pound dog isn't easy, but if you do it right, Lulu actually provides pretty good cover.

We stop behind a tree about fifteen yards away. Lulu lies back down in the grass while I press up against the tree. I can't hear anything, so I reach for the receiver in my messenger bag and put the buds in my ears. I play with the volume until I can just make out Ryan's voice.

"You need to chill. It's no big deal, okay?"

Tanner steps away from Ryan and rubs his eyes on his sleeve. "Have you lost your mind? You weren't supposed to kiss that girl. You know the rules."

My brain races to keep up. So Mary Chris and Ryan kissed? They've been all over each other all week so it was pretty much inevitable. But since when is Mary Chris "that girl"? And what kind of weird religion doesn't allow kissing?

Ryan looks up at Tanner. "She has a name."

I like Ryan more and more.

Tanner leans in closer, his voice a low growl. "Don't tell me you are starting to fall for her already? This is wrong on so many levels."

What? I knew Tanner was obnoxious, but he's even worse than I realized.

For a minute I think Ryan is going to hit him. At least that's what I hope for. Instead, Ryan slumps his shoulders. "I know."

"Maybe we should just go back to Irvine. It's not like there's anything for us to do here."

What? And Irvine's so great?

SPIES *and* PREJUDICE
•

Ryan runs both his hands through his hair. "Dude, we don't know that."

Lulu flops her head back down and snorts. Tanner turns and looks into the shadows, right where I'm standing.

"Who's there?" He walks toward the tree. I stand still and silent, frozen, like a trapped animal. When he finally sees me, his eyes widen. "Are you spying on us?"

I pull the earbuds from my ears, trying to look like I was just listening to music. "Newsflash. Not everything in this world is about you."

For a second, I think his lips curve into a smile, but it's there and gone so quickly I can't be sure. He bends down to scratch Lulu. She rolls over to give him direct access to her belly. Traitor.

Tanner looks up at me. "Then how do you explain the fact that you're hiding behind a tree listening to our conversation?"

He's so smug. "How do you explain the fact that you just happen to be at the same park I take my dog every Saturday? Are you following me?"

"You're the one hiding behind a tree."

I let out a sigh. "Maybe I'm waiting for someone who doesn't automatically assume I'm spying on him."

He stands, closing the distance between us in a heartbeat. Lulu lifts her head at the sudden movement. "I am not going to tell you this again. You have no reason to trust Drew Mattingly."

"Funny, I was just thinking the same thing about you."

Ryan walks up behind Tanner. "Hey, Berry."

"Hey," I say, but my eyes are still locked with Tanner's.

"You don't know anything about me." Tanner's voice is so quiet it's almost a whisper.

"I know enough." But my insides are a hot mess and I don't know anything at all anymore. I drop my gaze to his lips. Mistake. Now I'm remembering that stupid kiss.

Ryan puts his hand on Tanner's shoulder. "We should go." Tanner doesn't move. "Dude."

"Fine." Tanner turns away without another word.

"Nice seeing you too." I wave at his retreating form.

Lulu shakes her head, sending a line of drool flying across my shirt.

"You couldn't have done that thirty seconds ago?"

Lulu sighs and flops back in the grass while I watch Tanner walk the rest of the way to the parking lot. To make sure he actually leaves.

He does. Which makes me even angrier.

It's not until I hear the cheering from the baseball diamond that I turn to see my mark sliding into home.

Chapter 17

D ad and I have been circling around each other without saying much since our fight the other day, or I would've tried once more to get out of dress shopping with Shauna Waterson. At least I manage to convince Jason to come along so Shauna can't try to make this some kind of audition for the role of stepmother.

After wandering the formal section for all of five seconds, Shauna holds up a hanger with a pink monstrosity that is all puffs and ruffles. "What do you think?"

I shake my head. Oh no. Please let me find a dress and get out of here quickly.

Jason holds up a dark cherry gown with a skirt that poofs out at the waist.

"No." I hold up a simple black dress that will hit me mid-calf. "I like this one."

Shauna and Jason shake their heads in unison. I'm being double-teamed.

"That looks like something my grandma would wear," Jason says.

Shauna looks almost sad. "Oh honey, you need something special. That dress is fine for a nice dinner out, but this is Homecoming."

I cling to the dress. Jason is supposed to help me out here, but instead he's bonded with Shauna over their matching blue pearl nail polish, and I've got no chance of getting out of here with anything even remotely tasteful.

Shauna looks at the dress Jason still holds. "Ooooh. This is more like it." She presses the pink dress into my hands. "Don't say no until you try them on."

I take the dresses into a small fitting room, ignoring Jason's arched eyebrow.

I try on the black one first. If I like it, I won't have to bother with the other two. Of course, I have to figure out how to get it on. Do I step into it or pull it over my head? I manage to wiggle into it, though it takes another five minutes and a nearly pulled muscle to zip up the back. No wonder I don't wear dresses.

Shauna's voice carries across the dressing room. "Berry! Are you dressed? I want to see them all!"

I glance in the mirror. There's a swath of lace across the front that gives the dress a Morticia Addams quality that suits my mood, but even I have to admit that the dress looks like something a grandmother would wear. A goth grandmother, but still. There's definitely something depressing about it.

It hits me that the last time I wore a dress was at a funeral. Has it really been eight years? I guess my dad wasn't really the type to dress me up in frilly outfits and take me to tea. He was more the type to throw me in the back of the car with a sleeping bag and take me on stakeouts.

No way I'm coming out in this. Knowing Jason, he'll take a picture and keep it for blackmail.

I somehow manage to contort myself to reach the zipper without dislocating my shoulder. It takes me even longer to wrestle myself into the pink dress, as I try to figure out where my arms and head go in the midst of all the ruffles. There's only one sleeve, and it's capped with a giant ruffle that scratches against my cheek. When I look in the mirror, I see a giant pink puffer fish staring back at me. My face looks kind of green against the cotton candy pink.

"Berry!" Shauna knocks on the fitting room door. "Are you in the pink one? I want to see."

I open the door a crack, but she pushes it all the way open. She takes one look at the dress and shakes her head. "Maybe pink's not your color."

I don't know whether to be relieved or horrified that she thinks the color is the worst part of this train wreck.

"Try the red one."

I close the door and stare at the last dress on the hanger. I've never owned a gown, but gown is the only word for this one. The top is trimmed with gold thread and the skirt flows all the way to the ground. I step into the skirt and the fabric settles around me with a soft whoosh. I pull the sleeves over my shoulders and zip up the back without too much difficulty.

When I finally look in the mirror, I catch my breath. I don't look real. The bodice hugs my curves right down to my waist before fanning out in soft lines that don't poof at all. The gold threads shimmer in the harsh light of the store. I look like a life-sized Barbie doll.

Who is this girl in the mirror and where did she come from? She's a stranger to me, but somehow I know I've missed her.

"Berry!" Shauna's voice booms louder. "We're waiting."

I use my tee shirt as a towel, wiping my eyes. I can't let Jason see me crying over a dress. Talk about blackmail photos.

I brace myself with a deep breath and avoid looking in the mirror again before I open the dressing room door and step out into the store.

Shauna's hand comes to her mouth. "Oh!"

Jason's jaw drops to his chest. "Wow, Strawberry. You clean up well."

Tears sting at the corners of my eyes again.

Shauna nods her head. "Oh yes, honey. That's the one."

I disappear back into the room as quickly as I can. Once the dress is safely back on its hanger looking deceptively poofy, and I've turned back into Berry Fields, I let myself sink onto the bench.

It's not just my mother whom I lost eight years ago. Somewhere along the way I lost the girl who dreamed of wearing beautiful dresses and dancing with handsome boys. The girl who wasn't embarrassed to be called Strawberry or play with dolls.

It's just a dress.

I curl up in a ball and stare at it like it's a ghost.

I knew coming here was a bad idea.

Chapter 18

Shauna tries really hard the rest of the day. First, she buys me enough makeup to support a small family of clowns. Then she and Jason squeal over a pair of gold heels that they promise will be perfect, but pinch my toes when I walk. I do my best to nod and smile and just get through it.

Okay, I want to like her, and I might even be able to manage it, if it weren't for the fact that she's dating my father. Throw in the fact that she's Collin's mother, and the poor woman doesn't have a chance. She already has two strikes.

By the time I get home I'm exhausted. I lie on the couch and barely close my eyes when the doorbell rings. Lulu runs to the door and barks until I get up and open it.

Drew Mattingly grins at me. "I tried to call, but you didn't answer."

I lean against the door frame. "I was trying to take a nap."

"Sorry. I figured you'd want to hear this. I found the witness to your mother's accident. She lives in Lemon Grove."

I'm instantly awake. "What? How?"

"A little Internet research and a few phone calls."

Lulu presses her nose through the door to sniff Drew.

He holds his hands up and backs up. "You couldn't just have a Chihuahua?"

I grab Lu's collar, holding her back. "Lu's friendly. She just wants to say hello."

Drew keeps his distance. "I'll pass. Anyway, I just wanted to tell you that Heather Marrone agreed to meet us at Sconehenge on Tuesday night."

My stomach clenches into a gnarled knot. I know Drew is just trying to help, but it all seems like too much too soon. "Just like that?" I should be excited to talk to the one person who witnessed the accident. Maybe she saw something important. All I know about her is what I've read in the paper, but part of me wonders if she's the one who told the police that it looked like a suicide.

Drew still has one eye on Lulu. "Yeah. Cool, right? So I guess we'll see each other at school on Monday?"

"Do you want to come in?" He's already stepping away, like he regrets coming here in the first place.

He shakes his head. "I should go."

"Is it the rumors?"

"What?"

I don't know how to explain. I wasn't imagining him flirting with me all week. And last night when he held my chin, I thought he might kiss me. Except he didn't. And today, he shows up at my house but doesn't want to come in. Maybe he really does think I'll beat him off with a stick. "I just thought you might want to hang out."

"I'm the guy who hides in the library, remember?"

"Oh." Right. He doesn't want to get close to anyone. It was stupid of me to think that I was an exception.

He laughs. "I'm kidding." Drew looks at Lulu again and backs away. "In case you haven't noticed. I'm not exactly hiding from you. If you were paying attention, you'd see I've gone to extraordinary lengths to get you out to dinner with me on Tuesday."

"Finding the woman who witnessed my mother's death is a move?"

He laughs. "I prefer to think of it as a romantic gesture."

I'm pretty sure I blush. "So Tuesday?"

He backs up a step from the door and bows lightly. "At your service."

I think I want to like him. He's the first person in a very long time that I've invited in. I do want to like him, so what's holding me back?

After Drew leaves, I call Mary Chris and invite her over for my famous grilled triple-cheese sandwiches. I'm halfway through my second sandwich before I get the courage to ask her what I've wanted to since I called her.

"So?" I ask. "What's with you and Ryan?"

Mare blushes. "He's cute, right?"

"If you say so."

"You don't see it?"

I shrug.

"Because you're too busy checking out his brother."

"What?"

Mare's face turns serious. "Don't. You can block out the rest of the world, but I'm your best friend. Don't even think about keeping secrets from me."

I'm pretty sure my face burns. Did Jason tell her about my search for the letter? "I was going to tell you." Just not until I knew what there was to tell.

"I can't believe I had to hear it from my dad!"

Her dad? But Mr. Moss thought I was making out. Oh. She thinks I'm keeping secrets about Tanner. "It was just a kiss. It didn't mean anything."

"It was not just a kiss. It was your first kiss. Did you think you could just pretend it didn't happen?"

"Can't I?"

"No!" But Mare is smiling now. "So? How was it?"

"Okay."

"Okay?" Mare points her sandwich at my chest. "You've never lied to me before. Don't start now."

Too late. Way, way too late.

I try to think of words that will make what I did make sense. *I was just trying to find out why your dad has a letter with my mom's name on it that he didn't want someone to find.* No. *I just invited Drew over to cover for me while I snuck into your dad's office to go through his stuff because I still can't accept that my mother didn't leave me on purpose.* No way. *I kissed Tanner so your dad wouldn't find out I was spying on him.* No, no, no.

"Fine," I say. "Kissing Tanner was kind of amazing." I give her this small truth, and hope it will tide her over until I know if there's even anything else to tell.

"I knew it!" Mare hugs me hard enough that it hurts.

"And you were going to tell me about Ryan when?"

It's Mare's turn to blush. She talks animatedly about how much she really connects with Ryan, but I only half-listen. I'm still thinking about the secrets I keep buried.

By the time Tuesday night comes around, I'm a basket case. When I get to Sconehenge, Drew is already there, at a table near the back of the restaurant underneath one of the giant fake rock structures. I start toward him, but stop when I see Tanner two tables over, leaning over a basket of sweet potato fries between him and Ryan. I change my path across the restaurant to avoid walking by him.

I slide into the seat next to Drew, trying not to look at Tanner. The waitress sets a Diet Coke in front of me without asking me what I want. I stir the drink with my straw absently.

Drew pats me lightly on the knee. "This will be good. You need to know, right?"

I nod my head. He's right. I need to know.

A woman with bright red hair walks up to our table and holds out her hand. "I'm Heather."

I don't know what I expected, but this woman is not it. Her hair frizzes out in every direction at once. She's too thin and too pale, which only accentuates the dark circles beneath her hollow eyes. Her clothes are small enough to be children's clothes, yet they hang on her tiny frame.

She sits down across from Drew and offers a closed-mouth smile. When she looks at me her eyes turn pitying. "You must be the daughter."

The daughter of the dead woman. "That's me."

The waitress comes back and Heather orders a burger and fries. When the waitress leaves Heather focuses her tired eyes on me. "Aren't you having anything?"

I shake my head. I have nothing to say to this person. It takes all my effort to keep from getting up and walking out of the room. I'm not ready for this.

Drew squeezes my knee, holding me in place. "Thanks for talking to us. As I said on the phone, we just want to know what you remember about the accident."

Heather shakes her head. "Oh, it wasn't an accident."

I stand up too fast, sending a fork clattering to the floor.

"Berry." Drew puts a hand on my arm.

I pull my arm away and walk as fast as I can out of the restaurant. I thought I wanted the truth. I thought I needed to hear it.

The truth is I need the lies more.

I hear footsteps behind me, but I don't look back. I keep going until I'm across the parking lot. I rest my hands on the hood of my car and concentrate on slowing down my breathing. In. Out. In. Out. In.

"You okay?" The low thrum of Tanner's voice swirls around in my chest with the night air.

I turn around to face him. "Stop following me."

"You were upset. Did Drew do something?"

"Don't make this about Drew."

Tanner puts his hands in his pockets. "Sorry. I don't mean—are you okay?"

"No." My whole body trembles. It starts as a tremor, but gathers steam quickly. I hug myself to make it stop, but my body shakes of its own volition.

Tanner steps forward and puts his hand on my shoulder. "Do you want to talk about it?"

"No."

His arms come around me and I do nothing to stop it. I bury my face in his shoulder, shaking. He smells like cinnamon and fabric softener and for some reason this makes him seem more human.

He lowers his head so his mouth brushes my hair. "Better?"

I don't want to answer. I just want to stay here and pretend that none of this is happening. Eventually, I stop shaking, but I don't move away. For now, I'm safe. It's classic Stockholm Syndrome, finding comfort in the arms of the person who torments me.

"Can I ask you something?" Tanner's mouth is next to my ear. His breath sends a hot blast down my neck.

I nod into his shirt.

"Why do you hate me so much?"

I want to say that it's because he's arrogant and has done nothing but insult me and my friends. I want to say something that will make him leave me alone for good. Instead I say, "I don't hate you." It might even be true.

His lips move against my hair. "I don't hate you either."

Tanner's arms fall and I'm standing on my own. I'm not shaking anymore, but I miss the warmth of him. I miss the smell of cinnamon and Tanner.

"Who was that woman?"

"She saw my mother die." It sounds even worse when I say it out loud.

"What?" Tanner's face gives nothing away. I can't tell if he's shocked or just curious.

"It's kind of sick, right? Interviewing the woman who watched your mom die? I thought I could do it, but as it turns out, I guess I can't."

"Why was Drew there?"

I shrug. "He's helping me."

"Helping you?"

"Do you even know how to talk to people without sounding like you're cross-examining them? This is really none of your business."

"So you keep saying."

"Maybe I wouldn't have to keep saying it if you'd leave me alone."

Tanner steps closer. There's still a few inches between us, but his body heat hovers in the air between us. It's somehow more potent than when he was holding me. "Is that what you want?"

He waits for an answer that never comes. I can't bring myself to say the words that will send him away any more than I can utter the words that might bring him closer. I clutch the side of my car.

We stay like that as the seconds stretch into a minute. Tanner lifts his hand, reaching for me, then drops it to his side. "Just be careful, okay?"

"Okay," I say, but Tanner has already turned his back on me. He walks into the restaurant without a glance in my direction.

It's a half an hour before the red-haired woman walks out of the restaurant and climbs into a beat-up Corolla. Drew follows a few minutes later.

He sees me leaning against my car and jogs up. "Hey."

"Hey."

"I hope you don't mind that I went ahead and talked to her. I figured you'd want to know what she said."

I do want to know what she said. I am sick. "Thanks. I wasn't ready."

Drew watches me. "We don't have to do this now."

"I want to get it over with. Tell me."

"I'm not sure how."

"Tell me."

Drew takes a breath and then it all comes out in a rush. "She lied. She never saw anything."

I'm dizzy. "That's impossible. She said it wasn't an accident. She talked to the police."

"Someone paid her to talk to the police, Berry. She wasn't even on the bridge that day."

"How do you know she's not lying now?" Another dead end. That's all it is. The woman who saw everything isn't talking.

"I don't. But I believed her. It fits with the note you found. Someone wanted the police to think your mom killed herself."

My knees are wobbly. I lean against the car for support. As much as I thought I wanted to believe that someone killed my mother, the thought makes me want to puke. "Who? Who paid her?"

"Some guy she met in a bar in Chula Vista. She doesn't remember much about him now. He paid her ten thousand dollars to say she saw the car go over the edge and call the police."

I slip down the side of the car until my butt hits the pavement.

"Do you know what this means?" Drew kneels down beside me.

I wrap my hands around my knees. I know exactly what this means. Someone wanted the police to think my mother killed herself. Someone covered their tracks. "We have to keep looking."

Chapter 19

At school on Friday, Drew promises to meet me at the dance by ten. I was already planning to go with Mary Chris and Jason, so it's not like I'll be alone or anything. Still, as fake dates go, this one pretty much bites.

Dad kisses me on the cheek on his way out the door with his suitcase. "Don't stay out all night."

"I could say the same thing to you. But that would be weird."

"Call if you need anything."

"I won't." I don't know whether I'll need anything or not. But I won't call. I'm not about to interrupt Dad's romantic getaway. I'd rather pretend it's not happening.

Dad stops in the doorway. "You're sure you'll be okay?"

I could make him stay. I could tell him I need him here and put an end to this weekend with Shauna Waterson. It's tempting, but something stops me. "I'll be fine, Dad." As long as Mr. Moss doesn't catch me going through his office.

Dad smiles and hugs me before heading out the door.

I grab the dark cherry dress and drive over to Mary Chris's house to get ready.

Jason greets me at the door. He's wearing a pair of black pants that taper at the ankles and a red satin shirt that looks vintage.

"What, no tux?"

"Not that you can see."

"Invisible tux? Wow. So elite no one even knows it exists."

Jason laughs. "Wrong. It's a tuxSpeedo."

"Please tell me you are not planning to parade around in a tiny bathing suit with a bow tie."

"Buzzkill." Jason leads me upstairs. "Mary Chris is freaking out about her updo, even though it looks fabulous. Tell her she looks amazing. She thinks Ryan's going to change his mind about her. Like that would happen."

"Ryan's coming?"

"She didn't tell you?" Jason's smile is evil. "Then I'm guessing she didn't tell you about Tanner either?"

"What about Tanner?" I'm going to kill Mary Chris if she's done what I think she's done.

"Mary Chris might've invited him to come with us."

This is what I get for allowing myself to be so distracted. Left to their own devices, my friends are a dangerous pair.

We make our way up to Mare's bedroom. Her hair is swept up in a pile of loose curls that make me think of a cross between Scarlett O'Hara and Mae West. Still, Mare pulls it off. She's bent over a cell phone on her desk, wielding a tiny screwdriver.

"Tell me the truth, Berry. Do I look like a poodle?"

"You look gorgeous." Mare always looks gorgeous.

"Really?" Mare picks through a pile of motherboards and wires on her desk, pulling out a small white box with wires sticking out in every direction.

"Really."

"I told you." Jason winks at me from across the room.

I slip into the bathroom to put on the dress that Jason picked out for me last weekend. I leave my hair down, letting the blonde waves fall past my shoulders.

Mary Chris lets out a squeal when I walk back into the room. "Where is my friend and what have you done with her?"

Jason waggles his eyebrows at me. "Tanner is going to be drooling all over himself."

"That's his problem. I already have a date."

Jason and Mary Chris look at each other and back at me.

"What? Drew is meeting me at the dance later."

"Later?" Jason narrows his eyes.

"He had some family thing he couldn't get out of." It sounds even lamer when I say it out loud.

"Family thing?" Jason rolls his eyes.

"Forget I said anything. Wait. Tanner doesn't think he's going to the dance with me?"

Mary Chris and Jason both stare at the ground.

"You guys! That's completely unfair. I'm already going with Drew." There's a buzz in my stomach that I can't begin to control.

Mary Chris hands me the cell phone she'd been working on. "It's not a date. We're going as a group."

"Fine." There's no point arguing. I turn over the cell phone in my hand. It's heavier than it should be. "Wait. Is this what I think it is?"

Mare grins. "Just hold the face over the document and hit pound, nine, nine to activate the scanner. It will read the entire document and save it to the drive in less than a tenth of a second. It will save it as a PDF, but can be easily converted to a searchable TIFF file. Pretty good, right?"

I flip it over in my hand. It's more than good. It's amazing. "You're a freaking genius, you know that?"

"That's why you pay me the big bucks. What's it for anyway?" Mare tries to sound casual, but she's fishing.

Jason stares at me, daring me to tell her the truth.

At the moment, it's so I can spy on your dad.

I can't bring myself to say it. "Trust me, you're better off not knowing."

"Plausible deniability?" At least Mare doesn't seem angry that I'm keeping something from her. Somehow that makes it worse.

"It's for your own protection." What she doesn't know can't hurt her. At least that's what I tell myself. I tuck the cell phone into the small gold purse Shauna bought to go with my dress.

Jason won't make eye contact. It's easy for him to say I should tell her. He's not the one who's about to break into Mare's father's office and go through his desk.

We head downstairs and let Mare's mom take our pictures in the living room while her dad sips a tall coffee and watches from a distance. He smiles and acts like a doting father, but every now and then I think I catch a flash of what looks like a warning in his eyes. I'm sure it's just my guilty conscience letting my imagination run wild. He can't know I'm looking for the letter.

The doorbell rings and Mrs. Moss grins. "That must be your ride." She opens the front door to a short man in a poor-fitting suit. "At least you'll arrive in style."

"You got us a limo?" Mary Chris starts jumping up and down. It doesn't matter how perfect her life is, Mare is always genuinely surprised when things go her way. "This is so awesome!"

"You've got the limo until midnight." Mr. Moss looks pointedly at the driver.

Mare's smile fades. "Wait. This is a trap, isn't it? To make sure I'm home by curfew."

Mr. Moss laughs. "I'm not above a little subterfuge." Is he looking at me? I swear Mr. Moss looks directly at me.

"It's great." I grab Mary Chris by the wrist and rope her into a hug. "Thanks."

Since the front door is open, Tanner and Ryan walk into the house like they've been coming here all their lives. At least I think Ryan walks in. I only see Tanner.

He's dressed in a dark suit and a crisp white shirt with a light blue tie that matches his eyes perfectly. The cut of his jacket emphasizes his broad shoulders and tapers down to a fitted waist. But it's not the way he looks that takes my breath away. It's the way he looks at me.

He stares across the room, past Mary Chris, past her parents, past Jason. His eyes burn into mine.

Jason elbows me in the side.

I elbow him back. "Stop." But I'm smiling. I can't stop smiling.

Tanner crosses the room and stands directly in front of me. "Wow."

"You should see the shoes." I lift the skirt up and stretch out my foot to reveal the gold strappy heels that match the gold threads perfectly. Pinched toes or not, they look pretty cute.

"I wasn't talking about the dress."

"Oh." I watch Tanner watch me. My cheeks grow warm. "You look nice."

Tanner pulls at the knot in his tie. "I think I'm being strangled."

"It's very James Bond."

He smiles. "My mom would love that." He catches himself, giving me a worried look.

"It's okay." People always think I'll freak at the mere mention of someone's mom. I can handle the fact that other people have mothers. It's not like she's all I think about. Still, I can't help thinking that my mom would have liked seeing me in this dress too. She would've taken a million pictures and forced Tanner to pose with me in every one.

It's my turn to catch myself. There is no alternate universe where my mother is alive. There is no alternate universe where Tanner is my date to the dance. Besides, I already have a date. With Drew.

Someone should clue in Mare's mom, who herds us over for a picture on the staircase before I can move away.

"I'm sorry," I whisper as she urges Tanner to put his arm around me.

Tanner's hand slips around my waist. "I'm not."

I try to concentrate on Mrs. Moss's stage directions. Bend my head to the left, smile bigger, drop my shoulder. But the truth is I'm barely aware of her or the rest of our audience. I'm barely aware of anything but the strong arm around my waist and the heat that pours from Tanner into me as he whispers in my ear.

"At least she didn't assume I was with Jason."

Did Tanner Halston make a joke? "Trust me. Jason would be a better date."

Tanner's lips brush the soft patch of skin just below my ear, sending a shiver down my spine. "I doubt that."

"That's it." Mrs. Moss looks at us expectantly.

Tanner's hand still holds me to him. Neither one of us moves.

Jason holds up his cell phone and snaps a picture.

He gets a blackmail photo after all.

Chapter 20

The dance is in full swing when we get to the Valle Vista Country Club. The clubhouse has huge windows that probably have great views of the golf course in the daytime, but now they just look out into the dark. The wall of black is somehow fitting.

Mary Chris and Ryan go right out into the middle of the dance floor and start to dance.

Jason spots a group from the drama club. "What do you want to bet I can convince Clay to give Polonius a song in the second act before the night is over?"

"Tell me you're not Polonius?"

Jason shrugs. "What? I need a song." He darts off.

Stranding me.

Tanner fiddles with the knot around his neck, looking as uncomfortable as I feel.

"Do you want to dance?" The words come out of my mouth before I've had a chance to think about them. I already regret asking him. It's a stupid idea.

He looks down at the wood floor. "I don't dance."

It hurts more than it should. "It's called the Homecoming Dance. Not the Homecoming hide-in-the-corner-and-brood." I gesture to the dance floor, where Mary Chris and Ryan are bumping hips and laughing. "Must be a shock for you. All this merriment."

Tanner takes one look at Mare and Ryan and openly scowls.

Better. I just need to remember what an arrogant fake he is. "Why are you even here?"

Tanner finally looks at me, but his eyes are soft, not icy at all. "Maybe I like brooding in corners with pretty girls in fancy dresses who take my breath away."

I back up a step. When did he get so close? "You'll have to brood alone for a while." I straighten my spine and turn away from him, looking over my shoulder before I walk away. "I came here to dance."

I walk faster than I would have thought was possible in these heels. I don't know where I'm going, just that I need to put as much distance between myself and Tanner Halston as I can.

A slow song starts, and the couples on the dance floor move closer together, clearing a path for me. I'm nearly to the other side when a hand grabs my elbow. I spin to break the contact and come face-to-face with Tanner. "Are you following me again?"

"It appears that way."

"Why?"

He takes a breath. "I changed my mind." Tanner looks down at the dance floor and wipes a palm on his thigh.

It's all I can do to keep my eyes from following the path of his hand. "You changed your mind?"

Tanner looks uncertain. "This is stupid. I don't know what I'm doing here."

"Are you asking me to dance? 'Cause here's a tip. You might want to edit out the commentary about it being stupid."

He shakes his head, and for a second I think I've gotten it wrong, that he's not asking me to dance at all. But then he holds out his hand to me.

I should leave him hanging. I should turn around and walk away. Far away. How is it that I know exactly what I should do where Tanner Halston is concerned, but I can't quite bring myself to do it?

I place my hand in his, and I can't prevent the warm tingly pulse that travels through the rest of my body. "I thought you didn't dance."

"I might be terrible."

"Stop the presses. Tanner Halston is terrible at something?"

"It happens." His other hand finds my waist.

I bring my palm up to his shoulder and we are close enough that the heat coming off his skin moves through our clothes. The part of me that wants to be even closer is appeased when he steps into me, following the music.

Except I have to move a half a beat early to avoid his foot. "You are kind of terrible. Keep your feet still."

He stops altogether. Not just his feet, his whole body is frozen. "This isn't dancing."

"We'll get there. One thing at a time. Start with your hips." I bring both my hands to his waist and slide them lower. "Here."

He sways and I go with him. "Good. Now, step slowly. That's it. And turn slightly as you step."

He turns and steps right on my toes.

"Ow! Okay, forget the stepping for now." I laugh and bring my hands up to his shoulders. We barely move. He stops dancing.

"I told you I didn't dance." He smiles at me, and I have to remember to breathe.

"You're doing fine." Better than fine. We find the slowest beat of the song, swaying together. The movement brings us close enough that I have to slide my hands around his neck to keep them from getting trapped between us. Every beat of the song pushes us along, nearer to each other. His palm moves against the bare skin between my shoulder blades. I should be embarrassed by the way the hard lines of his chest press against the softness of mine, by the thigh that rests between my own, but I'm not. I'm pretty sure that I'm the one who's pulling him closer.

His breath whispers along my neck, its warmth coming faster as I curl my fingers in the fine hairs at the base of his neck.

"Berry," his lips brush across my neck as he says my name.

"Hmm?" I rest my head against his shoulder.

"The song's over."

I lift my head and look around at the couples walking on and off the dance floor as the music changes to a thumping bass. What just happened? I know better than to let myself lose track of my surroundings. Fields' rule number seven: be aware of what's going on around you at all times.

I stand up straight and push off of his shoulders. "This is the part where you're supposed to thank me for the dance." My breath is ragged and my voice cracks just a little.

"Thank you." Our eyes meet and I see a spark in his gaze that ignites a fire deep inside me. Then he spins on his heel and disappears through the crowd of dancers.

I was wrong before.

This is what it's like to be stranded.

I need fresh air. The patio outside is crowded with couples who came outside to be alone, only to discover that a hundred others had the same idea. At least the air is cool, and I let it wash away the last traces of heat from my body.

Much better.

"Berry, Berry, Berry. You are really messing with me." Collin Waterson slides next to me, his eyes glued to the line of cleavage bared by my dress.

"If I was messing with you, Collin, you'd be face-first in the punch bowl with a knee in your back."

"Sounds crazy." Collin finally looks at my face. His eyes are shot through with red.

He lurches forward, reaching for my wrist. "I need your help with something."

I jerk my hand away. "Why don't you try asking someone who might actually want to help you?"

Collin shakes his head, staggering backward. "Can't. You're the only one." He stumbles forward again, his hand moving toward my chest.

I duck my shoulder and twist away so that he falls into a planter and grabs a handful of dirt instead of any part of me. I walk away, blindly at first, but eventually I follow a lighted path that lines the fairway.

Collin trails me, staggering a few feet behind. "How much longer are you going to keep running from me?"

I turn to face him. "That depends. How much longer are you going to keep pretending that I am in any way interested?"

"This is getting old, don't you think?" Collin stops in front of me. Too close.

"Yes, I do."

He moves faster than I expect, and I'm not ready for it. His arms come around me, pulling me against him, trapping my arms with his. "So let's do something about it."

"Let go." I stomp at his foot, making contact with his instep, but I'm off balance, so my foot just glances off his.

"Kiss me first. I just need to see something."

I turn my head to the side and try to get a better stance to break away. "Let go."

"Come on. I'm the only guy at this school who will even touch you." Collin laughs against my cheek like he's just made the funniest joke of all time.

"Let her go." Tanner walks up the path toward us, his eyes narrowing on Collin.

As Collin twists to look at Tanner, I finally get some weight on the ground, giving me leverage to raise my knee into Collin's thigh. I make enough contact that he loosens his grip on my arms. I elbow Collin in the chin, which is enough to send him flying backward.

I charge after him before he can get his balance, grabbing his arm and twisting it around his back.

"Had enough?" I growl in Collin's ear.

"That hurts." His voice is a squeak.

I let go of his arm.

Collin struggles to regain his balance, rubbing his arm. "Ouch." He glares at me through bleary eyes. "I don't know why I bother."

Tanner watches Collin walk away, not turning to look at me until he's sure that Collin is safely back inside the clubhouse. His grin is absolutely wicked. "Watching you take him out might be the hottest thing I've ever seen."

We stand there watching each other. The cool air does nothing to stop my rising temperature. I try not to think about how much his smile affects me. I change the subject instead. "Mary Chris said you were homeschooled?"

"Something like that."

"So McHenry is your first real school?"

He nods.

"When you said you didn't dance, is that because you've never been to a dance before?"

"Are you trying to embarrass me?"

"No. This is called small talk. We ask each other questions about our hobbies, school activities, that type of thing. Did you at least play sports or something?" He's way too fit to be a couch potato.

"I've had some martial arts training."

"Seriously? Is there a level below white belt? Because I think one of the first things you learn in any system is how to avoid someone else's feet."

"Sparring is different than dancing."

"I know how to spar."

"No kidding."

"What else do you do? I'm pretty sure you're not a gamer." He said Rockstar Hero wasn't his thing. Was it because he'd never played before?

"Video games? I've played some. Mostly first-person shooters and simulations." He lets go of his tie. "Who's giving who the third degree now?"

He's right, but for some strange reason I want to understand him. To know him. "You want to go somewhere?"

Tanner raises his eyebrows. "I'm pretty sure the answer is yes, but I think I should ask what you have in mind before I commit."

"Dragon Holes." It occurs to me that Tanner didn't want to go before because he doesn't know how to play. That can be fixed. "We can take the limo as long as we're back by ten." For my date. I don't mention that part. It doesn't seem relevant. "Of course, there is a very real possibility I'll beat you."

"So I saw." Tanner's lips curve into that take-your-breath-away smile. "Still, I think I'm up for getting out of here."

"Tell me that after I drum you at medieval mini-golf."

We find the limo in a back corner of the parking lot. I give the driver directions and climb in the back. As Tanner slides into the seat across from me, I consider telling him about my date with Drew. So he doesn't get the wrong idea about this little outing. Set the boundaries right up front.

Tanner runs a hand through his hair, making it stick out in several directions at once. "You'll have to teach me how to play."

"You really should get out more."

"You should invite me more often."

My lips curve up in a smile before I can stop them. Forget boundaries.

Chapter 21

Y ou'd think that people would have better things to do on Friday night, but Dragon Holes is packed. We have to wait ten minutes for a gang of middle schoolers to finish the first hole and another group waits behind us.

I explain the rules and demonstrate with a first shot that ricochets off the concrete wall and heads under the miniature castle just before the drawbridge comes down.

"The drawbridge blocks the entrance?" Tanner sets his red ball in the depression on the right where mine had been. "Isn't that counterintuitive?"

"Just go with it. There's a water-breathing dragon on eighteen."

Tanner's tie hangs over the club as he leans forward, and he whips it back over his neck. He hits his ball too hard, sending it careening off the wall, over the drawbridge, and into a pit that will dump his ball behind a low wall that blocks any direct path to the hole.

"Not bad," I lie.

When we walk around the castle, my ball is a foot from the hole, while Tanner's is predictably trapped in no-man's-land.

Tanner groans. "I stink at this."

"You'll be fine. It takes at least three holes before you can really expect to master the art of the game."

Tanner laughs. The hard lines of his face soften all at once. I want to make him laugh like that again.

By the time we get to eighteen, he's gotten the hang of it and we're all tied. Tanner lines up his ball with the dragon's mouth.

"The trick is to hit the ball when the mouth is shut," I say as he addresses the ball. "That way it will be open by the time your ball gets there."

Tanner looks over his shoulder. "Are you helping me?"

"I'm teaching you to play, remember?"

"That was before we were tied and your personal pride was at stake."

I laugh. "My personal pride was pretty much eviscerated when I asked you to dance."

His eyes turn serious.

Did I say too much?

"I made you feel like that?"

My mouth is dry, so I just nod.

He reaches for a strand of my hair near my face and smooths it with his fingers. "Don't let me."

An eighth grader with the sides of his hair shaved in a faux hawk leads his friends up the path from seventeen. "Get a room!"

Tanner glares at the guy, then drops his hand, and turns back to his ball.

What did that mean? Don't let him what?

Tanner makes a smooth stroke while the dragon's mouth is shut, timing it so the dragon's mouth is wide open just as the ball sails through. I hear it fall into the cup on the other side.

"Nice." I pick up my skirt and line up my ball on the tee.

I don't have to see Tanner to know he smiles. "Best you can hope for is a tie."

I wish for that to be true. Something tells me that where Tanner Halston is concerned, I'll never be on an even playing field.

I hit the ball too soon. Tanner laughs as my ball bounces off the closed mouth of the dragon and water spurts from the dragon's nose.

"Yes!" Tanner pumps his fist in the air.

"You're not supposed to gloat."

"Oh, I'm definitely gloating."

"Fine. But don't expect me to feel bad for you when I beat you at laser tag." Some sick part of me wants to stay in this fantasy world where Tanner Halston plays mini-golf and laughs at my jokes.

Tanner nods toward a group of kids strapping on laser shields. "Care to fill me in?"

"Basically we shoot a bunch of eighth graders with laser guns. You up for it?"

"Definitely."

I strap a large plastic laser sensor across my beautiful dress and arm myself with a laser pistol.

Tanner picks up a pistol and tests the weight in his hand before holding it up and taking a few test shots. He puts the pistol down and picks up a larger rifle, going through the same routine. Okay, he's obviously watched too many episodes of *Cops and Lawyers*. He tries a third gun, finally settling on the rifle after looking through the scope a second time.

We're put on the red team along with two brothers who give us condescending glares. We'll see who's smirking when the clock runs out. I might look like a princess in a party dress, but I know how to fire a gun. And I'm guessing that Tanner's first-person shooter video game experience might come in really handy. I stare back at the taller brother and wink.

Faux Hawk sneers at us from across the way. He and his buddies make up the green team.

Tanner leans into me as each team is sent through different doors into the dark game room. The room is a maze of low walls and mirrors. The walls are painted black and accented with a trail of neon that provides just enough light to see, although everything looks oddly distorted.

"Stay behind and follow my lead." He directs the brothers to opposite sides of a low wall. "Wait here."

Tanner gestures for me to follow him down a dark hallway. He really does look like James Bond in his dark suit with a gun in his hand. I can't stifle a laugh.

"Shh." Tanner peeks around a corner. "They'll have to come through here. They won't see us until we've gotten in a couple shots. You take the first and second guy, and I'll get the two behind. Don't shoot until all four of them have come around the bend."

"Have you done this before?"

Tanner shakes his head. "The room from the outside was a

square. Since there are only two entrances, it makes sense that each are opposite routes to the center. They expect us to engage there, but that eliminates any advantage for either team. We have to let them come find us."

We lean back against the wall, guns poised to shoot for several minutes. I try to concentrate on the area the green team will come through, but all I can think about is Tanner's arm touching mine as we wait.

Tanner's lips brush my ear. "Being alone with you in the dark is getting to be a habit."

"Watch the door," I say, but I'm already turning my head toward him. For a second I think he might kiss me. At least I might want him to.

"Forget this," brother number one says from behind us.

Brother number two brushes by. "We're going to massacre the green team."

Tanner shrugs and focuses back on the opening as they race through it. "You're walking into an ambush."

"I think we know how to play laser tag." The brothers disappear down the black hallway.

A few seconds later we hear the frantic beeps of a firefight followed by the blaring of three sirens. Tanner points to two lighted red X's on the wall, and one green one. "At least they took one of the bad guys out on their suicide mission." A time clock ticks down. Now we're losing and running out of time.

"Where's the Homecoming queen?" Faux Hawk's whiny voice carries down the hall. "I say we take out the pretty boy and see if she wants to switch teams."

I stick my finger in my mouth in the universal sign of puking.

Tanner shakes his head. "They won't take me."

This is just a game, but there's a moment of panic when the first guy rounds the corner. He's a shadow in a sea of fake fog, but the green dot on his target blinks at me. I aim my pistol, waiting. The second guy comes behind him. I'm supposed to wait for the last guy, but they're getting too close. In a few steps they'll see us and we'll lose our advantage. I step forward and start shooting, hitting the first guy twice before he even raises his gun.

The second guy starts shooting blindly down the hall, but Tanner steps forward and takes him out in three rapid-fire shots. Number two's siren goes off and another green X lights up on the wall. Number one aims at Tanner and scores a hit, but I jump in between and nail him with a third shot, causing another siren to blare.

"Where's Faux Hawk?" I ask, gun poised and ready to shoot as adrenaline thunders through my veins.

Tanner gestures for me to get behind him. "He sent in the cannon fodder to gauge where we were. He won't be far."

"Do we wait?"

Tanner shakes his head. "We've lost the element of surprise. We have to go find him."

"There's two of us and only one of him. I can go ahead and draw him out."

"I'm not letting you do that."

I walk around him. "Yes, you are." I point to the timer between the rows of X's. We only have a minute left. "It's now or never."

Tanner follows me down the narrow hallway and around the

corner to the large room in the center. There are more places to hide here. A thick layer of fake fog hangs in the air. I gesture for Tanner to stay put at the entrance as I walk straight to the center.

"Come out, come out wherever you are." I think I hear footsteps to my right, but when I turn my head there's nothing. I tell myself it's just laser tag. No one's really going to hurt me. But my heart races as though the guns are real.

I raise my gun and point it in the direction of the sound.

There's a louder noise behind me. Faux Hawk gets two shots off before I can turn around. Direct hits. I duck behind a low wall, firing blindly as I go.

Tanner runs through the room firing. I hear two more hits, but no siren, so Tanner must have gotten in at least one shot. Tanner slides up next to me. "I told you it was a stupid plan."

"You didn't say it was stupid. You said you weren't going to let me do it." Tanner's hand reaches for my arm as he pulls me behind a column. "At least now we know where he is."

Tanner grins at me. "So we do."

He moves forward, his laser gun at the ready. The kid comes out from behind a low wall, gun blazing. Tanner drops to the ground and rolls on his side, angling his gun and getting off a single shot that hits the kid squarely on target. Faux Hawk's siren goes off and the lights come up inside, signaling that our game is over.

Faux Hawk doesn't look at us as he leaves the game.

Tanner pulls himself up from the ground slowly, brushing dust off his shoulder.

I take his laser gun. "You're really good at this."

"Some parents take their kids mini-golfing. Mine took me to paint ball."

"Paint ball? Isn't that kind of intense?"

"It was the way we played."

I dust off the back of his jacket with the palm of my hand. "When did your parents get divorced?"

"They didn't."

They didn't? "How do you have a stepbrother then?"

"We're not really related. Ryan's parents moved to Spain for a job six months ago. Ryan moved in with us to finish out high school."

I'm surprised Mary Chris hasn't mentioned this to me yet. It's probably my own fault for not paying enough attention to her crush on Ryan, but I should know this anyway. It's my job to know about people. This thing with my mother has thrown me off my game more than I realized.

My hand still rests on Tanner's back, even though I've stopped brushing off the dirt. He turns around and I drop my hand to my side.

Tanner leans forward, his mouth near my ear. "Next time listen to me when I tell you not to do something."

"Next time trust me when I say I'm going to do something."

Tanner laughs again. "So you agree there's a next time?"

The sirens go off again inside the game, saving me from having to answer.

The limo waits for us outside. This time we slide in next to each other, so we're both facing forward.

Neither one of says much as we drive back to the dance. I try to

SPIES *and* PREJUDICE

•

figure out how to explain about Drew. I can't reveal our plan to break into Mr. Moss's office, but I can't let Tanner think it's a real date either.

Just as I open my mouth to say something, Tanner reaches across the seat and takes my hand. "Thank you," he says, still looking straight ahead. "That was the most fun I've had in a really long time."

I stare down at our hands between us. My traitorous fingers lace with his like it's the most natural thing in the world. His thumb strokes along the top of mine, trailing down to the inside of my wrist.

"You're welcome," I say. And I let myself wish that the limo would somehow miss the turn and just keep driving.

It's a pointless wish. The limo turns into the parking lot a minute later, flashing its lights on the students gathered out front. Tanner lets go of my hand as the driver opens the door on my side.

"Listen," I say, "I should explain something."

"You don't have to explain. Let's just start over." Tanner smiles at me. "Starting now."

I barely step out of the car when Drew runs up. "There you are." He loops his hand through my elbow and guides me back toward the dance. "I thought you stood me up."

I look over my shoulder, but I don't see Tanner behind me.

I don't see him anywhere.

Chapter 22

D rew's hand doesn't leave my elbow as he guides me inside to the dance. "Where were you anyway? I've been waiting over a half hour."

I look behind me again, but I still don't see Tanner. "Turns out going to a dance without a date kind of bites." Not half as much as coming back to the dance to meet your date. I need to talk to Tanner. Why didn't I just explain in the limo when I had the chance?

"You're right about that. I've spent the last fifteen minutes trying not to look too pathetic, standing by myself on the curb." Drew leads me back inside the dance. "You look great. Well worth the wait."

"It's not a real date, remember?"

"Tell yourself whatever you need to. If I recall correctly, we already have plans to sneak off together later."

"To break into Mr. Moss's office and find the letter from my mother. It's every girl's romantic dream."

Drew's arm slides around my waist. "You know it."

I start to laugh but stop before any sound comes out. I feel the chill at the back of my neck before I see Tanner a few feet away. His eyes look dark in the poor lighting, his expression darker still.

I need to explain. Tanner will understand once I've told him what I'm trying to do.

Drew pulls me closer. "Does that guy ever lighten up?"

"He's not so bad once you get to know him."

"Somehow I doubt that." Drew leads me to a table where Jason sits with the theater crowd. You can always spot the theater crowd. Just look for the sea of bad dye jobs and black eyeliner.

Drew squeezes me tighter.

"You don't have to keep your arm around me."

"Just keeping up appearances. We've got to look the part if anyone's going to believe it when we sneak off later." There's a spark in his expression that sends off all kinds of warning bells in my head.

"Drew, what I said before about not really dating—"

"I get it. Don't worry. I'm the guy who doesn't want any ties to this place, remember? I can't help it if spending time with you makes being here just the slightest bit bearable."

"Just the slightest?"

"Yeah, don't let it get to your head." He grins, and I can't help but laugh again.

How does Drew manage to turn around even the most awkward conversations?

Jason is in the middle of a heated debate about whether Polonius should have a duet with Ophelia in the second act of *Hamlet*. The guy arguing against it has obviously heard Jason sing.

Jason winks at me as I sit down. Drew scoots his chair closer to me and leans forward so his lips are next to my ear. "You have some strange friends."

I kick him under the table. "Says the guy with no friends who hides in the basement of the library."

A slow song comes on and I'm relieved that Drew doesn't ask me to dance. My dance with Tanner was a lifetime ago, but just thinking of it makes my stomach do little flips. It's dangerous to think of Tanner this way. Things would be so much easier with Drew. He'll leave me, but I'll see it coming. There's no chance of him getting too close. On second thought, Drew might be perfect boyfriend material.

I reach for Drew's hand. "Do you want to dance?"

"I thought you'd never ask." Drew's Cheshire smile is almost enough to make me take back the invitation.

Jason stops mid-Polonius rant and asks a silent question with his eyes. Since when is Jason the arbiter of who I date? There's nothing inherently wrong with Drew. I lead Drew out to the middle of the floor and slide my arms around his neck.

Dancing with Drew isn't awful.

He's strong without making me seem weak. He holds me at a respectable distance, not too far and not too close. My feet are perfectly safe. I might even enjoy it if it weren't for one glaring problem.

I feel nothing.

"Are you okay?"

I look up at Drew. "What?"

"You just shook your head. Is something wrong?"

"It's fine." I step closer to Drew, so we're almost touching. "This is nice."

"Nice?" Drew lowers his chin. "You know how to hurt a guy."

"I'm sorry. What I meant to say was this is beyond amazing and I'll die if you don't kiss me right here in the middle of the dance floor." I throw my head back in mock surrender.

Drew pulls me the rest of the way to him, laughing. "Don't tempt me."

He's too close. Claustrophobic. Boxed in and trapped. I focus on breathing. It's just Drew. We sway for a few beats and I try to relax. I just need to get used to the closeness. I need to find a way to let him in.

I close my eyes and try to imagine something warm, a hot summer day, a roaring fire, molten lava. It helps some. It's kind of . . . nice.

"I hate to interrupt." The low tone of Tanner's voice startles me. I jump back from Drew, putting as much distance between us as I can.

"Sorry?" The heat that had been so elusive a few seconds ago is here with such force that my face is on fire.

The hard line of Tanner's jaw is fixed. He conveys nothing. "Mary Chris sent me. Everyone's waiting in the limo."

Drew slips his arm around my waist. "We'll be right there."

Tanner lifts his chin in a dismissive nod and walks away.

The sinking rock in my stomach chases away the warmth and leaves me trembling as I watch Tanner's back until it's no longer visible in the throng of people.

Drew laughs in my ear. "I see what you mean about Tanner. He's so much more fun when you get to know him."

Chapter 23

J ason keeps everyone entertained on the ride back to Mare's house
with his near perfect impression of Donald Trump. He pushes his
hair back across the top of his head and explains how we are riding in
the most luxurious limo in the history of limos.

Tanner stares out the window, completely ignoring Jason. Ignoring me. He hasn't looked at me once even though he's sitting directly
across.

I resist the urge to push Drew's hand away from where it rests on
my knee, trying not to think about how it felt when Tanner held my
hand just thirty minutes earlier. A lifetime ago.

Jason kicks my shin lightly to get my attention. "You're the tie-
breaker for our movie marathon. *X-Men* or *Lord of the Rings*?"

"James Bond." I watch Tanner. He has to look over here eventually.

"*Lord of the Rings* it is." Jason sounds triumphant.

"That's not what she said." Ryan has his arm around Mary Chris.

Jason rolls his eyes. "I don't know why you're bothering to put up

a fight. I'm fairly certain you guys will disappear before the first movi
ends."

Mary Chris blushes.

Ryan grins. "Fine. But until then we're watching *X-Men*."

Tanner finally turns away from the window to glare at his brother.

It's just what I need to remind me why I don't like him. I don't lik
Tanner Halston. I don't like Tanner Halston.

He starts to say something but stops himself. Then he finally look
at me. For a second I see something else in his eyes that makes m
heart beat faster, a primal acknowledgment.

I might like him a little.

Mary Chris's house is dark when the limo pulls into the driveway.

"Are your parents home?" Drew asks.

"They're spending the night at a bed and breakfast on the beach."

Drew reaches for my hand and squeezes it. All according to plan
At least I hope that's what he's communicating.

Tanner sits up straighter. "Your parents are out?"

"Yeah," Mare says. "You don't look happy. Do you need a chaper
one?"

"Not me." He stares at my hand in Drew's.

It's not like I'm cheating on Tanner. We're not even together. S
why do I feel like I'm no better than the men I spy on?

Everyone piles into Mare's family room and stakes out a spot on th
large couch. I hang back, a nervous twinge fluttering through my stom
ach. For the first time tonight, I focus on the reason I'm here in the firs
place. I'm really going to do this. I'm going to break into my best friend'
father's office and find out what my mother was doing before she died

Once the movie starts, it's Drew who gets up first. I give him five minutes before I follow. No one seems to pay attention. Not even Tanner, who hasn't glanced at me once since we came inside.

Drew stands outside Mr. Moss's office. "You sure you can do this?"

I pull a bobby pin from my small purse and set to work on the lock. I fumble for a few minutes as I search for the slot in the back. "Stop staring. You're making me nervous."

Drew leans closer. "I can't help it. You look kind of hot when you're breaking and entering."

"Get over it." The pin finally catches, and I give it a twist until the lock clicks over. The knob turns easily in my hand.

We slip into the office. A small desk light illuminates the room just enough to see. Drew shuts the door and locks it.

"What are you doing?" I try to ignore the prickle at the back of my neck. It's normal to be nervous. Drew is harmless. He's here to help.

"Making sure no one comes in."

I don't waste any time on the loose papers on the credenza. I go straight to Mr. Moss's desk. The bottom drawer is locked. I kneel down and slip the bobby pin in the lock while Drew flips through the documents on the desk.

"What are we looking for?"

"The letterhead will say 'Caroline Fields.'"

"That's your mother, right?"

"Was." I'm not sure why it's important for me to correct him, but it is.

The lock under the desk is smaller, and it takes me longer to find the indentation inside the locking mechanism, but eventually I do. The door pops open as soon as the lock clicks.

My mom's letterhead sits right on top.

The air disappears from the room. I thought I was prepared to see it in person, but seeing her name in bold green font makes everything seem so real. She might be dead now, but she had lived. She had been a mother, a wife, a psychologist. She touched this paper.

My hands shake as I lift the pages out of the drawer. The letter is addressed to Michael Moss.

"What is it?" Drew kneels down next to me.

I shake my head as I fumble for the scanner in my small bag. I press pound, nine, nine and watch the face of the phone light up. I hold it over the letter, listening to it whir and click as it reads the first page in an instant.

Drew leans over my shoulder.

"Back off, okay?" My hands still shake as I flip through the pages and scan them as fast as I can. I catch a few words here and there. Enough to see it's some kind of report about a study she was doing involving some new drink.

It's just a work letter.

Mr. Moss may want to keep the information secret, but it's not me he's hiding it from. It's just work. So Mom worked for Mr. Moss before she died. That tells me exactly nothing about how she died.

I slide the letter back in the drawer exactly where I found it and click it shut.

"We should go." I don't bother keeping the disappointment from my voice.

"Wait a few minutes. You're upset." Drew puts his hand on my shoulder and lets his hand trail down my arm. "It's going to be okay. You need to know."

Needing to know and finding out are two very different things. "What if I never find out the truth?" The possibility is suffocating. "What if there's always this hole inside of me?"

Drew slides his hand down to my own. "Let me help you."

"How?"

He leans and rests his forehead against the top of my head. "Let me in."

I close my eyes. "I want to." I do. I want to let Drew hold me and tell me everything is going to be okay. But that's all. It's not fair to either of us when it's clear that Drew wants to take this somewhere I can never go. I am just not girlfriend material. "But I can't."

Drew doesn't move. "Give it time, okay? I'll wait."

"Until you move back to San Jose in December?" I mean for the words to hurt him, but it doesn't make them any less true.

He sighs into my hair. "Until you're ready."

The click of the lock on the door is soft, but unmistakable. "Someone's coming."

Drew grins. "I guess this means you have to kiss me."

It's our cover. Mr. Moss is going to think I'm some kind of boy-crazy kissing fiend. It's only slightly better than him finding out I'm spying on him.

I lean forward, but before I can touch my lips to Drew's, the door swings open and Tanner's voice fills the room. "Don't bother. I know why you're really here."

Chapter 24

I step away from Drew and clutch my purse behind my back instinctively as I move away from Mr. Moss's desk.

Tanner walks forward with his hands in his pockets. "Let me guess. Drew convinced you to help him get into Michael's office by telling you the information could save a lot of people. Sounds noble, but I bet he didn't tell you that his employer is planning to use the same information to create its own version of the drink."

"What are you talking about?" I wish this dress had pockets. I consider shoving the small purse down the V at the back of my dress, but the fabric clings to my skin and the purse will just look like an alien growing out of my spine.

Tanner stares at Drew. "You didn't tell her?"

I look between them. "Tell me what?"

Drew leans back on Mr. Moss's desk. He looks slightly amused that Tanner busted in on us. "Yes, tell her what?"

"Guess that's a no." Tanner holds his watch to his mouth and talks into it. "They're in Moss's office. Get in here."

"Is that like a walkie-talkie? Who are you talking to?"

Before Tanner can answer, Ryan comes into the room with Mary Chris close on his heels.

Mary Chris looks from Drew to me and back again. "What's going on? How did you get in here?"

Tanner's icy eyes zero in on Drew. "Ryan and I work for a corporate security firm. Someone broke into Moss Enterprises and stole some information a few months ago. They didn't get what they were after, but they got a taste, so we expect them to try again. It's not uncommon for an operative to try to get close to family members or their friends to get inside. We're here to make sure that doesn't happen."

"Make sure what doesn't happen?" I watch Tanner's face, but he gives nothing away. He looks so angry and perfect and better than the rest of us.

"Him." He points to Drew. "We're here to make sure no one uses you or Mary Chris to gain access to Moss's secrets."

"Are you kidding me?" Mary Chris backs up a step, wide-eyed. "Ryan?"

Ryan looks down at his sneakers. "We're trying to help."

Mare's face goes white. "You're here to spy on me?"

I want to kill them both. I've been trained better than to believe in coincidences, yet I've ignored them all because Tanner Halston and his stupid smile set me on tilt. Of course Tanner and Ryan didn't just happen to approach us at Sconehenge during my stakeout. They didn't randomly show up at McHenry and worm their way into Mary Chris's good graces. They didn't happen to be at the park last Saturday or nearby when Drew set up the meeting with Heather Marrone. They're here to spy on us.

Tanner's wearing a smug expression that makes it easy for me to remember why I hated him in the first place. "Let me get this straight. The reason you've tried to hang out with me is because you wanted to keep an eye on me?" I look over at Ryan, who won't look at any of us. "And you. Was this all a game to you?"

Ryan finally looks up. He looks terrified. "It's not like that."

Drew steps up beside me and puts his arm around my waist. "It's exactly like that. You two have been taking advantage of Mary Chris and her friends from day one, right?"

Mary Chris looks like she's going to throw up.

"We've been protecting them from people like you." Tanner finally takes his hands out of his pockets. They're balled into fists.

Drew laughs. "Thankfully, the make-out police are on the scene."

Tanner's face turns beet red. "Don't bother denying it. You sent Berry into this office last weekend to do your dirty work for you. And when that didn't work, you convinced her to break in for you. You're sick."

I shake my head violently. Tanner has it all wrong. "You just broke the number two rule of investigations. Never jump to conclusions. Haven't you ever heard of confirming your facts?"

For the first time since he came in the room, Tanner looks less than confident. "I was here, remember? You were snooping around for him. You used me as cover when Michael walked in."

Okay, it's weird that Tanner calls Mr. Moss "Michael." "Please tell me you're not some thirty-year-old pretending to be in high school."

Please tell me I didn't kiss some old guy and like it. "How old are you?"

"Eighteen."

At least there's that. "Well, super sleuth, guess again. Drew has nothing to do with this. Searching Mr. Moss's office was my idea."

A squeal comes from across the room. Mary Chris covers her mouth with her hands. Her eyes are huge. Hurt.

No.

This is not how I wanted Mary Chris to find out I am investigating her father.

Tanner looks confused, but I can't even enjoy being right. I need to try to explain and pray that Mare understands.

"I'm not trying to steal any corporate secrets," I start. "Mr. Moss has a letter from my mother. She died eight years ago in an accident that was ruled a suicide. I never even knew my mom did work for Moss Enterprises, but she did. Just before she died. I thought maybe the letter would tell me something more about her. I asked Drew to help. He was helping me. Not the other way around."

Drew puts his arm around me. "Sorry to disappoint you guys."

"What's behind your back?" Tanner tries to look over my shoulder, but I lean into Drew, blocking his view. He stares at me, holding out his hand.

I bring my hand around slowly, showing him the small handbag. "It's just my purse." I glance at Mare, pleading with my eyes. She knows I have the scanner.

Mary Chris looks down at the floor and then back up at Ryan. It's one thing to discover Tanner has been playing us, but she really likes Ryan.

And she loves me.

Tanner holds out his hand, and I give him the purse because it's not like I can just make a run for it.

"Didn't your mama ever teach you not to go snooping in a lady's pocketbook?" Drew asks.

Tanner's icy eyes focus on Drew, and for a second I worry that he might hit him. I've seen Tanner handle a gun. He knows a thing or two about hurting someone.

Drew wisely keeps his mouth shut as Tanner unzips the small bag and looks inside. He pulls out the bobby pin and sets it on the table. He takes out the cell phone and turns it over in his hand.

I look at Mary Chris, but she won't look at me.

I hold my breath for what seems like forever as Tanner flips on the phone. It's not that I'm afraid of being caught. I've already confessed to looking for the letter. But I can't bear to lose it before I've even had a chance to read it.

Rescue comes from an unexpected source. Ryan puts his hand on Tanner's shoulder. "Dude, let it go. I believe her."

Tanner looks at me. Looks through me. "I don't know what to believe."

"Try the truth." I hate that I have to defend myself to Tanner. He's no one but some hired rent-a-cop who couldn't figure his way out of a cardboard box. "Drew is my friend. He's here because I asked him to be."

Mary Chris finally steps forward. "You asked him to come here to spy on me?"

"Not you. Your dad." Okay, that doesn't sound good either.

Mary Chris takes the fake phone and the purse from Tanner. She drops the phone into the purse like she can't stand to touch it. She holds the purse out to me with two fingers. "I hope you got what you came for."

Is she giving me the scanner?

There are tears in her eyes and I realize Mare is asking me to make a choice. Take the scanner. The scanner that she made for me with the letter I stole from her father. Take it and leave.

Or give it back. Walk away from this whole thing and choose our friendship.

I stare at the little gold purse that Shauna and Jason picked out for me last weekend. Inside is a business letter. A letter that probably won't get me any closer to the truth about my mother's death. But it might get me closer to the truth about her life.

Mare still watches me, holding out the purse. Mare, who has never given up on me, even when she should have. Mary Chris, who never minded that I was the stray that never found a more permanent home. Who stayed with me through the darkness and accepted the stranger who came out on the other side.

I should be able to put my mother's death behind me. I thought I had.

The lives you think you're saving aren't worth your own.

But this is about more than whether my mother left me. Fields' rule number four: there are no coincidences. Death threat plus death equals murder.

I step forward and take the purse from Mary Chris. I don't miss the pain in her eyes. We both know I've chosen the letter over our friendship.

My fingers tighten around the bag.

There was never any real choice.

I made up my mind the second I came into Mary Chris's house last Friday with a plan to search her father's office.

I've already betrayed my best friend. The sick part is that I can't seem to stop.

Chapter 25

Mary Chris doesn't look at me as I walk out of the room. The skirt of my gown trails behind me, a river of crimson. Which is fitting considering all the blood that's been spilled.

I have to drive Drew to his car at the country club, so I don't have time to wallow.

I wait until we're safely out of the gate at the end of Mare's long driveway before I say anything. "I'm sorry I dragged you into all of this."

"Are you kidding? That was kind of awesome. So what were those guys? Corporate spies?"

I shake my head. "Don't sound so impressed. My guess is they're contract security detail. Not very good, considering they just blew their cover based on a hunch."

"I can't believe they thought I was some kind of spy. That's kind of cool."

I want to slam on the brakes and throw Drew out of the car. Doesn't he realize what any of this means? My best friend hates me.

The real Tanner is the guy who thinks I'm nothing amazing. The guy who was just hanging around to make sure I didn't betray my best friend. Which I did.

I take a deep breath. "Why did you offer to help me?"

"What?"

"Why did you offer to help me?" I'm getting paranoid. I shouldn't let Tanner get to me like this, but the truth is, now that I think about it, none of this makes any sense. Why would a guy who doesn't even like people go out of his way to help me find out about my mom? Why would he set up an interview with the woman who witnessed my mom's death without talking to me first? "Most people would just say, 'Yeah, you should totally look into it.' They wouldn't offer to help."

Drew smiles. "Are you kidding? I'm pretty sure that most guys would do pretty much anything if it meant they'd get to hang out with you."

Is he serious? Is this all some kind of game to him? My heart is already tangled up in loss, and this last bit with Mary Chris constricts the knot so tightly I barely breathe. "This matters to me." My whisper is barely audible.

"I know." Drew looks out the window. "I meant it when I said I'd help you find out what happened to your mom." We pull up to Drew's red hatchback, but he doesn't move to get out of the car. "Do you want me to follow you home? Someone should be there when you read the letter."

He's trying to help, but all I can think of is his line about hanging out with me, and I don't want to be alone with him tonight. "I'll be fine. You can come by tomorrow if you want."

Drew leans forward like he's going to kiss me, but I turn my head to the side at the last minute so his kiss lands squarely on my cheek. "Good night," he whispers against my skin. Then he gets out of the car and I'm finally alone.

It's a relief to pull into the garage of our quiet little house. Dad's car is gone. I try not to think about what Dad and Shauna might be doing in Palm Springs together. There should probably be some law about parents dating while their kids still live at home.

When I open the door from the garage into the house, it opens wide. Okay, this has never happened in the history of Lulu. I move down the hall to the alarm, which is not even flashing. Dad has never forgotten to arm the system. I take out my pepper spray, leaving the lights off.

"Lu," I whisper.

Slurp, slurp, clunk. The noise comes from the kitchen. Slurp, slurp, clunk. I tiptoe down the hall in the dark, peeking into my bedroom on the way, but it's still and quiet. I cross over to the living room, sprinting behind the couch to the archway that leads into the kitchen.

The slurping is louder now, wet and monstrous. A streetlight on the corner illuminates the floor through the sliding glass window. Lulu lies on her side, licking and slurping at something on the floor. I let out a breath and turn on the light.

Lulu lifts her head and tilts it toward me. There's a huge T-bone on the floor next to her, with tiny pieces of gristle and meat still attached to it. Her head flops back down in a puddle of drool as she goes back to licking and slurping at the bone.

SPIES *and* PREJUDICE

•

I pat her on the belly, but aside from lifting her paw to give me better access, she doesn't acknowledge me as she continues to slurp on the bone.

"Did Dad leave you some leftovers?" Maybe they went to dinner before making the drive to Palm Springs.

I start flipping on lights, first the living room, and then the hallway. Before I'm done, I've turned on every light in the house. It's silly. Dad works most nights so it's not like I'm afraid of being alone. Everything that's happened tonight has me on edge. I'm not used to getting caught.

I set the gold purse on the kitchen table and stare at it for a few minutes. My new best friend. I finally pull out the scanner, releasing the memory card from the phone shell and carrying it over to the desk in the living room.

There's just one problem. The desktop computer is gone.

I look back over at the alarm panel, and then back again at Lulu and her giant bone.

I reach for my pepper spray again. Someone broke into my house and took the desktop. I know the house is empty, but I check every room again anyway, my blood rushing in my ears. Everything is different, now that someone's been here. My home feels like a cage at the zoo, the windows blackened, but doing nothing to stop me from being aware of invisible eyes on the other side of the glass.

After searching the house a third time, I can't stand it anymore. I can't spend the night here alone. I consider calling Jason, but I'm sure he's still over at Mare's house. And she probably needs him more than I do. If he's even talking to me now.

I could call Drew, but he would get the wrong idea.

I can't call Dad. He already told me not to look into this. He'll be furious. Plus he's almost two hours away.

I could call the police, but they would just make a report and disappear again. And let's just say the police at my door is not an image I want to relive.

So I do something I regret almost immediately. I call Tanner.

Chapter 26

Tanner doesn't ask questions. He says he'll be right over, and fifteen minutes later he is. He's changed into a pair of jeans and a long-sleeved tee. I'm overdressed in my red gown, but it's not like I've been comfortable enough to change.

Tanner walks the perimeter in the front yard after he checks every room in the house again. He makes me stay in the house, relegated to watching him from the window while Lulu pants after him like she's his dog, nuzzling his hand whenever he stands still long enough. He searches the yard at least six times before he finally deems it clear.

It should make me feel better to know the thief is gone, but it doesn't. He's still out there somewhere. He could be anywhere, which is somehow scarier than if he were still here in the living room. At least then I could fight back.

Tanner comes inside, Lulu trailing behind him. "You're sure you're alright?"

"I guess. Just shaken up." An understatement. The more I think about the theft, the more wound up I get. I sit on the couch, my arms folded against my chest. Tanner is here in my living room and I need to fight with someone. "Why did you come?"

"You called me, remember?"

Fair enough. I'm still trying to wrap my head around exactly why I called him. He manipulated and used me. And Mare too. "How could you let Ryan use Mary Chris that way? Did you think she wouldn't help you?" Even as I ask the question, it leaves a sour taste in my mouth.

He raises his eyebrows. "Said the mouse to the rat."

"You were helping Mare's father." Not spying on him. "She would've helped you."

"The less people who know about what we're doing, the more effective we are."

"And now?"

Tanner shrugs. "Now we go back to Pemberley."

"Pemberley?"

"Our home."

"Your house has a name?"

"Our company. It's a family business." He looks up at the ceiling. "My parents are going to kill me for botching this one."

"You didn't exactly botch it. No one was trying to steal secrets from Moss Enterprises to begin with."

"Right."

"Wait. You still think I was trying to steal from Moss Enterprises?"

"Not you. Him."

"Him? You mean Drew? No way. Unlike some people, Drew didn't come looking for me. I found him."

"You found him?"

"In the back corridor of the library." Drew had been at school for weeks before I ran into him.

"And you were there because?"

"Because I go there sometimes." I leave it at that. He doesn't need to know about the dozens of times I've read the same newspaper article that I can't bring myself to print out.

"Exactly."

"Can we drop this?" Drew did not use me. Tanner did.

Tanner sighs and sits down on the couch next to me. "Any idea who did this?"

I look at the empty space on the desk where our computer used to be. "Could be one of our marks trying to destroy the evidence before we turn it over to his wife."

"You don't sound convinced."

"I'm not. Most of these guys are so flagrant I'd swear they want to get caught. And I can't think of any of them who would risk a theft like this."

"Who else might want your computer?"

I don't want to think about who else might want our computer, because there's only one person who comes to mind. The person who wrote the death threat to my mother. "I don't know."

"Where's your dad?"

"Palm Springs until Monday."

Tanner closes his eyes. With his eyes closed, Tanner looks deceptively innocent. Nice even. "I'm staying with you."

I don't argue with him. I can't handle being alone right now. I take a breath. "Okay."

He opens his eyes slowly, watching me. "Okay?"

The energy in the room changes in a heartbeat. The air around us is still and hot, so thick I choke on my own breath.

"On the couch," I say, trying desperately to clear my head. I already know how safe I feel in Tanner's arms. Having him here now is dangerous.

I don't move closer, but I don't get off the couch either. I realize my mistake too late. Tanner's hand comes up to my cheek, his thumb dropping just below my chin. My pulse thunders beneath his thumb. "It's late," I say. I mean for it to be an exit line, but it comes out like a purr, an invitation.

"Then I probably shouldn't do this," he says.

"Do what?" I whisper as Tanner leans closer.

"This," Tanner says against my lips.

His kiss is soft and tentative, asking. He pulls away, just a tiny bit, waiting for my answer. I don't hesitate. I close the distance between us and kiss him back, slowly at first, savoring every second this time.

His hand drops to my shoulder, sliding down my arm, pulling me the rest of the way to him. I loop my hands around his neck and bring him even closer.

Our kiss builds slowly, warming me from the inside out until every part of me is on fire.

Tanner's weight presses into me as we lay back on the couch. "We should stop," Tanner says, his breath ragged. His lips press against my ear and his tongue dances along the line of my jaw.

"Yes." But I'm not sure if I'm agreeing with him or urging him on.

SPIES *and* PREJUDICE

•

I kiss him again, harder and more insistent. His hand finds my knee and inches higher, tracing circles that brand my skin.

Just as his fingers reach my thigh, Tanner breaks the kiss and pushes himself up on his elbow, creating a distance between us. "We have to stop, Berry. This is against the rules."

"Whose rules?"

"Pemberley's." Tanner sits up and leans back against the couch. "Mine."

"You have rules about this?"

Tanner nods. "It's why I've been so annoyed with Ryan. He's been too close to Mary Chris from the start. It's a major distraction. The job has to come first. Always."

I prop myself on my elbows, suddenly cold. "The job? Is that what I am? A job?"

"Of course not. Protecting the formula is the job. You're the distraction."

"I'm the distraction?"

"I can't explain it. I mean I was supposed to get close to you. I just wasn't supposed to feel anything."

I sit up, pulling my skirt down around my ankles. "So you were just supposed to swoop in and string me along until your job was finished?"

"Something like that. It should've been easy. I mean you're only sixteen, and you were wearing those ridiculous glasses."

Is he seriously telling me how I was supposed to fall all over him so he could keep an eye on things for Mr. Moss? "Those ridiculous glasses take high-resolution photos from fifty feet away."

"Still ridiculous." Tanner runs his hand through his hair. "I don't get it. You're too young. Way too headstrong. So damaged."

I clutch my knees to my chest, setting my chin on the soft fabric. The pain that fills me is at once familiar and strange. Grief, I know well. This other thing is a different kind of heartbreak. I bite my lower lip, but it still trembles. "You think I'm damaged?"

"No. I mean yes. This is coming out all wrong." Tanner looks up at the ceiling, clenching his jaw. "You keep everyone at a distance, Berry. You don't even believe you can love someone."

His words hit me so hard that I have to fight back or risk getting beaten to death. "Maybe that's because I'm surrounded by ego-maniacs who don't need *distraction*."

My shot hits solidly. Tanner actually flinches. "Well, it did kind of ruin my first field mission. My parents think I'm a complete imbecile who's going to lose it whenever there's a halfway decent-looking girl around. All this time I've been on Ryan for Mary Chris and I'm the one who let things get too far. I should've been able to do this without feeling anything more than sorry for you."

"Right. How could you possibly feel anything but pity for some pathetic motherless child who doesn't even know how to properly swoon in the presence of your royal hotness."

"This isn't going right." He runs his hand through his hair again. "I'm trying to—just listen. I think—I know it's crazy." Tanner turns his head so his blue eyes meet mine. "I might be falling in love with you."

I spring to my feet so fast I almost trip over my skirt. "Don't bother. It's a complete waste of time. I can't love anyone, remember?

SPIES *and* PREJUDICE
•

And even if I could, I'm positive it wouldn't be a guy who thinks I'm only halfway decent and blames me for his own stupidity."

Tanner stands up to face me. We both just stand here, staring at the invisible wall between us. "I don't blame you, Berry." He looks down at the floor. "I blame myself."

At least now we can rule out the L word. "I might not know much about love. I might not even be capable of it. But you don't have to worry. You're not falling in love with me." I wait for him to meet my gaze. "I'm pretty sure it's not love if you have to beat yourself up over it."

Tanner doesn't say anything as I walk down the hall to my room. He lets me go.

Chapter 27

In the morning Tanner is gone. Lulu is curled up on the couch where he sat last night, her head resting on a blanket folded into a neat square. I scratch the soft spot behind Lu's ears, but she doesn't lift her head.

"Trust me, Lu, he's not worth pining over." Not that I can't relate. I spent most of the night trying to figure out how things got so far with Tanner that he could hurt me so easily.

I curl up on the other side of the blanket and rest my head next to Lulu's. There's a faint hint of cinnamon that's only tolerable because it's overpowered by Saint Bernard breath.

The worst part is that he was not exactly wrong about me. I can't pretend I'm not damaged. It's worse than that. I'm broken. I proved it last night when I took the scanner from Mary Chris.

I close my eyes and try to remember my mother. Not the professional photograph in the paper, or the picture of us at a wedding that hangs in my room, but the real her. The woman who helped me learn to read and made peanut butter and banana sandwiches every time I got a perfect score on my spelling test. The woman who drove me to judo class when all the other girls in my class were playing soccer or taking ballet. I try to remember, but there's nothing there but a vague image of a faceless woman in the place where my mother should be. How is it that I can remember what she did, and not remember what she looks like beyond a few faded pictures?

Lulu whines and sets her chin on my head.

"You would've liked her," I whisper.

I must fall asleep, because the doorbell wakes me. Lulu wags her tail like crazy at the front door, and I let myself think it's Mary Chris before I'm awake enough to remember that it won't be.

Jason stands dressed in a pair of skinny jeans and an oversized terry cloth bathrobe, holding a tray of coffee.

"What's with the jammies in the daytime, Hef?"

"It helps me get in character."

"What, no bunny slippers? 'Cause I'm pretty sure that Polonius was a fuzzy slipper kind of guy."

"Who isn't?" Jason holds the tray of coffee over his head while he makes his way past an overenthusiastic Lulu.

I reach for a cup. "Does this mean you don't hate me?"

"Hate you, no. But this is the part where I get to say I told you so."

"Like I could've asked Mary Chris to build me a scanner so I could snoop around her father's office."

"Just like." Jason sets his coffee on the table and grabs the other end of the rope toy hanging from Lulu's mouth. "My laptop's in the car if you want to see what you got."

"How do you know I don't have a computer?"

"Tanner told me about the break-in. Didn't he tell you? He asked me to hang out with you until your father gets back on Monday. I'm your bodyguard."

When did Tanner tell Jason about the break-in? "I don't need a bodyguard. But if I did, I think I'd go for someone who doesn't wear towels as outerwear."

"Says the girl who thinks throwing on a black hoodie is accessorizing." Jason pulls harder on the rope in Lulu's mouth. "I swore I wouldn't let you out of my sight, so you're stuck with me. I can't say no to that guy. His eyes are dreamy."

"You always were a sucker for a pretty face."

"The washboard abs don't hurt either."

"You've seen his abs?"

"Not in the technical sense, but it's implied. So how did the thief get in?"

"I'm not sure. The alarm was disarmed but not damaged. Lulu was plied with a porterhouse, and the only thing missing is the desktop. Whoever did this knew exactly what they were after. It was a surgical strike." Somehow that doesn't make me feel any safer.

"Anything on the computer you're worried about losing?"

"Most everything we have is backed up to an off-site server. We probably lost some recent work reports and photos. A bunch of personal drama that no one will care about except those involved."

"Not true. I'm always interested in personal drama." Jason finally pulls the rope toy from Lulu's mouth and tosses it down the

SPIES *and* PREJUDICE

•

165

hallway. Lulu trots after it. "So spill. I want details. Did he spend the night? It sounded like he spent the night."

"Don't get excited. He slept on the couch."

"You're killing me, Berry. I can't believe you let him spend the night and didn't make a move."

I feel my face flush.

"Oh my God! You totally did!"

"No!" Only because Tanner ended things when he did. Stupid, stupid girl. The wound is still too fresh to dwell on, but I do it anyway. "He called me damaged."

Jason understands immediately. He closes the distance between us and folds me in his arms. "I never liked him anyway."

"Liar," I say into his shoulder.

"Fine. I don't like him now."

"Thanks." I rest my head against the rough cloth of his robe. "Did you really wear this thing to Starbucks?"

"Drive-thru."

"The things you do for your art." I take a breath and let go of him. "Can I see that laptop you brought?"

Jason goes out to his car and comes back with his arms loaded with two backpacks and a computer bag.

"How long were you planning on staying?"

"What? One bag is clothes. The other is skin care. Stage makeup can do a lot of damage to the pores."

I take the computer bag from him and point him in the direction of my dad's room to unpack. I waste no time finding the memory card and popping it into the computer.

TALIA VANCE

•

The letter flashes on the screen, but I don't read it right away. Part of me wants to keep her out for a little longer. The ghost of my mother is not exactly a friendly ghost.

It's just a report on some sort of psychological testing of participants who were trying a new energy drink called Juiced that Moss was planning to launch. There's a boring summary of reactions to taste tests and colors, and some self-reported energy levels. Things don't get interesting until page five. A small percentage of participants began to behave erratically after a few weeks. At least two showed signs of psychosis, complete with hallucinations and paranoia. One became violent. The majority of the participants had no adverse side effects, but all showed signs of addiction after four weeks. My mom was going to recommend against final FDA approval.

Is that why someone wanted her dead? Because she discovered a problem with Juiced? *There are no coincidences.*

What had that woman told Mr. Moss in the parking lot when she gave him the letter? Now that they knew the product was real, they would come after it. Tanner and Ryan were here to protect the formula for Juiced.

The lives you think you're saving aren't worth your own.

Someone wanted Mom to stop her plans to go the FDA. And now someone wants the formula for Juiced.

Jason walks back in the living room. "What's first on the agenda? A stakeout of some poor sap who doesn't know his wife is on to him yet? A trip to the mall to get some color into your wardrobe? Spa day?"

I close the laptop. "Witness interview."

"Oooh. Sounds very *Cops and Lawyers.* Who are we interviewing?"

"Heather Marrone."

"Should I know who that is?"

"She told the police she saw my mother's accident."

Jason's eyes go wide. "For serious?"

"If you're not up for it, I can go alone."

"Nice try. Bodyguard, remember?"

"Fine. But lose the bathrobe."

Jason glances down at something on the table. "What's this?" He holds up a piece of paper with some handwriting scrawled across it.

"What?" I step forward.

"He left you a note!"

"Tanner?" Who leaves notes? There's a reason that people prefer e-mail and texting to leaving notes lying around. It's so messages don't fall into the wrong hands. Tanner really is terrible at the whole spy thing. Jason holds the note just out of reach. "There's this thing called privacy."

"Fine." Jason hands it to me. "But I expect you to tell me everything."

I stare at the handwriting, which is almost too perfect to belong to a guy. Homeschoolers must spend a lot of time on penmanship.

Berry,

> *I messed up everything and I'm sorry. I do blame myself, but not for the reasons you think.*

> *I meant it when I said that last night was the most fun I've had in a very long time. It was. I can't remember the last time I went out and just played like*

that. Maybe never. But when Drew showed up I lost it.
I couldn't stand the way he kept touching you in the
car. I wanted to clock the guy right there. And when
you followed him into Michael's office, I nearly did go
insane. All I could think about was how you kissed
me there.

I thought telling you the truth would make you
see through him. And maybe help you see me. Not just
my cover. It was stupid. I ended up blowing the entire
mission before we caught the guy with anything. Worse,
I hurt you.

I took Lulu for a walk. Jason will be here at ten. He
promised to stay with you until your father gets home.
Please be careful.

For the record, I don't believe for a second that
you can't love anyone. I said you don't believe you can.
There's a difference.

Tanner.

I stare at the words until they bleed together. Then I read them
again. Tanner botched his mission because of me. He's more of an
idiot than I thought.

I should shred the letter before Jason gets his hands on it again.
I can't explain why I fold it up and tuck it into the pocket of my jeans.

I can't explain why I read it again as soon as Jason goes into Dad's
room to change for our trip to Heather Marrone's house.

I can't explain why I wish for Tanner to be right about me.

Chapter 28

Heather Marrone is easy to find. A simple Internet search is all it takes to find her online beauty products store and a number to call for a free makeover with purchase. The woman in the pictures bears only a passing resemblance to the woman I met at Sconehenge. With her hair blown straight and a thick layer of makeup, she looks like someone who should be wearing tight sequined dresses and hanging on the arm of a game show host.

Jason comes out of the bedroom wearing a form-fitting jacket over his tee shirt.

"Is that my jacket?"

He spins in a circle. "What do you think?"

"I think you have to stop taking shots at my wardrobe choices."

"So I can wear it?"

"That depends. You up for a makeover?"

"Does Polonius have a solo in act three?"

"They're letting you sing?"

"I am SL-ain!" he bellows.

"You sing about being murdered?"

"While being murdered. It's a singing death scene. Cool, right? So are we going to Elizabeth Arden, or do you want to do one of those glamour things where they make your hair all giant and give you cat eyes?"

"Neither." I flip around the laptop so he can see the picture of Heather and her retouched white teeth.

"Yikes!"

"Will you come? It's in Lemon Grove."

"Only if you promise me that you will let me take your picture after."

"Promise."

Heather Marrone lives in a weathered house behind a Walmart. The grass has enough weeds that it probably can't be called a lawn anymore. An overweight tabby lifts its head as we walk up the steps to the front door, but doesn't make a move from its perch in the windowsill.

The door swings open before we can ring the bell. Heather takes one look at me and her face drops. "Do I know you?"

"We met for a few minutes at Sconehenge?"

"That's right. You're the daughter?"

I don't flinch. "So I am."

She looks from me to Jason. "Does this mean you're not going to get the makeovers? 'Cause I already broke the seals on the starter kits."

Jason steps forward. "We're definitely getting the makeovers."

Heather looks skeptical, but she opens the door the rest of the way and ushers us past a tired living room decorated in Salvation Army castoffs, except for a shiny black flat-screen television braced against the wall. We stop at a plastic table covered in a plastic tablecloth, with cosmetics laid out in perfect rows.

Heather's face is caked in layers of makeup that only partially mask her sallow skin and the dark shadows under her eyes. She was probably pretty once, but now she looks more like the living room furniture, faded and threadbare.

Jason sits down and immediately starts cataloging the skin care products. "Does this redness minimizer really work?"

Heather finally smiles, showing off tobacco-stained teeth. "Like magic."

I settle in next to Jason and let Heather go through her spiel about the importance of skin care and beauty at any age. Jason nods along with such enthusiasm that I half expect him to holler out an "amen" every now and then.

I let Heather slather my face in moisturizer and apply copious amounts of mascara while Jason oohs and ahhs over a particularly noxious smelling cleanser. I wait until she's almost done helping Jason with an exfoliating mask before I say anything. "Can you tell me about the man who paid you to say my mother drove off the bridge?"

Heather shrugs. "I already told your friend everything I remember. The guy picked me up at a bar near Miramar. I needed the money and I knew better than to ask any questions or to pay too much attention to details."

"What did he look like?"

"Cute enough. He wore a baseball cap, but I remember his eyes. They were baby blue. Like the sky."

Jason grins at me through his green mask. "Sounds like Dreamy."

"Tanner was ten. How old was the man you met?"

"Older than I ought to give the time of day, but like I said, he was nice to look at."

Okay, so Heather must've majored in vagueness in beauty school. Her knack for dancing around details probably made her the perfect fake witness. I keep trying. "How were you paid?"

"Cash. Up front. All I had to do was call the police the next day and tell them I saw the car go over. Easy peasy. And they found that car right where he said. No one asked any questions until your boyfriend started poking around."

"He's not my boyfriend. Wait. You were paid to talk to the police the day *before* the accident?" The implication of this grabs me by the shoulders and shakes me so hard my brain rattles. If someone knew about the accident in advance, Mom's death couldn't have been suicide. It couldn't have been an accident. If someone knew it was going to happen the night before, it means only one thing. My mother was murdered. "You have to go to the police. Tell them what really happened."

Heather sits up straight, every muscle in her body visibly tight. "That will be sixty bucks. Twenty more if you want the redness mini-mizer."

I don't get up. "The police think my mother killed herself because of what you told them. Don't you realize what this means? Someone knew my mother was going to die before it happened. Someone did this to her and let the police think she killed herself." Let Dad and me think she killed herself. "Please."

SPIES *and* PREJUDICE
•

"I already said too much."

I've lost what little trust I gained by letting her make me up like Little Miss Carnival Sideshow, but I press forward anyway. "Help me find who did this to her."

Heather stands up. "I don't need some cub trying to be a bear turning my life inside out. You got no idea what you're in for, but one thing's certain. This is nothing to do with me."

Jason peels the rest of the green mask from his face. "Maybe Ms. Marrone could agree to think about it for a little while?" His attempt to give us both an out is admirable but futile. I won't take no for an answer. Not on this.

"It doesn't matter." I lay three twenties on the table. "If you won't tell them, I will."

Heather might look weak, but she grabs my arm hard enough to make me gasp. "You can't! No one will believe you." I'm pretty sure Heather's face pales, but it's hard to tell under the thick coat of makeup. "You should go."

Jason pulls another twenty from his pocket. "Not without the minimizer."

Heather scoops bottles and tubes from the table and puts them in Jason's arms. "Take them all. Just get out of my house." She looks like a trapped animal, ready to bite first and ask questions later. We're not going to get anything else from her today. One more push and we'll be lucky to get out of this house in one piece.

"We're going," I say, grabbing Jason's sleeve and pushing him toward the door.

"Please," Heather says, her voice barely a whisper. "I know you miss your mama. But you're just a girl. You best not get involved."

I stop at the front door. "Why not?"

Heather stares at the floor. "If this guy really made your mama disappear, what makes you think any of y'all will be safe?"

"I don't." Aside from the fact that someone broke into my house last night, I'm pretty sure I stopped feeling safe the moment I found the note in my mother's storage locker. Who am I kidding? I stopped feeling safe the moment the policeman came to our front door to tell my dad that she drove off the Coronado Bridge. It's a relief to have an enemy besides her ghost. Even if he is just a nameless man with sky-blue eyes.

"What are you fixin' to do?" Heather's eyes flit back to the flat-screen television.

I follow her gaze to the giant screen, so out of place in the fading little room. Fields' rule number sixteen: never trust a paid witness. And this one's already proven she'll lie for cash.

"Ten thousand dollars to lie about witnessing the accident?" Someone's paid her much more recently. "How much to lie to me?"

At first Heather looks offended, but she quickly regroups. "Does it matter? You can't go running to the police telling tales, now can you?"

"I don't know. It seems like it was pretty easy for you."

"I'll deny it all." She folds her arms across her chest, more sure of herself now that she thinks I doubt her story about lying to the police. That's the part I believe. It doesn't explain why she's talking to me now.

A tube of concealer falls out from beneath the waistband of Jason's jacket as he reaches for the doorknob. "We should go."

I don't move. "Just one more thing. Who paid you this time?"

Heather flips her hair back over her shoulder and levels her eyes at me. "Ask your boyfriend."

Chapter 29

I don't slow down even though Jason is clutching the handle over the passenger door so hard that he's in danger of cutting off the circulation to his fingers. I can't believe I let myself get taken in by Drew's line about wanting to help me. I can't believe I let myself get taken.

Twice. First Tanner, now Drew.

I turn to Jason. "Tell me you haven't been hanging out with me since seventh grade as part of some devious scheme to get inside information on Mary Chris's dad."

Jason's gaze stays focused on the road. "I've actually been hanging out with you to find out your secret recipe for macaroni and cheese with those little hot dogs in it."

I floor the gas to get around a blue convertible. "I'll save you the trouble. You cut up the hot dogs and mix them in with the packet of flavoring. Satisfied?"

"Do you cook them before or after you cut them into little pieces?"

I bring the car back down to more normal speed. "I'm not giving all my secrets away."

SPIES *and* PREJUDICE

·

Jason finally lets go of the hand grab. "Then I guess I'll have to keep hanging out with you."

"That and you promised Tanner you'd be my bodyguard."

"I can't let Dreamy down. Where are we going anyway?"

"First, I'm going to throw myself on Mary Chris's mercy. Then I'm going to tell Drew off. I wish I were a guy so I could punch him in the teeth."

"That's never stopped you before."

"Maybe I've matured." If I don't count taking down Collin at the dance last night. I keep that part to myself.

"As your bodyguard, I'm going to step in here and say that maybe you should stop and think a bit before you go confront a suspected corporate spy and tell him off. I'm just saying."

Jason's kind of right, but not for the reason he thinks. If I confront Drew now, I'll have no chance of actually catching him in the act. Which is kind of my thing. "Fine. What are the chances of Mary Chris helping me nail the guy?"

Jason shakes his head. "Give her some time, okay?"

"So what am I supposed to do now? Just go home and sit around knowing the person who killed my mom is out there somewhere?"

"You could go to the police."

"You heard Heather. She won't back me up."

"Only one way to find out for sure."

"They'll call my dad." Not that I can leave Dad out of this anymore. He'll be angry when he finds out I've kept digging, but he'll understand once he hears the whole story. He'll want to catch the guy himself.

"You're awesome, Strawberry. But if what Heather said is true . . . I just think that maybe we should let the police handle it."

"You're my bodyguard, not my dad." I turn left at the next light anyway. I need to talk to the police. Just not for the reason Jason thinks.

Inside, the police station is a linoleum-themed horror, kind of a cross between a hospital and the DMV. We're shuffled from desk to desk, before being left alone in a sterile waiting room made only slightly more homey by the presence of plastic chairs and lukewarm coffee.

Jason turns up his nose as he takes a sip. "I thought cops were supposed to be coffee connoisseurs."

"And everything else on *Cops and Lawyers* is so realistic."

We're ushered back to a tiny conference room, while we wait for an investigator to come talk to us. The chairs are only slightly harder than the waiting room. It's like this place was designed to drive people away.

Finally, a large-framed policeman enters the room and sits across from us, straining the buttons on his khaki shirt. His thin blond hair is combed across the top, in a pointless effort to mask his expanding forehead. His name tag says "Officer K. Hickle."

"My shift is almost over so make this quick." Even the cops want out of this place.

"We're here to review the investigation files on the death of Carolyn Fields. She's the woman who drove off the Coronado Bridge eight years ago." I say it quickly, my attention focused on his shirt. I try not to look at his badge.

"I know the case." He leans forward, and the middle button of his shirt practically screams at the pressure. Grease stains dot the khaki fabric.

"Great. So just get us the files, and we'll let you get home to your double cheeseburger and fries." The badge. It's like a beacon in the fog, its shiny silver face calling to me. I look. And I immediately regret it.

The day my mom died was unremarkable. It wasn't until it started to get dark, and Mom hadn't come home, that things felt weird. Mary Chris and I were playing Scrabble over the Internet. She was winning. The doorbell rang and then the man with the badge came inside. I remember thinking the badge was pretty, the way the light from the foyer reflected off the silver face, and that I wanted one of my own. Then my father fell to his knees, and the man with the badge kept talking. I stared at the badge, focusing on the silver light, imagining it would transport me to another world. One where I would be safe. Where my mom would be safe. It didn't. It just kept on shining, mocking me.

The fluorescent lights dance in Officer's Hickle's badge until he crosses his arms across his chest, covering the silver. He probably means for his stance to be intimidating, but he's doing me a favor.

"We're not at liberty to disclose those files."

Okay, so he's one of those guys who thinks I'll believe whatever he says because he wears a uniform. Tell it to someone who respects authority. "There's this thing called the Freedom of Information Act. Perhaps you've heard of it. The case is closed so we won't be compromising any investigation. And it's been more than five years. I don't see the problem."

His lip twitches. "How old are you?"

"I'm a citizen. I'm entitled to request the reports."

He shakes his head. "You can request 'em. The files are in storage though. It will take a few weeks to get them back. I'll have Barb bring you the paperwork." He looks at me again. "You're the Fields girl, right?"

"I am."

"You might not like what you find."

"You know what's in the files?" Did he work on my mom's case? He does look dumb enough to conclude her death was a suicide on the vague words of an at-home beautician. "Then you should know my mother was murdered."

He looks resigned, and I can almost believe that he understands exactly what I'm getting at. "Never proven."

"You think she was killed too?"

He doesn't deny it. "Investigation's closed."

I keep pressing. "Why was it ruled a suicide?"

"Look. There was a witness. And there was nothing wrong with the car. In the end, the death threat was just a coincidence."

There are no coincidences. "What if I could prove the witness was lying?"

Hickle stands up, letting his arms fall to his side. Exposing the shiny silver badge. "If I was you I'd wait until you see the files before you get all up in arms about reopening the investigation."

"Why?"

He looks down at his feet and shakes his head. The seconds drag out before he finally raises his eyes again. " 'Cause I'm pretty sure you don't want to send your daddy to jail."

Chapter 30

I stand up to face Hickle, sending the plastic chair skittering across the gray linoleum. The sound barely registers as my head fills with white noise. "What are you talking about?"

Hickle waves me off. "I'm trying to tell you that you won't like what you find when you go digging through those files. I've already said too much."

Before I can say anything else, Hickle turns and walks out of the room.

Jason stands up and puts a hand on my shoulder. "We should go."

"He's lying. He's trying to bully me into backing down. He doesn't want me exposing his shoddy investigation."

Jason nods, but he's not a good enough actor to cover up the fact that he's not sure I'm right.

"You weren't there. Dad was devastated when she died." My knees tremble, and I have to grab the table to keep myself upright.

Jason puts his arms around me. "The police always think it's the husband, right? It's Death Investigation 101. They always look at the people closest first."

Whether he got this from some cheesy crime drama or not, I want to believe him. I need to. "Maybe."

"And they closed the file. That means they ruled him out as a suspect."

Except I know the suicide theory is wrong. And Dad was furious when he found out I knew about the death threat. Inside, everything is twisting.

I get that a murder investigation could be dangerous. I'm sure Dad doesn't want to think about Mom now that he has Shauna making goo-goo eyes at him. But what if the reason he wants me to back off is because he's hiding something?

I want to punch myself for even thinking it. I might not trust that Mom didn't leave us on purpose, but I've never doubted Dad's love for her. I saw how much he missed her. Still, there's no question that Dad has left out some very important details.

Jason rubs his hand on my back. "The guy Heather described was not your father."

He's right. The man that Heather described was not Dad. He wasn't Mary Chris's father either. He was someone else. "You know you're kind of brilliant for a bodyguard."

"Yeah, most people think we're all brawn."

"We need to get into Moss Enterprises. Find out who else was working on the Juiced launch."

Jason stands up straight. "You're kidding, right?"

"Drew will help us."

"Drew? What happened to telling him off?"

"He's helping me because he wants the formula, right? He'll keep helping me as long as he thinks it will get him closer to what he wants. And in the process he'll get me closer to what I want."

"What about Mary Chris?"

"I'll talk to her. This could clear both our fathers."

Jason shakes his head. "You're kind of smart for a girl who's about to do something really stupid."

I punch him lightly in the shoulder.

"Ow!"

Oops. Not so lightly. "Sorry. Are you in?"

"I have a bad feeling about this."

"The free makeup wasn't enough for you?"

He shrugs. "Throw in the jacket and you've got a deal."

"Done."

By the time we get to Mary Chris's house I have a plan all worked out. Thankfully, Mare's mom doesn't know any better than to let us in.

Mare sits on the couch in her family room, guitar controller in hand as she expertly works her way through a Green Day song. She grins at Jason, but her smile falls when she sees me behind him. I wave sheepishly.

She misses the next few bars of the song, and the life bar on the game starts flashing yellow and then red before timing out. She turns to Jason. "I don't want to talk to her."

"Just let me explain," I start.

Jason holds up his hand. "Here's the deal. You two are my best friends and I can't handle much more of this fighting. It's damaging to my psyche. Mary Chris, I know you're upset. I also know that Strawberry is really, really sorry. The sooner we put this behind us, the sooner I can get back on track to graduating high school without permanent psychological harm."

Mare sets down the guitar controller and sighs. "I'm listening."

I tell her everything. I start with the letterhead I saw her father take from the woman in the Sconehenge parking lot, take her through the death threat I found in my dad's storage unit, and explain about the participant study my mom was doing for Moss Enterprises on Juiced. By the time I tell her about Drew and the payoff to Heather Marrone, her shoulders slump forward in what I hope is surrender.

But when she looks at me her eyes are hard. "Why didn't you tell me this before? I would've helped you. Did you think I wouldn't?"

"I don't know. Maybe. I didn't know how your father was involved." I stare at the carpet. "But it turns out it's my father who might be."

"What are you talking about?"

I tell Mare about our visit to the police station. "We need to find the man who paid off Heather."

"We?" Mare shakes her head. "I can't believe you. You're supposed to be my friend. But you take advantage of my friendship to spy on my family behind my back. You used the scanner I made to do it. Then you come here to try to make up with me so that I'll help you with some crazy scheme to catch a guy who probably doesn't even exist."

"He exists." It's the only part of her statement I can contradict.

"According to the woman who claims to have been paid to talk to you in the first place."

Mare's right, of course. I can't be sure that Heather is telling the truth about the man who paid her off. Nothing is true just because I want it to be. I gave up on wishes years ago. But now I don't have to sit around and wish. I can find out the truth. "I need to know." I'm not sure how to describe the hole inside me, so I don't. I shouldn't have to explain. Mary Chris knows exactly how different I am from the girl I used to be.

Mary Chris closes her eyes and opens them again. This time the hurt I see in her face isn't her own. Somehow Mare's pity stings a thousand times more than her anger. "Maybe you should let it go. Nothing will change what happened. Don't let your obsession with something that happened eight years ago drive a wedge between the people you have left."

I feel like I've been slapped. I rub my cheek even though Mare is still seated on the couch several feet away. "Please, Mare. I need you to understand. This is important to me."

"I know how important it is to you, Berry. Important enough that you were willing to walk out of my life, if it meant you got to keep whatever you stole from my dad's office."

I have no answer. She's right.

"I can't help you. No one can. It won't bring her back. There's no fix for this."

Am I so broken that even my best friend is done trying to fix me? How many bridges can I burn before I end up all alone on my little island?

I run from the room, past Mare's mom, and out to my car. When Jason doesn't immediately follow, I drive away.

Tanner's words from last night are there again, seeping into my skin and taking up permanent residence.

Damaged. Damaged. Damaged.

Chapter 31

I drive in endless circles, past Sconehenge, past the park, past school, past Sconehenge again. I stop when I see Tanner and Ryan standing outside a beige sedan in the parking lot. They're arguing about something, and I want to get closer, but I don't want to be seen. It only seems fair, to spy on the spies.

After about ten minutes they finally get in the car. I know a thing or two about tailing a car. There's an art to it. Staying two to three cars back isn't always possible, and if you get too far behind you can get left at a light, but Tanner gets on the freeway and gives me plenty of cover as he heads north.

I can't let the car out of my sight, but even I have trouble concentrating on it. He may be a horrible spy, but the car is perfect. Nondescript and unremarkable. Not too new, and not too old, just another car on the road. It doesn't help that I'm still trying to process everything that's happened. Less than twenty-four hours ago, Tanner and I were playing miniature golf in our formal wear, pretending to be normal. What a crock.

Now at least I know that there's nothing left for me but uncovering the truth.

Tanner and Ryan veer off the freeway near a business park in Irvine. They pull into the parking lot of a five-story office building with no sign out front. There are ten or twelve cars in the parking lot even though it's a Saturday.

I park on the main road, watching as Ryan and Tanner unload suitcases from the trunk of the car and wheel them into the first-floor entrance. A uniformed guard holds the door open for them and then closes the door firmly behind them.

I get out of my car and walk around the building, a blue glass structure with sleek lines and an imposing steel frame. It's beautiful and sharp at the same time, standing apart from the smaller corporate buildings that surround it.

There's a lobby with a large front desk manned by two well-muscled men in black pants and matching yellow polo shirts. They have matching haircuts, cropped military close. Any doubt that these guys are meant to keep people like me out is resolved by the large guns hanging from their belts.

So walking in the front door is probably not an option.

I circle the building once, seeing nothing but my reflection off the blue glass. On the surface I still look reasonably put together, even with the thick layer of makeup, but if I look a little closer I can almost see the wheels coming off. It's a relief when I get to a stucco wall with no windows in the back.

I should go home. It's not like I really want to talk to Tanner. The sooner I forget last night the better. The sooner I forget him the better.

I'm nearly halfway across the parking lot when I see him.

Tanner stands by my car, leaning against the driver door. He waits for me to get across the street before he speaks. "Who's the stalker now?"

"Ha." One-syllable sarcasm is all I can muster at the moment. My heart is pounding in my ears. Tanner's hair sticks out in several directions at once, like he's been running his fingers through it all morning. I stuff my hands in my pockets so I'm not tempted to reach up and smooth it out. Or bury my hands in it and pull him closer.

"You should avoid changing lanes when you're following someone. It calls attention to your car."

"Double Ha." Three syllables. Better. I step closer before I can stop myself. It's like there's an invisible string that pulls me to him. I step to the side and lean my back against the car so I don't have to face him. "You work here?"

"You know I can't tell you that."

"So that's a yes."

Tanner laughs. I still love the sound of his laugh. I focus on what matters. He thinks I'm halfway decent and damaged.

"Why are you here?" Tanner asks.

I'm afraid of the answer. Technically, I'm here to find out if Tanner knows who might threaten my mom over an energy drink. I am not here so I can see him one last time. I am in no way here to hear him laugh. "The million-dollar question."

"Can I phone a friend?" he asks, rubbing the back of his neck with his palm.

"That would require having one."

He looks sideways at me. He looks hopeful. "I'd like to think I do."

"That's only because you've apparently got a thing for crazy girls. You'll come to your senses eventually."

"And you know this how?"

"Two years of trailing guys with poor judgment."

"Not all guys are like that."

"I know." I do. Near as I can tell, my dad was a good husband to my mom. He loved and cared about her. It only made things worse when she left us. I try to change the subject. "Mary Chris hates me now."

"I'm pretty sure she hates me too. She won't even talk to Ryan."

"How's Ryan?"

"He'll be fine. It's a job hazard."

So all that stuff about falling in love with me was just a hazard of the job? "You guys just disappear and leave the wreckage behind, while you move on to the next job?"

"I don't know how it works. I'm just trying to figure it out as I go."

"But the plan is to move on, right?"

He turns sideways, so his chest is nearly touching my shoulder. He's too close, but I don't move away. I'm frozen. Like those people who stall their car on the train tracks but make no move to get out of the car while the train bears down on them. I understand them completely. It's not that they want to get hit by the train. The hesitation comes from trying to get your brain to engage when every nerve in your body is flooded with adrenaline at once. It's pure panic.

Tanner's eyes search mine. "I thought that's what you wanted."

It is what I wanted. It's what I want. Isn't it? "Yes." The word slips from my tongue.

Tanner falls back against the car with such force that the car bounces. It's a bit like waking from a dream, this sudden crash back to reality.

"You were right about Drew."

"Did something happen?"

"Not like you think. I found out he paid the woman who witnessed my mom's accident to talk to me."

"I should've waited until I had something on him."

I throw him a bone. "I'll get something."

Tanner spins to face me. "No."

"What do you mean, no?" Does he seriously think he can tell me what to do? "You're not the only one who was trained to do this. I've got more than one botched mission behind me."

His watch buzzes on his hand. He brings his wrist to his mouth and talks into the face. "Tell her I'll be there in five minutes."

"Her?" I ask.

"My mom. I was expected for the debriefing ten minutes ago." He doesn't look happy at having to face his mom. "This isn't like spying on someone's boyfriend, Berry. These people are dangerous."

Spoken like someone who's never been caught holding a memory card that will destroy a man's family. "I can handle Drew Mattingly."

"You don't know that. And we still don't know who he works for."

"Then how do you know they're dangerous?"

"Because they're after something that can hurt a lot of people."

"The energy drink? It sounded like it worked like some kind of caffeine on steroids."

Tanner's jaw falls. "How do you know that?"

"Not the only one who was trained to do this?"

Tanner watches me, letting the silence grow in the hopes that I'll talk to fill it. It's a simple interrogation technique that's surprisingly effective. Unless the interrogee knows exactly what you're doing. I keep my lips firmly shut.

After a few seconds Tanner falls prey to his own attack of silence. "That stuff is potent, but the herb that's used is virtually undetectable."

"Okay, but wouldn't the side effects be pretty obvious once it got into the marketplace?"

"Not necessarily. Most people will only get a minor kick, like drinking a few cups of coffee. Only a few will have a violent reaction, and that will occur so gradually that it could be years, maybe decades, before anyone makes the connection with Juiced."

"So the product's destined to fail in the long run."

"But in the short run, it will sell like crazy. And a lot of people will be hurt along the way. Not just the people who go nuts. Their victims."

Why is he so sure it will sell? Then I remember what the letter said. "And it will sell like crazy because people will become addicted to it." The implications of my mom's letter are bigger than I thought. The drink may make a few people go crazy, but there is a reason someone might still want to get it to market. There's a reason someone might want my mother dead.

"You saw the letter."

"Busted."

Tanner pushes his hand through his hair so hard that it stands straight up.

"If it makes you feel any better, I'm pretty good at what I do."

"Yeah, no." His watch buzzes again. "I'm coming," he says into it.

"If it's so dangerous, why doesn't Moss just destroy the formula?"

"Maybe because he trusted my family to keep it safe."

I don't miss the fact that he uses past tense. "Are you in a lot of trouble?"

"I'm about to find out just how much. I might not be allowed back in the field until I'm twenty-one."

I shouldn't feel guilty. Tanner botched his mission all by himself. "Maybe you could go to college or something."

He shakes his head. "Probably not."

"Why not? You could major in mercenary studies."

Tanner bites his lower lip to keep from smiling. I try not to stare.

"I'll be okay. It's you I'm worried about. Which reminds me, where's your bodyguard?"

"I ditched him. Have you heard him sing?"

He nods. "Just lay off the Rockstar Hero and you'll be fine."

"He's got a song in the school play. There's no stopping him."

"Earplugs then. You shouldn't be home alone."

"I won't be." I don't add that it's because I'll be looking for a way inside Moss Enterprises.

"Do me a favor?" Tanner's face is so close that for a second I think he might kiss me. His eyes are half-closed and his lips part so slightly I might not notice if I weren't watching them so closely.

"What?" The word is strangled in my throat.

His watch buzzes again. His eyes fly open and he stands up.

straighter. He's still right next to me, but he feels a mile away. He reaches for his watch and hits a button without saying anything. He looks back at me. "Let this go. Please."

I step away from the car. Away from him. He has no idea that he's just asked me to do the one thing I can't ever do. "Drew won't hurt me."

Which is more than I can say about you.

Tanner puts his hands in his pockets and takes a step toward the office building across the street. "Just be careful."

"I know what I'm doing."

Tanner smiles. "You don't."

"Well, I'm not going to lose it over a guy and blow my cover before I have anything, if that's what you're worried about."

"That was low." He doesn't stop smiling.

"Have a nice life, Tanner Halston."

He lifts his chin and walks the rest of the way across the street. He starts jogging once he gets to the parking lot, running all the way to the office building. He moves unconsciously, in perfect strides that nearly float above the ground.

I wait until he disappears inside before I allow myself to close my eyes. I try to memorize the angles of his face and how they soften when he smiles. How he looked when I thought he might kiss me. I cling to the memories while I still have them. I know too well how good-bye can steal more than just the future.

Chapter 32

S aturday afternoon is always quiet at Sconehenge, but today the place looks positively vacant, with the wait staff outnumbering patrons by three to one. Since there are only three servers, I sit alone with my Diet Coke and manage to draw glares from all three of them for interrupting their social hour.

Drew shows up right on schedule, wearing an easy grin that doesn't look the slightest bit forced. Either he thinks I'm going to help him get exactly what he wants or he's really good at this. Probably both.

When I called him on the way back from Orange County, I tried to invite myself over to his place, but he immediately came up with a plausible reason I couldn't (his father was hosting a barbecue for all his new coworkers). Right. No way was I letting him into my house alone now, so I had him meet me here.

He takes a seat across from me. "Last night was kind of insane, right?" He has no idea just how insane it all turned out to be.

"Can we not talk about it?" I ask.

"Yeah, of course. Rumor is your friend Tanner already skipped out. I guess Mr. Moss rethought the whole high school security team." He laughs.

"How did you hear that?" I wonder if I would've caught Drew's slip, if I didn't already know what a snake he is. Probably. It's not like Drew has friends.

"I wanted to talk to him. It's not every day someone accuses you of being some kind of spy, right? Anyway, he's gone."

"So this rumor was started by who, you?"

"Right here, right now. How does it feel to be in on the ground floor?"

I can't help admiring the skill with which Drew weaves his lies. Quickly and with enough charm to make you gloss right over the holes.

"So what was in the letter?" His voice is perfectly modulated, with just the right mixture of idle curiosity and genuine interest.

I give him the details, even though I'm fairly certain he already knows. It's the same leaked letter that Pemberley recovered for Mr. Moss a few weeks ago.

"It sounds like a motive," he says.

"I've been thinking about that. If someone wanted my mom killed so they could get Juiced past the FDA, why isn't Juiced in stores?"

"Good point." Drew picks up a menu. "Maybe they're just waiting for the right time." The menu shakes in his hands.

Drew's words send a shiver down my spine. I assumed that I was wrong about Mr. Moss because the drink was shut down. But what if it wasn't? What if it was just postponed? What if Mr. Moss needs to keep his secret safe so he can release the product himself?

SPIES *and* PREJUDICE

•

I take a breath. "We need to get into Moss Enterprises."

Drew looks up from the menu. "How are we going to do that?"

"I don't know. But what if you're right? What if the formula for Juiced is still there? What if they're waiting for just the right moment to get it past the FDA?"

"What are you saying? That we steal the formula?"

Wow. Drew is really good at this. He plants the seed and then makes everything seem like it's my idea. He made me think I asked for his help, when he was pushing me to find out about my mom from the beginning. And now he gets me to suggest finding and stealing the formula he's here to get.

"I know it sounds crazy. I'll understand if you don't want to help."

Drew shakes his head. "I'm not letting you do this by yourself."

"Jason will help."

"Jason? He knows about this?" Drew looks genuinely concerned.

"He's my friend."

"I know. But isn't this kind of dangerous? I mean your mom might have gotten killed for knowing about Juiced."

I nearly choke on my soda. It hasn't occurred to me that I might've put Jason in danger by telling him about my mother's letter. It's all ancient history. Unless someone really does want to release the drink now. If so, the information is every bit as dangerous as it was when my mother first discovered it.

And I've just told the enemy that we know.

Chapter 33

J ason paces in the parking lot of Moss Enterprises. "I can't believe we're doing this."

"You can wait in the car if you want." I already tried to get Jason to stay home, but he insisted on coming.

"Oh no you don't. You've already bailed on me once today. Someone has to keep an eye on you."

"Drew will be with me."

"Hello, Drew is a two-faced fake, remember?"

"He wants the same thing I do."

"Until you find it."

"I'll figure it out." I can't let Drew leave with the formula, but I can't worry about that part now. I reach inside my messenger bag and finger my pepper spray.

A car turns into the lot, its lights illuminating Jason's white tee shirt.

"Put on the hoodie," I say.

Jason shrugs on the black jacket. The car parks farther up the lot. It's not Drew's hatchback. It's Mary Chris's Lexus.

Jason watches Mary Chris get out of the car and walk toward us purposefully. "We are so busted."

Mare's blonde hair is tied up uncharacteristically in a tight bun. "You guys weren't seriously going to try to break into my dad's company?"

I glare at Jason. "You told her?"

"Not exactly."

"Define not exactly."

Mare raises her palm. "It doesn't matter. Be glad he did. Don't you think it will be easier if the boss's daughter is with you?"

"You're coming with us?"

Mare takes a breath. "I've been thinking about what you told me all day. If your mom died because she was working for us, then I need to find out what happened as much as you do."

"It's not your dad, Mare. He hired Pemberley to keep the formula from getting into the wrong hands."

"It's not your dad either, Berry. I've known him since I was five. He couldn't have killed your mother. He would've died for her."

"Truce?" I hold out my pinky finger.

Mare clasps my finger with hers. "You can trust me with the truth."

"I know."

Drew's car finally pulls into the lot. He's dressed all in black, like an emo kid. He takes in the three of us. "We can't all go in. It's going to be hard enough for one or two of us."

Mary Chris holds up a key chain. "Unless one of us has the key."

"Mare, you can't. What if we get caught?"

"We'll tell them we came in to party."

TALIA VANCE

•

"You're kind of brilliant. Devious but brilliant."

Mary Chris takes us to a side door that leads to a corridor connecting two buildings. There's a large warehouse to our right, but we head down the hallway to the main office building. The hall is brightly lit with florescent tubes, even though the office is empty.

"Two security guards patrol the building and grounds, but they're stationed up front most of the night." Mary Chris leads us up some stairs and past a large conference room, before stopping at a set of double doors. "This is my dad's office. Anything sensitive is kept in here."

"How do we get in?" Drew gives the door a push, but it's locked. He looks at me. "What do you think? Can you pick a dead bolt?"

Mare rolls her eyes and dangles the key chain. She steps in front of Drew and tries a series of keys until one of them clicks into place and the latch turns. "Voilà!"

We step inside. Mare turns on a light switch as the door closes behind us. Mr. Moss's office is even larger than his home office. Two leather couches frame a huge abstract painting covered in blue and red splatters. To the right is a desk that curves around in an L-shape. The computer has two huge flat-screen monitors. There are neat stacks of documents in boxes labled "in" and "out." A bookshelf holds a series of business and marketing guides. Behind his desk is a poster-sized photo of Mary Chris and her mom, looking over the chair like angels.

Mare glances at the photo and then looks away. She's just let us into her dad's private sanctuary. She watches silently as Drew heads straight for the desk and flips on the computer monitor. The enemy is in the safe house.

I follow Drew and look over his shoulder as he tries a series of passwords without remembering to ask us for input. In his over-excitement, his hands fly over the keyboard. He forgets to pretend to be a high school student.

After about ten tries, Drew's brow creases. "I don't suppose you know your father's password too?"

Mary Chris shakes her head. "It's not the kind of thing he talks about over dinner."

Jason fingers a series of DVDs next to the flat screen. "Try *Close Encounters.*"

Drew looks up from the computer. "Nope."

"*Jaws? E.T.? Schindler's List?*"

"Stop with the Spielberg references." Drew looks at Mary Chris. "I need something concrete."

"Every DVD in this place is a Spielberg movie. Keep trying."

Drew taps something into the keyboard. "Nothing."

"*The Sugarland Express,*" Mare says quietly.

"What?" Drew looks at her expectantly.

"Spielberg's first movie."

"We're in!" Drew's face lights up as the monitor glows white and Mr. Moss's desktop flashes on one of the monitors.

Drew clicks on the document library and begins scanning through the files. "These are all encrypted."

Mary Chris steps forward. "Let me see." She leans over the desk and starts clacking away on the keyboard. Watching Mare hack into her father's computer system is too much. She thinks she's helping me, and she is, but I hate that she's helping Drew too. "What are we looking for exactly?"

"Something to do with an energy drink called Juiced." Drew watches the screen flash as Mare types in codes.

"This one!" Mare clicks on a file and a title flashes up on the screen. "Juiced Project—Closed Files."

Footsteps tap on the tile outside the door. "Shh!" I say. "Do you guys hear that?"

Everyone freezes. Drew reaches into his pocket and pulls out a thumb drive, casually inserting it into the computer and pushing a button. The files download with a whirr just as a key turns in the lock on the door.

Mare throws herself in Drew's lap.

Jason lies down on the couch and pretends to read the back of a DVD. I just stand there frozen, waiting for the train to come.

The door opens and a tall man with dark brown hair bursts through. At least I think his hair is brown, at the moment all I see is the gun in his hand.

Mary Chris laughs from Drew's lap. "Hi, Dave!"

The man, Dave, glances over at Mare, but the gun is still pointed squarely at my chest. "Mary Chris? What is this?"

"You know, it's not polite to hold a gun on my friend." Mary Chris looks completely calm.

Dave looks at the gun in his hand and sets it back in the holster on his waist. Now that the gun isn't aimed at my chest, I can finally look at his face. Dave is older than my father, but not much. He still has all his hair and a square face that probably looks good on camera but is kind of boxy in real life. I can't stop staring at his eyes.

Eyes as blue as the sky.

Chapter 34

He stares at Drew and Mary Chris draped across the chair. The monitor is black. When did Drew turn it off?

"What are you kids doing up here?" Dave walks toward the desk, where the papers are still stacked into neat little piles.

"What does it look like? We're having a party."

Dave crosses his arms. "You know you're not allowed in here."

"I won't tell if you won't." Mare raises her eyebrows. "I'm sure Daddy won't be happy to hear that a couple of high school kids snuck in right under the nose of his chief of security."

Chief of security. Blue Eyes is the chief of Moss's security? I step toward him. Part of me wants to throw myself on him and punch him until he's unconscious. Only the gun at his waist keeps me rooted to the floor.

"You have to leave." He addresses Mary Chris, but his eyes dart over to me, like he senses my barely contained threat.

Mare throws her head back and spins the chair around. "Party pooper." She's really convincing.

"If you leave now, I'll keep this between us." Blue Eyes waits as Mary Chris stands up and takes Drew's hand.

"Come on, guys."

Jason stands and comes beside me. "You okay?" he whispers.

"I think so." My left leg shakes with adrenaline. All I see is my mom's killer.

The four of us walk out of the office and wait while Blue Eyes locks the door. He follows us all the way out to the parking lot.

The gun is behind me. Did he use a gun to kill my mom before he pushed her car off the bridge? Was the gun that had been pointed at my chest the same gun? All at once I can see my mom clearly, not the one in the pictures, but her, her face frozen in fear as he holds the gun to her forehead.

I reach for the pepper spray in my messenger bag. "Hey, Dave," I say, taking a step toward him.

Jason catches my arm, holding it down before I can pull out the pepper spray. "Don't."

"Let go of my arm."

"I can't. I'm still your bodyguard."

Dave takes one last look over his shoulder and then jogs back to the office building with his hand on his holster. His jog is graceful for someone so big. I'm reminded of Tanner even though I've managed to avoid thinking of him since I left Orange County. My heart aches a little as I watch my mother's murderer disappear into the darkness, though whether it's for her or Tanner, I can't tell. Maybe both.

It's what happens when you love people.

They leave.

"Wow!" Mary Chris says. "That was close."

"You were amazing!" Jason gives Mare a hug. "You should consider trying out for *Hamlet*. Our Ophelia has really bad hair."

I turn to Drew. "Did you get anything?" I don't look away, daring him to deny it.

He pulls the thumb drive from his pocket and waves it at us with a grin. "Only one way to find out. Let's load up the laptop."

"Not here." Mare looks back to where Dave disappeared.

We pile into cars and head to my house, where at least we'll have some privacy.

Jason waits until we're halfway home before he asks me again if I'm okay.

I almost blow the question off, but I can't bring myself to do it. "I don't know. Dave fits the description perfectly of the guy who hired Heather Marrone to say my mom drove off the bridge. He still works for Moss. He's still going about his business like nothing happened."

Jason nods, but still doesn't say anything.

"Do you think Mare's dad knows?"

"No way."

"But if Dave wanted to release the drink, he could've just taken the formula himself. Why is he protecting it?"

"I don't know."

I can't stop picturing my mom with the gun at her forehead, imagining how scared she must have been.

"How did you know I was going to Mace him?"

Jason grins. "I've seen that move before. Just before you sprayed

Collin Waterson at Kennedy Patton's 'While the Parents Are Away' party in eighth grade."

"Why can't anyone let that die?"

"'Cause it was epic. Besides, beating him up at Homecoming is not exactly the kind of thing that will make people forget."

"You heard about that?"

"Collin might have told me."

"What? When?"

Jason blushes. "Sometime between the walk on the golf course and the make-out session."

"You and Collin?"

"What? He's sweet. He's just a little confused right now."

"No kidding."

"You have to promise to keep this super tip-top secret, okay? I don't think Collin is ready for the world to know."

"Tip-top secret. Got it."

"I mean it."

"I can keep secrets."

"No offense, Strawberry, but you're kind of known for exposing secrets."

Okay, so I have a reputation for beating guys up and revealing skeletons they'd rather keep buried. No wonder Tanner was the first guy to even try to kiss me. It's the way I thought I wanted things, but kissing turns out to be kind of amazing. At least kissing Tanner does.

I try to remember his face, just to see if I can. He's still there, but even now the sharp edges of his face are blurring.

As we pull into my driveway, I recalibrate. I have to focus on getting the thumb drive from Drew before he can copy it. I know how he'll play it. He'll get it uploaded on his laptop and let Mary Chris encrypt the files. Then he'll make a big show of giving me the thumb drive, but he'll already have saved everything to his computer.

Inside, I hand Drew Jason's laptop before he can get his own out of his computer bag.

"Thanks," he says, not appearing thrown at all.

I watch Drew watch Mare hacking through the files. I know the moment Mare gets the file open because Drew's lip curves into a sly smile. I'm seeing him for the first time, not his cover, but the guy who's here for one reason and one reason only. I know exactly how he feels right now, enjoying the little rush that comes the moment that you're going to get what you came for. He reaches for the keyboard but stops when Mare calls my name, as if he's just remembering that this is still my show.

I sit down at the keyboard and skim through the files. There's a lot of preliminary sales figures, marketing materials, and a national ad campaign, and some e-mails about the same. After a half hour, my eyes are blurring, but I stop on a document marked "confidential." I read through it and then read through it again. It's some kind of list, but I don't understand half the words on the page. "What is this?"

Mary Chris comes up behind me and reads the document. "It's a glucose-based formula. It looks like the base for the energy drink."

Drew looks over my shoulder. "Where's the rest?"

Mary Chris stares at him. "The rest of what?"

Drew lowers his voice. "If this is the base, what about the flavor and energy components?" Translation: where's the good stuff? Where's the part that makes people addicted?

Mare scans the page and flips through the rest of the documents in the electronic file. "There's a note here. Part two is its own file. Hang on." Mare freezes on a document and reads. "There's an identification code with a server address. Once we identify the server, we can trace the computer where the rest of the document is stored remotely. If these files are any indication we'll still have to get to the hard drive. The formula's kept on two separate machines for extra security."

Drew nods his head. "So we have to go back."

"We can't. Dave Preston will have the entire building on lockdown after our little party stunt." Mare goes back through the files I just skimmed. "There's nothing about your mother here."

I try not to be too disappointed. I don't know what I expected to find. Certainly not a memo detailing the plan to murder her and make it look like suicide. Still, it bothers me that only Drew gets what he wants. Not that I'm going to let that happen.

I take the thumb drive out of Jason's laptop and close my hand around it. Simple.

Drew stares at my hand, watching me cross the room to where Lulu lays stretched out on the floor snoring. "I need that back," he says, his voice so casual that I would never suspect how much he wants the files if I didn't already know better. "My English paper is on there."

"Oh." I look at the little black drive. "I can't ask you to take this. It might be dangerous. I'll e-mail your paper in the morning."

"Great," he smiles, and for a second, I think this was too easy. "Does this laptop have Scrivener?"

Jason shakes his head. "No."

Drew walks over to me and holds out his hand.

"We can download it," I counter, closing my hand back around the drive.

"No point risking viruses." Drew's eyes narrow as he waits.

Lulu lifts her head, suddenly awake. She blinks sleepy eyes up at Drew.

"Traced it!"

We both turn to look at Mary Chris.

"The other half of this file is on a computer in the north end of the warehouse." Mare's smiling, but I want to strangle her for telling Drew exactly where to find the rest of the formula.

Drew grins at me. "Genius."

My first instinct is to run. Lulu sits up, forming a canine wall between us.

Drew backs up a step. "Um, Berry, you might want to call off your dog."

I don't want to call off my dog. I think I want to sic my dog on him, even though as near as I can tell she's just panting and drooling. I'm not knocking it. Death by Saint Bernard drool would be a nasty way to go.

"What's going on?" Jason walks over to us, in full character as bodyguard, with his shoulders back and his neck stretched tall.

"Berry was just going to give me my English paper so I can finish my homework tomorrow." Drew's voice is strained.

Lulu growls and flashes her teeth. Whoa. She actually looks kind of Cujo-y.

"Not according to Lu," I say, trying to make a joke of it and failing miserably.

Drew backs up another few steps until Lu finally goes back to panting. I stay firmly behind her. He picks up his computer bag, and for a second I think he's given up. That he's going to leave.

He doesn't move toward the front door. Instead, he reaches in his bag and turns to face me.

For the second time tonight, I stare down the barrel of a gun.

Chapter 35

L ulu lays down at my feet, content now that Drew has retreated to the other end of the room. She's oblivious to the fact that the danger has increased exponentially.

"You brought a gun into my house?" I say it before I can stop to think that chastising the man with the gun might not be the best plan.

Drew looks nervous. "I don't want to hurt anyone. I just need the drive."

"Why?" I tighten my grip on the hard drive.

"You wouldn't believe me if I said I was trying to stop Moss from unleashing Juiced on the public, would you?"

"Put down the gun and I might be willing to listen."

"Can't. Give me the drive." His hands shake and the gun drops lower.

"You won't shoot me."

"Strawberry." Jason steps toward me. "Give him the drive."

Drew almost smiles. "I won't shoot you." He lowers the gun further. "I can't say the same about Cujo here."

My lip starts to tremble. "No."

Mary Chris closes the laptop. "Please. Give it to him."

I step around Lulu, putting myself between her and Drew's gun. I keep walking to Drew, closer and closer, until the gun is nearly touching my shirt. I hold out my palm, offering up the little black thumb drive.

Drew closes his fingers around it, his fingers brushing against my palm with such familiarity that I feel like a complete idiot. I trusted a stranger with my secrets. With Mare's. Drew opens his mouth to say something, but I hold up my hand to stop him. I glance at the gun between us, the cold weapon that says more than anything that could ever cross his lips.

When I look back at Drew, his eyes are wet. "I'm sorry," he mouths. Then he throws the computer bag over his shoulder and disappears out the front door.

Jason collapses on the couch.

"I can't believe he threatened Lulu." I go over and give her a big hug and a kiss on the nose. "Who threatens a dog?"

"Do you think the gun was real?" Mary Chris opens the laptop and starts punching some keys.

"Does it matter? He got the drive. I'm sorry, Mare. I shouldn't have included him. You did all the work. For what? So some corporate spy could get one step closer to stealing your dad's formula?"

Mare grins up from the computer. "What he got was the script for *Hamlet, the Musical*. Not worth all that drama if you ask me, but I'm not one to judge."

Jason sits up straight. "*Rock Opera*. And if that script gets posted online somewhere, I am a dead man."

I glance over Mare's shoulder. "How did you do it?"

Mare taps out a few more clicks on the keyboard. "I figured he'd try to get out of here with the file, so I erased the drive and loaded it with the script as soon as I got the files uploaded to the laptop."

"You couldn't have used my chemistry notes?" Jason still looks panicked.

Mare shakes her head. "Sorry. I just grabbed a file that was close to the right size. You only have like two pages of notes."

Part of me wants to jump up and down and hug Mary Chris, but the part that's just had a gun pointed at it for the second time today is less enthusiastic about this latest development. "He'll come back."

Mare looks up from the computer. "There's nothing left for him to get. I've deleted the file and ran an elliptical program to scrub the machine so there are no echoes of it on the hard drive. The only copy of that file is the one in my dad's office."

"He won't know that." I hate that I've put Mary Chris and Jason in danger. Because there's no question now that's what I've done. "And he knows where to find the second piece of the puzzle."

"About that." Mare pulls the pin that holds her bun in place, letting her hair fall around her shoulders. "I might have lied."

"What?" I have to hand to Mary Chris, she's good at this spy stuff.

"It is kept in another computer at Moss Enterprises, but it's nowhere near the warehouse."

"At your house?" I guess.

"Nope. The guardian keeps it closer."

Blue Eyes. "It's on Dave's computer?"

Mare nods. "That's what it looks like. There was a firewall a mile thick, and Dave is the only one who has the kind of information that would warrant that level of security."

"You're not sure?"

"Won't know for sure unless we get inside."

Mary Chris is thinking of going back into Moss Enterprises to hack Dave's computer? "You guys can't help me anymore. This is getting complicated."

"We're already in." Mary Chris reaches into the pocket of her jeans and hands me a folded piece of paper.

The paper is handwriting paper with one-inch lines and a dotted line in the middle like we used to use in first grade. Creases have left permanent marks in the paper. As I unfold it, I recognize the large block letters, slanted slightly to the right. The handwriting of a much younger me. "You still have this?"

She nods. "I figured it's about time I cashed it in."

The large handwriting at the top says "U. O. Me." Below it is a single sentence: "I talked your mom into getting a kitten for your birthday."

The U. O. Me was something that Mare invented in first grade after she got her mother to buy me an annual pass to Disneyland so I could go with her year-round. It blossomed into a friendly competition, each of us trying to outdo the other in breadth and scope so the other would have to come up with something as good or better in return. I helped Mare get Oscar, and the ball was in her court. But a new note never came.

"You didn't forget." I turn the paper over in my hand.

"I almost had your mom convinced that you should have a puppy." She doesn't have to say the rest. Two weeks after Mare's eighth birthday, my mother was dead. "I didn't know what to do . . . " Her voice trails. "After."

"I know." And I do. My heart had been ripped right out my chest and there was nothing anyone could do. Mare couldn't bring my mom back, and for a long time that's all I wanted. Then my dad disappeared into his bedroom, and I had to learn to shop and cook and keep what was left of our family alive. There was no time for games. "You don't owe me anything."

Mare smiles. "I won't after we find out what happened to your mom. And when we do, you're going to owe me big-time."

"I can't let you do this. It's your dad's company. That man, Dave, might be a murderer. And Drew, well, you saw the gun."

"You should know better than to think you can stop me. Besides, I kind of killed it tonight."

"Kind of?" Jason sits up on the couch. "You pretty much rocked it. Except for letting the *Hamlet* script out."

"We don't know what we'll find. Your dad—"

"Didn't kill anyone," Mare finishes. "Neither did yours. But there's only one way to know for sure. We prove it."

"I'm in," Jason says. "But I want a bigger role in the next heist."

"Fine, but no singing." I fold the note and stick in my pocket, right next to the one from Tanner.

My phone rings, but it's a number I don't recognize. I pick it up. Before I can say anything Drew's voice comes through so loud, I'm sure Mare and Jason hear every word. "Where is it?"

"Moss Enterprises. Mary Chris wiped the drive and the laptop."

"This isn't a game. I'm running out of time. You have one week."

"I don't work for you."

"It's not a request. Berry, if I don't get that formula, innocent people will die."

"Is that a threat?"

"You're in enough danger without me threatening you. What do you think happened to your mom, Berry? They killed her before she could get the truth out. I'm not going to let that happen again. We want the same thing. To stop whoever did this."

"That's where you're wrong. I want to put away the man who killed my mother. I don't care about some stupid energy drink."

"We can do both."

"You held a gun on me. You threatened my dog. If I ever see you again, you better run as fast as you can."

"You think Tanner's your friend?" Drew's voice is uncharacteristically hard. "He's protecting the information your mom was killed for trying to get out."

"You think this is about Tanner?"

"Isn't it?"

I hang up on him. I can't believe he tries to make this about Tanner. Tanner may have been here to spy, but I'm pretty sure he'd never pull a gun on me.

"Did you hear that?"

Jason nods. "So what's the plan? Are we going to get the second file?"

"Not for Drew." I set the phone on the table, wanting to put as much distance between it and me as I can. I keep seeing that gun. Pointed at me. Pointed at Lu.

"We'll get it for Berry." Mare reaches for my hand and squeezes it.

There's no talking Mare out of something when she sets her mind to it, so I don't bother trying. I take her hand and force out a smile.

Chapter 36

Mary Chris spends the rest of the weekend on the computer trying to break through Internet firewalls at Moss Enterprises. Jason howls and screeches his way through his death scene in the living room. Lulu stretches out on the couch and watches it all in between naps. I spend half my pathetic college fund to replace the desktop and get our software loaded. As far as I can tell, we're left alone.

I'm left alone.

In quiet moments when no one's looking, I try to remember Tanner's face. His laugh. The way his fingers left a trail of fire along my skin. I should be trying to forget, but the thought of forgetting him terrifies me more than the fact that he's somehow managed to work his way into my life. This is all wrong. I am not supposed to miss him.

At school on Monday, I go to the library. Drew's secret study room is empty. I suspected it would be, but it's a relief to know for sure.

The woman behind the periodical counter sets down her magazine and reaches for a box of disks. I don't do anything to stop her.

She hands me the CD from eight years ago, and I take it to the computer in the corner.

The ancient computer whirrs and grinds itself awake. I scroll down to the day of the accident. The pictures are right there where they always are, the article telling the same story. Woman drives off Coronado Bridge. I wait for my throat to close, but it doesn't. It's not panic or even sadness that grips me as I read the article, it's anger.

"I'll find who did this to you," I say to the woman in the picture.

And I will. I just need to find a way to do it that doesn't involve putting Mary Chris and Jason in harm's way.

Dad is home when I get back from school. He looks up from the monitor. "You want to explain what happened to our computer?"

"Virus." The lie comes too easily. It must run in the family. "Even the Geek Squad couldn't save it."

"I told you not to download anything without talking to me first. What was it? Some new text spoofing software? You know we can't approach marks under false pretenses."

I let the lecture slide right over me. I watch Dad's eyes. In his anger there's frustration, but no trace of violence. Dad is not a killer.

"Why do the police think you killed Mom?"

Dad's face changes in an instant. One second, he's stern father and the next he's deathly pale. "What?"

"The police think you had something to do with Mom's death. Is that why you didn't want me to look into it?"

The color is back in his cheeks tenfold. He clenches his fists. "I told you leave your mother's death alone. I told you that note had nothing to do with it. How dare you go behind my back? How dare you disobey—"

"I deserve to know the truth. I'm part of this family too. She was my mother. You have no right to keep me from finding out what happened."

"You're a child, Berry."

That might be the biggest lie of all. "I haven't been a child for a very long time."

Dad watches me, his eyes full of pity. Ah yes, the look. "I'm sorry."

Everyone's sorry. No one knows how to help me. I know how. The truth will set me free. "Tell me what happened. Please."

"If I do, will you promise to drop this?"

No way am I caving to parental extortion. I shake my head. "I can't. I think I know who killed her."

"What?"

"A man who works for Moss paid Heather Marrone to say she saw Mom drive off the bridge."

Dad shakes his head. "You can't trust a paid witness. Even if it were true, it wouldn't mean he killed her. He could have been just trying to keep the police from looking too closely at the company."

"He hired her the night before the accident, Dad. The man knew she was going to die before it happened."

"What?" Dad drops his head in his hands. He stays like that for at least a minute. It's not until I see his shoulders shake that I realize he's crying.

Even during that dark year, he never cried in front of me, but now it's getting to be a regular thing with us. I don't know what to do. I kneel on the floor beside him and put my hands on his knees. "Dad?"

When he looks up his eyes are red. "I'm sorry, honey."

"It's okay." It's not. Seeing my dad cry is horrible. It tears at my insides in a way that I didn't think was possible anymore, shredding up pieces that are buried so deep they should be untouchable.

He shakes his head. "You don't understand. I'm the one who wrote the note."

The note? The death threat? It's impossible. Dad was an insurance fraud investigator. He had nothing to do with Moss Enterprises. "I don't understand."

"There were rumors about the security team at Moss's company. Never confirmed, but they were known to make problems disappear. Your mom found out something that threatened the entire product line she was working on. She was a problem."

"She found out the drink was addictive."

"You know about that?"

"I saw Mom's report."

For a second I see something like pride in his eyes, but he covers it quickly. "She was just doing what they hired her to do, but her manager got upset and told her to keep the information to herself until he figured out the best way to handle it. When it looked like the product launch was going forward anyway, your mom threatened to go to the FDA herself."

"And they threatened her?"

"No. That's what worried me the most. I thought they might skip the threat and just wait to see if she kept their secret. Not that they would let her say anything."

"So you threatened her yourself?"

He looks away. "I was afraid. Your mother thought I was being paranoid. She was also stubborn. Like you. I thought if she understood the threat was real, she would drop it."

"But she didn't?"

"I thought she did. She was terrified. She thought they were going to hurt me. She thought they were going to hurt you. You were only eight. I felt awful, but I didn't think they would do anything as long as she kept quiet, and I thought the note would keep her quiet." He looks down at the floor. "I had no idea what I had done until it was too late."

"You didn't do anything. You were trying to protect her. You couldn't know they would still hurt her."

"They didn't hurt her, Berry. She killed herself. She killed herself before they could hurt one of us."

"No." I've spent the last eight years wanting to believe that her death was an accident, hating myself for not trusting that her death wasn't a suicide the way my father did. No wonder I couldn't believe him when he said she would never kill herself. It was all a lie.

"I'm sorry," he says again.

"Stop saying that!" I stand up on shaky legs. "She didn't leave us. If she was really like me, than she would've fought back."

"Either way, it's because I pushed her."

"How can you say that? Moss's chief of security knew she was going to die before it happened. He's the one who's responsible. He's the one who should pay."

"Stop." Dad stands up so we're back on even ground. "Revenge won't bring her back. And if anything happens to you, your mother will have died for nothing. I know you're growing up and I can't stop you from doing anything you set your mind to, but I'm asking you, Berry. Please. Leave this alone."

Traitor. She died for the truth. She died rather than risk the lives of countless people by allowing Juiced into the marketplace. How can Dad expect me to cower in the shadows and let this go? "Her death will mean nothing if we don't expose her murder. If she was willing to die for the truth, we owe it to her to get it out there."

"I can't lose both of you." Dad's voice is choked.

"You won't." I'm breaking the number nine rule of Fields Investigations. *No promises.*

"I never should've let you get so involved in my business."

"I don't think I gave you the choice."

Dad smiles for the first time since I walked in the door. "Your mother would be proud."

Of all the things my Dad says, this is the one that makes me cry.

Chapter 37

By Friday, Mare has gotten through the firewall to Dave's computer, but as she suspected, everything on the hard drive has an extra layer of security. We won't be able to access anything without going straight to the source.

My dad gives me some space, though it's not clear if he's letting me make my own decisions or just busy with work and Shauna. Either way, the effect is the same. We both need some time after our talk Monday.

Mare wants us to try to get into Moss Enterprises again on Saturday night. I agree, but only because I plan to be in and out of there long before. I don't have the mad skills needed to break through the cyber security, but I'm pretty sure I can get in and out with the computer itself. And if I can't, I'll be the only one on the line.

Jason slides into the seat next to me in chem. "Guess who might have a date tonight?"

"Tell me it's you and that you and Mary Chris have not been playing matchmaker again."

"I can't believe I'm saying this, Strawberry, but you might want to lay low for a little while. Your track record with guys hasn't been so solid."

"And yours is so great?" Collin won't even look at Jason. The side benefit is that Collin won't look at me either.

"It's looking up."

"So spill."

"Can't."

"I'm sworn to secrecy, remember?"

"Me too." Jason waggles his eyebrows.

"He talked to you?"

Jason grins so wide, I can count his teeth. He holds a finger to his lips.

I roll my eyes. "Just be careful." I'm not sure how I feel about Jason dating Collin. It's not just that I think Jason can do a whole lot better. It's the whole top secret thing. No matter how much people try to hide them, secrets have a way of getting out.

It's what I count on.

By the time, the last bell rings, I have a plan worked out for getting inside Moss Enterprises. It's risky, but it could work.

I spend the afternoon with Lulu at the dog park. She doesn't chase balls, but she enjoys chasing the dogs that do. I barely have time to shower and pack my messenger bag when the phone rings. I jump a little before I pick it up, but it's just Mary Chris.

"Hey," I say into the phone.

Mare's voice is a whisper. "Can you come over?"

I stare at my messenger bag, packed and ready to go. "Sorry. I've got a lot of homework to catch up on. I think I'm going to stay in tonight. Free myself up for tomorrow, right?" It's a terrible excuse. I've never had a problem doing homework at Mare's house.

"I don't think this can wait."

"You don't think what can wait?"

"The police are here. They just arrested my dad."

"For what?"

"Conspiracy to murder your mom."

"This is insane. I'll be right there."

I throw my bag over my shoulder and drive as fast as the four cylinders in my Camry will allow. Mary Chris stands on the front steps hugging herself.

"He didn't do it," she says.

"I know he didn't. Dave did."

"They arrested Dave too. I can't believe it. I mean, what if . . ."

"He didn't do it, okay? Do you have any idea why they arrested him now?"

"That beautician lady you talked to before. Heather?"

"Heather went to the police? Either I'm a lot more persuasive than I think I am or someone just wrote Heather Marrone a big check. Come on, let's go."

By the time we get to Heather Marrone's house it's after five. Mare is still too upset to get out of the car, so I go to the front door on my own.

Heather answers the door but doesn't open it all the way. "You? I have nothing to say to you. I did what you wanted. You'll get no more favors from me."

"What did you tell the police?"

"Why don't you ask them?"

"I'm asking you."

"Well then, you must be planning on buying some moisturizer. I have a case I need to unload."

I nod. At least my Christmas shopping for Jason will be done early.

Heather opens the door all the way and ushers me inside. "Five minutes."

"What happened?"

"I told them the truth. About the man who hired me. Like you wanted." She walks back to the kitchen, coming back with a cardboard box. "Eighty bucks for the lot. I suggest you get on your way."

I don't bite. "What else did you tell them?"

Heather's eyes dart to the floor and back. How did anyone believe a word this woman said? "What makes you think I told them anything else?"

Because they didn't just arrest the man who paid you off the first time. "I know you were paid again. Don't worry, I won't tell anyone. Just tell me what else you told the police."

"Nothing."

I stay silent watching her, waiting. It doesn't take long before she jumps in to fill the silence. "I just gave them a copy of some letter."

"Some letter?" There's only one letter that I know for certain Drew has. The letter from my mother to Mr. Moss. The same one that that woman handed Mr. Moss outside of Sconehenge. The letter that provides a motive for murder. "This wouldn't happen to be a letter from Caroline Fields to Michael Moss, would it? A letter that talks about some tests for a new drink?"

"Did your boyfriend talk? He swore no one would find out."

Bingo.

She's just admitted that Drew is the one who gave her the letter and paid her off. The question is, why? "For what it's worth, I'm glad you did it. Thanks."

"Oh." She sets the box on the counter. "I guess you don't need to buy this stuff if you don't want it."

I pull the last three twenties from my wallet. "Will you take sixty?"

She nods and hands me the cardboard box. At least now I know why the police might think Mr. Moss is involved. It's not like he's been ruled out. I'm not sure how to tell Mare that he's a legitimate suspect at this point.

When I get back to the car, I try to explain how the letter combined with Heather's statement is enough to raise questions about how much her dad knew. Even Dave Preston was working for Mare's dad when he paid Heather to lie about my mom's accident.

Mare shakes her head. "We can prove Dave acted alone, right? There has to be something in the files."

My phone buzzes in the cup holder between us. I start to turn it off when I see the number from last weekend. "It's Drew."

Mare nods for me to pick it up.

"Hello."

"You're welcome," Drew says into the phone line.

Okay, I guess he expects me to thank him for getting Heather to come forward with the evidence of my mom's murder, but somehow a thank-you doesn't seem appropriate here. A get-out-of-my-life seems appropriate, but I swallow it. "What do you want?"

"You know what I want." Drew sighs into the phone. "But since I'm pretty sure I blew my shot with you, I'll settle for the Juiced files. How's tonight? I have a feeling that the security team is going to be otherwise engaged."

"I'm not stealing anything for you."

"Not just for me. We'll turn what we find over to the FDA. You'll be finishing what your mother started."

I can't trust a word Drew Mattingly says. Still. If we're both going after these files tonight, it will be better to work with him than against him. "I'm in. It will have to be later. Midnight. Where do we meet?"

He gives me the address of a hotel. It's the same country club where we had our Homecoming Dance. Figures Drew couldn't just stay at one of the cheap hotels near the freeway.

Mary Chris stares at me in disbelief. "You can't be serious. If you think I'm letting that guy near those files—"

"Don't worry. I'm hoping we'll have backup." No way am I facing off with Drew alone.

"Jason? I know he was your bodyguard last weekend, but honestly, I don't think he's up for this."

"Not Jason. How would you feel about a little side trip to Orange County?"

"Orange County?" Her jaw drops when she realizes what I'm thinking. "No!"

"You don't think Ryan and Tanner will want the chance to take down Drew and save your dad's company?" Who doesn't want redemption? Tanner will help us. What concerns me more is how much I want him to.

"Is that what we're doing? Because I was just planning to hack into a hard drive and retrieve a few files that will prove that Dave Preston killed your mother."

I shrug. "Two birds."

"Technically, it's three."

"That's why you're the computer genius, and I'm the girl who lurks in shadows and takes pictures."

Mare laughs, and for the first time since her father got arrested, I think maybe we're going to be okay.

"Mare?"

"Yeah?"

"No matter what we find, promise me one thing."

"No promises. Rule number eight. Or is it nine?"

"This is important. No matter what happened with my mom, we're still friends, right?"

Mare sits up straight. "You think my dad had something to do with it?"

I've botched it. "I don't. But right now we don't know anything for sure. And I just want you to know that it doesn't matter. I love you no matter what."

Mare looks out the window. "It's easy to say now."

Obviously not. I don't miss the fact that Mare is not saying anything.

"I mean it."

"Stop worrying about things that will never happen and start worrying about what you're going to say to convince Tanner Halston to come back to Valle Vista and help us stop Drew."

Not so easy to say at all.

Chapter 38

It's dark when we get to Pemberley. The parking lot is a sea of beige and gray sedans, each trying to blend into the darkness and be less noticeable than the next.

This time I walk right to the front door, but it's locked up tight. Maybe they really do close at night, but judging from the cars in the lot, I'm guessing there are still a few people here. Security work is not a nine-to-five job.

We head back to the car, grabbing my messenger bag from the trunk.

"What now?" Mare asks.

"Plan B."

"There's a plan B?"

"There will be." We head back around the building, keeping behind a row of bushes that rim the grass. I could always throw a rock at the glass or something, but I want to avoid setting off every alarm in the place if I can help it.

I've almost circled the building when I see a window tilted open on the third floor of the south side. It's the first window next to the stucco wall in back.

"We're in."

Mare follows my gaze to the window. "Are you insane? We can't get up there."

"Not both of us. I'll go in, find Tanner, and then meet you at the metal fire door we passed a few minutes ago."

Mare looks skeptical. "Is there a plan C?"

I rifle through my messenger bag until I find a pair of strap-on foot spikes, and buckle them around my shoes. The matching set of hand picks clinks in the bottom of the large black bag. I ordered them with my birthday money in sixth grade. I haven't used them since Dad had to pay our homeowners association for the damage to the stucco walls on our house, but I got pretty good at scaling the wall before I got caught. Of course that was forty pounds, eight inches, and two B-cups ago. At least the straps are adjustable.

I make my way back around to the stucco wall. I pause, giving myself one last chance to change my mind.

Maybe Mare's right. Maybe there is a better way to get Tanner's attention than breaking into a mercenary security headquarters. But if they're going to leave a window open right next to the one wall on the building that's not glass and steel, how can I help but at least take a peek inside?

I punch the left hand claw into the wall above my head, hoping I miss a stud. The claw sinks into the stucco just fine, and when I give a test pull, it holds. I kick in a foot spike with the opposite foot and step up into it. So far so good. The key is to keep moving. If I hang for too long in any one spot, the stucco will give way under my weight. I move hand over foot, trying to remember to use my legs instead of my arms to keep me moving forward. It's harder than I thought it would be, but I force myself forward, if only because there's really no easy way down once you start climbing. Finally, I can grasp the top of the base of the open window and lean on it to support my weight. It's a struggle to pull myself the rest of the way up, but eventually I throw my waist across and balance in the ledge.

I'm expecting an office, but the window opens into a room that looks more like a hotel room. A huge bed draped in navy blue bedding takes up most of the room. A small antique desk sits near the window, cluttered with papers and sketchbooks. A notebook is open to a charcoal drawing of a dog, possibly a German shepherd.

Posters of huge waves dot the wall.

I wasn't expecting to break into someone's bedroom. It seems wrong. Not that breaking into a corporate agency is the best idea I've ever had, but sneaking into a stranger's bedroom was not part of the bargain. It could be Tanner's room. The thought sends a rush of heat along my spine.

Okay, I am not going to sneak into Tanner's bedroom. There's something pathetic and desperate about climbing in through his window when I haven't been invited. I might be desperate, but there has to be another way to get Tanner's attention.

I'm about to reach for the pick and make my way back down when Ryan walks into the room.

His mouth curves into an easy smile. "Dude! How did you get up here?"

"I kind of climbed."

Ryan laughs. "Awesome."

Even with most of my weight on the ledge, the stucco beneath my left foothold starts to give. "Mind if I come in?"

He darts over and pulls me the rest of the way in. "What are you doing here?"

"Looking for Tanner."

"This is so cool. Tanner is going to freak." He talks like I'm here to hang out, completely ignoring the fact that I crawled in through his third-story bedroom window. "And his mom is going to have a flipping cow when she finds out you're here."

"I don't want to get Tanner in any trouble." I realize that it's true.

"Oh! Is this some kind of secret rendezvous or something? I was hoping to take you on a tour."

Just like that? What kind of high-level security company is this?

Ryan looks out the window behind me, and it occurs to me that he might be hoping I didn't come alone.

"Mary Chris is waiting for me down at the fire door."

Ryan's eyes light up. "She's here? She's not still mad at me? I wanted to tell her everything from the beginning. Tanner insisted we do things by the book, but I was going to tell her. I promise."

"You don't have to explain to me."

"We really messed things up, huh?"

"We all did."

Ryan's easy smile is back. "Not you. I loved watching you shoot down Tanner at that restaurant. I still watch that video file when I need a laugh."

"Video?"

He nods. "We were wired with a live audio-video feed."

I think back to some of my more embarrassing moments with Tanner. How much was being broadcast on live feed back to Pemberley? The kiss in Mr. Moss's office? Did Ryan hear Tanner call me damaged?

I must look stricken, because Ryan immediately reacts. "Oh! Sorry, I forget that people don't always like being filmed. It was just a few times. That first meeting. A couple of times at Mary Chris's house."

I feel myself blush. I rush to change the subject away from the Berry and Tanner reality show. "Mary Chris is waiting. Can you let her in through the fire door?"

"Yes!" Ryan practically dives out of the room and into the hall. He pokes his head back in. "Wait here. I'll just go get her."

"Okay." I wave at the empty hallway. I move over to the desk and flip through the sketchbook. Ryan's a talented artist.

I sit on the edge of Ryan's bed and unstrap the climbing spikes from my shoes. I stand up abruptly when I hear someone coming down the hall. I look up, expecting to see Ryan, but it's Tanner's lean frame that fills the doorway.

"A security sensor went off outside your window. Probably a bird, but Mom—" He stops when he sees me. We both stand motionless. He's nothing like my memories. He's bigger, more present. Real. His blue eyes radiate heat. Had I ever really thought they were cold? Everything about him is sharper, too sharp to be truly beautiful, yet somehow the effect is disarming. Slowly, his lips curve into a smile that reaches inside of me and promises things that can't be true, but make my heart skip anyway. "You're not a bird."

"You're not Ryan."

"You saw Ryan?"

"He just went to let Mary Chris up the fire stairs. You were next on the list."

Tanner steps the rest of the way into the room. The rest of the way to me. I stand with my back to the bed, my knees touching the edge. Tanner stops just a few inches away. He's too close to be polite, yet much, much too far. "Did something happen?"

I have to concentrate to keep from falling back, but I can't step closer without touching Tanner. I'm much too aware of the bed behind me. "Define *something*." I can't begin to explain everything that's happened in the last week.

He doesn't say anything at first. He lifts a hand, and for a second I think he's reaching for me, but it falls to his side again. "I didn't think I'd see you again."

The truth. Tanner was never coming back for me.

It's nothing more than what I've always known, but a little piece of me grieves anyway. This was a mistake. I may have spent the last week trying to remember him, but Tanner Halston had been safely behind me. He had moved on too, content to bury whatever aberration attracted him to me in spite of my many faults. Still, I'm here now, opening a door that is best kept firmly shut. "I shouldn't have come."

"Probably not." He runs his hand through his hair, forcing it up at an unnatural angle. "I'm in enough trouble as it is."

Stupid, stupid, stupid girl. He doesn't want me here. I'm an embarrassment to him, the manifestation of his mistakes. I should be relieved. There's no question that I am weak where Tanner Halston is concerned, and I can't slip up if Tanner keeps his distance. So why does my heart twist around until I can't feel anything but pain?

He steps away from me just as Ryan and Mary Chris walk into the room.

"Surprise!" Ryan grins. He looks from Tanner to me. "What?"

Tanner doesn't acknowledge them. He keeps his eyes on me. "Why are you here?"

I finally move away from the bed. "We need help." I fill Tanner in on Drew's plan to steal the formula and Mare's father's arrest.

Tanner nods his head. "So we know when and where Drew will strike. We can bring him in and make sure he never gets the actual formula."

"And maybe find something to help Mare's dad in the process."

Tanner isn't fooled. "And find out what happened to your mom? Berry, Mare's father has access to whatever's in those files if he needs help. And there might not be anything else to find."

"If Dave Preston killed my mom without Mr. Moss knowing, Moss won't know about the files either. Dave is head of security. Moss trusts him."

Tanner's face pales. "What do you know about Dave Preston?"

"He's the man who paid Heather Marrone to lie about my mother's accident the night before. He knew my mother was going to die before it happened. He's the one who should be in jail right now."

Ryan raises his eyebrows and looks at Tanner.

Tanner shakes his head. "There's got to be another explanation. Dave Preston isn't a murderer."

"You don't know that."

"I'm pretty sure," Tanner says. "I've known him all my life. He's my father."

Chapter 39

Dave Preston is Tanner's father? Now that he says it, I see the resemblance. Not just the eyes, but the strong jaw and the lack of identifiable social skills. "Your father is Moss's head of security?"

"I told you that we worked for Moss Enterprises."

"You failed to mention that your family has been under Moss's thumb for over eight years."

"Under Moss's thumb?" Mary Chris steps forward. "What's that supposed to mean?"

I stare at my best friend and I realize that she was right to avoid making promises that can't be kept. The anger that spills out of me may be primarily directed at their fathers, but the speed with which Tanner and Mary Chris leap to their dads' defense makes it impossible to separate my feelings into neat little boxes.

"I want to believe that your father is innocent, Mare. I've known him since I was five. He took me to Disneyland fifteen times in the first grade. He paid for me to go on the sixth-grade camping trip when my dad couldn't afford it. But the police have him in custody for a reason. My mom threatened to blow the whistle on one of your dad's products, and a few weeks later she turned up dead." I turn on Tanner. "And your father knew it was going to happen. How do you explain that?"

Tanner swallows. "I can't. But there has to be an explanation."

The wall between us is back in place, every brick sealed tight with mortar and bitterness. I can breathe for the first time since Tanner walked into Ryan's bedroom. "Fine. Let's do this."

Tanner buzzes someone on his watch. "Meet me in the conference room in five." He nods at Ryan. "Can you take them down to gear up? I need to talk to Mom."

Ryan grins at Mary Chris. "Follow me."

He leads us down a bare hallway that looks like a hotel corridor, except for the security cameras placed every few feet that follow our movement. Ryan ignores them, but I can't resist waving at whoever is monitoring us from the other side. Ryan scans a laminated badge in front of the elevator before pressing the button.

The elevator has eight buttons even though the building's only five stories tall. "Where do all these go?"

"I'm pretty sure I can't tell you. But don't worry. I'll show you." He presses the bottom button.

The elevator goes down, beeping through six floors until it finally stops on the bottom. The doors open to an empty concrete room that's not much bigger than the elevator. There's a huge steel door in front of us with a computer panel to the left.

"Welcome to Pemberley." Ryan holds his hand up to a scanner that reads his palm before the door slides back into the wall.

"Holy cave lair, Batman," Mary Chris says as we walk into a large room that looks like something out of NASA. There are rows of flat screens on the walls, broadcasting silent scenes. A group of men eating dinner at a fancy restaurant, a girl writing in a notebook at a desk, an empty alleyway. Two women in headphones sit at computer screens and manipulate the images on the main screen.

"This is the surveillance room. We can monitor the transmissions from our operatives twenty-four hours a day." Ryan wrinkles his forehead. "When we remember to gear up and go live."

"Those are live feeds? What kind of cameras do you use?" Mary Chris walks up to one of the monitors.

Seriously, the resolution is amazing considering the cameras are probably hidden in their clothing.

"I'll show you." Ryan leads us out through another door that requires a hand scan before it opens with a beep.

We step into a small warehouse, filled with rows and rows of shelves, each one overflowing with electronics, gadgets, weapons, and—accessories? I pick up a delicate tennis bracelet with a row of alternating emeralds and diamonds. "Are these real?"

Ryan laughs. "Of course not. They're hollowed out and filled with explosives."

Whoops. I set the bracelet down with decidedly more care than I picked it up.

Ryan leads us around the corner to another shelf. "These are the cameras you saw broadcasting in the surveillance room." He holds up a small round lens with a wire that attaches to a small transmission box behind it, and passes it to Mary Chris. "It's a button camera.

The lens slips over a standard shirt button and the box snaps behind. Pretty cool, huh?"

"It's so small." Mary Chris admires the lens. "It's lighter than the system I used for the spyglasses, and it streams live video. What else do you have?"

Ryan walks past a row of cell phones and stops at some pens. "Check this out."

I take the cap off the pen. It's just a pen. I scrawl it across my hand, leaving a line of blue ink. "What about it?"

He takes it from me and unscrews the bottom, revealing a hidden flash drive. "Wait." He unscrews the flash drive from the base, and beneath it is a small vial of powder.

"What is that?"

"Sleeping powder. Comes in handy when you want some uninterrupted computer access."

"Cool." Mary Chris grins at Ryan.

I walk toward a shelf full of listening devices, suddenly in need of some space. Mare and Ryan are so easy together. I'm happy for her, but maybe just a little bit jealous too.

I pick up a pair of earbuds. I guarantee these work better than the receiver I got online.

Ryan follows me. "You know Tanner likes you, right?"

I laugh before I can stop myself. "Trust me. He doesn't." He might have, once, but he's over it.

Ryan raises his eyebrows. "If you say so. You know he's never really had a girlfriend."

"What?"

"I just think you should give him some slack is all."

"I don't hate your brother."

Ryan grins. "That's what I thought."

"Nothing's going on with us." As I look around this room, the truth is impossible to ignore. "I'm just a mark. Tanner was doing his job."

"Marks don't usually get the grand tour."

"I'm guessing they don't usually break into your bedroom and accuse Tanner's father of murder either."

Ryan looks hurt. I want to take back the comment, but it's already out there, putting distance between us.

Ryan blinks. "We don't hurt people."

"I don't think your brother got that memo." Did I just admit that Tanner hurt me? I turn down another aisle, putting some distance between me and Ryan.

I lose my sense of direction as I round another corner. I stop before an array of firearms, ranging from pistols so small they could fit in the front pocket of my jeans to automatic rifles. I back away instinctively. If they don't hurt people, what are these for? The image of my mother sitting in an empty room with a gun at her head is back. Only this time it's Drew holding the gun. It's Drew pulling the trigger. It should be Dave Preston on the other end of the gun. Dave is involved in Mom's murder.

Voices carry through a wall up ahead. I can't make out any words, but I recognize the low thrum of Tanner's voice. I'm still holding the earbuds I found on the shelf, and I arrange them in my ears. At first, all I hear is the clatter of something that Mary Chris drops a few rows over. Then I hear voices.

A woman is talking. Her voice is familiar. "This better work. We'll be lucky if your father still has a job when Michael gets out of jail." It must be Tanner's mom. I'm sure I've heard her voice, but I can't place it.

"They're counting on the distraction of Moss's arrest to get access to the file," Tanner says. "This is our chance to catch Drew in the act and find out who's after the formula."

"That's what you said three weeks ago." Tanner's mom's voice is cold. She doesn't sound happy. "If I let you do this, you understand that failure is not an option. If those files end up in anyone's hands but ours or Michael's, everything we've worked for is over. You shouldn't bother coming home."

I recognize her voice now. It's the woman who met Mr. Moss outside Sconehenge. The woman who gave him the letter from my mother.

"I won't fail." Tanner sounds confident on the surface, but I can hear the way his breath quickens.

"And the Fields girl?"

"What about her?" Tanner's voice is hard. Is he defending me to his mom?

"She can't see those files. Ever."

There's a pause before Tanner answers. "She won't."

What? It shouldn't surprise me that Tanner is going to try to protect what's in those files. Especially if it involves his dad. But they're talking like the files need to stay away from me in particular.

The woman's voice is softer now. "Good. You've trained for this all your life. I'm trusting you to do this right. Do not let that girl interfere again."

I don't hear Tanner's response. Ryan walks down the aisle, prompting me to pull the earbuds out of my ears in a hurry. He hands me a watch like the one Tanner wears. "The watch has a shortwave radio that will keep you in radio communication with us." He fits a new earpiece in my right ear.

I don't say anything. My mind is still reeling from the conversation I overheard between Tanner and his mother. I know Tanner wants to catch Drew, and I'm happy to help him do it. But he still wants to keep me from the documents? There's only one thing I can think of that Tanner's family can't let me see: proof of my mother's murder.

Ryan outfits me with a button-cam, explaining again how the watch and earpiece work. He will monitor what we hear, so we're not distracted while we're engaged with the mark, shutting off our access to each other whenever he thinks it's necessary.

I hope Ryan doesn't notice that I'm shaking.

Tanner knows what happened to my mother.

He's not my boyfriend. He's not really even my friend. He's a spy who tried to get close to me to protect Moss's secrets. To protect his family's secrets. What makes me think I can trust him with anything? The fact that he makes my heart race?

I am such an idiot.

It's not like Tanner gave me any reason to trust him in the first place. But I was suckered in anyway.

That's the trouble with being damaged. It takes so little to break completely.

Mary Chris rounds the corner with Tanner close behind. Tanner doesn't meet my gaze as he unbuttons his shirt to install his own cam. At least he doesn't try to fake like everything's okay.

"What about weapons?" I ask, trying again to focus on the mission. Tanner is going to help me get to those files whether he knows it or not.

Tanner answers. "You're not certified to carry a weapon."

"Not true. I'm licensed to carry pepper spray. And I've got a brown belt in judo."

"Not black?"

"I might've gotten kicked out of the dojo after I beat up Mark Holberg in the sixth grade."

"I'm sure he deserved it," Tanner says dryly.

"He made fun of Mare."

Mary Chris laughs. "I'm pretty sure it was just his way of flirting."

"Dude, good for you." Ryan runs a camera through his own shirt. "Deserved. It."

Mare reaches out and punches Ryan in the shoulder, still smiling.

Ryan sticks a tiny earbud in Mare's ear before he looks back at me. "You have any training with knives?"

Tanner's camera is in place and he buttons his shirt back over his abs. Jason will be glad to know that he wasn't far off in his speculation about Tanner's physique. Tanner finally looks at me. "No knives. They can be used against you if you don't know what you're doing."

I plead to Ryan with my eyes. I don't want to face Drew without something to protect myself. A knife is no protection against a gun, but it's better than nothing. "I can handle it."

Ryan grins and tilts his head toward the back of the room. I follow him past a few shelves until we reach a row of knives of every size and shape. He holds up a curved blade with jagged edges. "I trust you'll know what to do with this."

"What's there to know? Point and slash. Got it." He hands me a holster that straps around my stomach. I strap the blade on and pull my shirt over it.

Ryan points to the camera on the button of my shirt. "Don't forget. I've got your back, but I can only see what's in the lens, so try not to cover it up."

"I'll try."

"Oh, I almost forgot." Ryan slips a green-and-white bracelet around my bare wrist. "The fuse is on the clasp. Just unclasp it and light the thick end. You'll have about twenty seconds from ignition to a small caliber explosion. It's good for getting through locked doors, that kind of thing."

"Are you sure you should be giving me this?"

"It's standard issue. We'll tell Tanner that's what we went to get. The knife will be our secret."

I like having a secret to keep from Tanner. If it doesn't make us even, it at least makes me feel back in control.

I might be desperate. But I'm going to do this on my terms.

Chapter 40

We pile into a black minivan that's outfitted with a mini-communications station, complete with laptops, flat screens, and satellite phones. Tanner and I sit in the back to review a schemata of the hotel where Drew is staying, while Mare and Ryan discuss the software capabilities of the satellite program from the front.

"You don't have to do this." I hear Tanner in stereo, here in the car and also in the little speaker in my ear. Like he's literally inside my head. "Drew's going to try to get those files tonight with or without your help."

And if I'm not there, there's no danger of my seeing those files. Thanks for the concern, buddy. "I need to do this."

"Okay." Tanner's voice is in my head again, a low thrum that travels under my skin. "How long have you been working for your dad?"

I think back to when it started. I went with him on stakeouts from the time he started taking on contract jobs, in the backseat of his car with a blanket and pillow and a DVD. In the daytime, he'd take me to restaurants, the park, hotels, wherever our mark went. I was great cover, and I loved every minute of it.

"Nine," I say. "Eleven when Dad first put a camera in my hands. Fourteen before I got my own assignments. How about you? When did you start training to do this?"

"Pretty much since I could walk and talk. Some kids got puzzles as toys, I got codes to break. I've been trained in weapons, covert ops, undercover work, and interrogation techniques."

"But no dancing."

"And no mini-golf." Tanner reaches for a monitor above his head and flips a switch, lighting up the west side of the hotel. "Drew's room will be right here."

I do my best to memorize the layout of the hotel grounds. "What does your mom do?"

"She's more of a public relations guru."

"Tanner." Ryan's voice is in my ear, and I almost jump out of the car seat and into Tanner's lap, but stop myself by grabbing the armrest instead. "You know the rules."

"Jesus, Ryan." Tanner smiles at me from across the car. Not his behold-how-gorgeous-I-am smile, but a smaller, more intimate one that makes my heart flip over in my chest. "I always forget he's there."

I have to force myself not to smile back. I can't let myself forget that Tanner and I are not on the same side.

"You already know too much." Tanner's eyes meet mine.

He has no idea.

Mary Chris interrupts from the front seat. "We've got live satellite feed of the hotel." Mare is in her element, surrounded by all this high-tech equipment. "Looks like Drew just left."

Tanner turns back toward the front of the car. "Maybe I can get a look around his room before he gets back. Find out who he's working with."

"I'll do it," I say too quickly. I'm not letting Tanner keep any more secrets from me.

Tanner rubs his hand over his eyes. When he finally looks at me, his eyes are pained. "I can't let you do that."

The van is silent. The silence stretches, and after a minute, I think no one is going to say anything. Then Tanner's voice is there, in the car and in my ear, so soft it's almost an echo. "If anything bad were to happen . . ."

"I've got news for you, Tanner Halston, Preston, whatever your name really is. Something bad already happened. My mom is dead."

Tanner closes his eyes and leans back in his seat. "Berry," he starts to say, but Ryan interrupts him.

"Dude."

Tanner turns to me, his face a mixture of sadness and something else. I can see the internal war he's fighting right there in his eyes. I want to touch him, this him, and my hand finds his arm and slides from his elbow to his wrist. He breathes a sigh, smothering it on an exhale, but I catch it through my earpiece, his breath igniting a small fire that spreads through me. He takes my hand.

I lace my fingers with his and lean my cheek against the cold leather of the headrest, watching him. I don't know how long we sit in silence, our eyes saying everything that we cannot.

He is going to betray me, but I won't let him stop me from finding the truth. We both know that we can never really be together. Yet, we're here now, our hands linked and our hearts clinging to the fantasy that we are a team. And maybe we are, for a few more hours at least.

Ryan turns the van into the parking lot of the Valle Vista Country Club. "We're here."

I practically leap out of the van. What was that? I know better than to hope for impossible things.

I almost jump at Ryan's voice in my ear. "Berry?"

"Yeah?"

"I'm glad Tanner found you."

"Yeah, well don't give him too much credit. I wasn't that hard to find. I've been living in the same house since I was born."

"You know what I mean."

The hotel is right on the golf course and is probably the most expensive one in Valle Vista. Ryan and Mary Chris stay in the van and monitor the perimeter so they can tell us when Drew gets back.

Tanner walks up beside me as we make our way inside.

The lobby is cold, with marble floors and marble walls and marble covering the surface of every table or desk. The patchwork of fresh flowers that adorn every table does little to warm up the room. I rub my arms with my palms until Tanner curls his arm around me and whispers in my ear. "Pretend we're together."

Pretend. My life is one giant game of pretend. Pretend you're not watching people. Pretend you're not here to sneak into a spy's hotel room. Pretend you don't feel anything as you lean into Tanner.

It's a useless show. The only person in the lobby is a girl behind the check-in counter who doesn't look up from the book she's reading. Tanner pushes me down a corridor to an empty hallway. He keeps his arm around me even though there's no one to see us here, and I do nothing to stop him.

We stop in front of a room near the end. He nods and finally takes his arm away from my waist, ducking back against the wall as I knock on the door.

"Drew?"

I don't hear any sounds from inside the room, but I knock again. Still nothing. "How do we get in?" The door has one of those electronic locks. "Do you have a master key?"

"Something like that." Tanner pulls a tennis bracelet from his pocket. "Explosives."

"That might attract a little more attention than we're going for."

He raises his eyebrows. "You have a better idea?"

The door is tucked into the frame, so it's not the kind of lock I can pick. I'll have to get us in the old-fashioned way. Manipulation. "Watch me." I walk past him before he can stop me. He starts to follow, but I hold up my hand. "Stay out of sight."

I head back into the lobby. The girl at the counter still doesn't look up from her book. I get closer and study the cover, one of those romance novels with the picture of a girl getting ravished by some guy in a ruffled shirt and ripped chest. What's with the ruffled shirts? It's not exactly masculine.

I lean over the counter, and she finally looks up, pushing a strand of black hair behind her eyes. "Can I help you?"

"I'm so sorry to bother you." I lean forward. "But I was hoping you could help me surprise my boyfriend." The girl perks up, setting the book on the counter as I talk. "I'm not supposed to be here until tomorrow, but I got in early. Drew is having dinner with his parents tonight, and I thought I'd surprise him by waiting for him in the room."

The girl smiles and taps at the computer in front of her. "Is your name on the room?"

I shake my head. "I'm not sure. It's Drew Mattingly, room 139."

"He's here, but there's no one else on the room, hon. I can't give you a key if you're not registered. It's against hotel policy."

It's not hard to look crestfallen. Tanner's voice is in my ear. "Nice try." But Tanner doesn't see the disappointment in the girl's eyes. She wants to help me.

"Oh. I wanted to surprise him. I mean, he'll be surprised when he sees me in the lobby, but I was hoping when he saw me, it would be more"—I look around the lobby, and even though there's no one else around, I lower my voice—"romantic."

"Hello," Tanner laughs in my head. "I'm sold."

The girl grins back at me.

"It's a little crazy, right?"

The girl shakes her head. "Not at all." She lowers her voice to a whisper. "I've always wanted to do something like that."

"Me too. Oh well." I start to turn away from the desk, but I don't take my eyes off the girl, letting the silence stretch between us.

Predictably, the girl fills it. "I can't give you a key, but maybe I could let you in?"

I can picture Tanner's smile as he talks in my head. "I had no idea you were such a romantic." It's all I can do not to tell him to shut up.

Tanner is smart enough to make himself scarce as the girl leads me down the hall and opens the door with a master key card.

"Have fun," she smiles as I slip into the room and flip on the light.

But the surprise is on me.

Drew sits up in bed, his eyes blinking. "You're early."

Chapter 41

Drew is out of bed and across the room in three smooth strides, his hand on my arm before I can reach for my knife or get out of the room.

I try to focus. My pulse is running the Kentucky Derby, but I need to stay calm on the outside. Not easy when Drew is wearing a pair of jeans and nothing else. "Hi Drew."

It doesn't help that Mary Chris is my ear, her voice edged with panic. "Tanner, Ryan! You guys need to get in there now!"

Then Tanner's calmer voice. "Berry, you're doing fine. He was expecting you anyway. Just go with it."

Drew tightens his hold on my arm. "How did you get in?"

"The girl up front let me in. She thinks I'm here to seduce you."

He smiles and steps closer so his bare chest is touching my shirt. I try not to flinch, but there's no preventing it. "Are you?"

"No."

"I'm just outside the room, Berry, on the patio." Tanner says in my ear. I have to fight not to look for the sliding glass door. "If you get a chance to unlock the slider, do it. But you're doing fine. Just keep him talking."

I force myself to lean in and press my lips next to Drew's ear. "I hate you."

He lets go of my arm and sits down on the foot of the bed. "I don't like dogs, okay?" He points to a jagged scar near his neck. "Don't take it personally."

Drew's not far enough away for me to get out the door, which is fine, since I'll have to take the back way if I'm going to run. I'm all too aware that there's no furniture in the room except the giant unmade bed. I'm not about to crawl in bed with him, so I hug the wall near a flat-screen television.

"Go ahead," Tanner whispers. "Ask him about the files."

"Don't press her," Mare says, her voice finally sounding something close to normal.

There's a curtain covering the sliding glass door. There's no indication that Tanner is so close. I'll have to walk past Drew to unlock the door. I don't move from my spot on the wall. "You're looking for the Juiced formula?"

Drew smiles in his nonthreatening boy-band way. "You make it sound so dirty. I'm going to the FDA, Berry. I'm shutting Moss down before he can hurt a lot of people."

"Lose the act, Drew. That formula is old news. The only reason you want the formula is because someone else is going to try to market it."

Drew puts a foot up against the wall, blocking any path by the bed. "You're not far off. Someone is going to try to market it. I'm here to stop them."

"You've got him talking," Tanner says. "Ask who he works for."

I step closer to the bed. "If that's true, then we want the same thing."

"Do we?" Drew leans back on his elbows, and it's all I can do not to roll my eyes. "That's what I've been trying to tell you."

I can feel how close he is to letting me in. Drew will tell me everything. I just need to play this out. I sit down on the bed next to him.

"Berry, what are you doing?" Tanner raises his voice in my ear. "Now's your chance to unlock the door. He's admitted he wants to steal the formula. Find out who he works for and we can take him into custody right now."

"Now?"

Drew laughs. "Slow down. We need a game plan."

I wasn't talking to Drew. I was talking to Tanner, who's gone silent. I can't let him take Drew down now. Tanner will never let me near those files. Drew will.

I lie on my side, propping myself on my elbow and resting my head in my palm. Drew turns on his side to face me. We're like friends at a slumber party, sharing secrets. "What do you think happened to my mother?"

"I have my suspicions. Someone wanted her out of the way because she figured out what was going on with Juiced. You have all the same information I do at this point."

"Why'd you pay Heather Marrone to go to the police?"

He shrugs. "You want to see the people who hurt your mother pay, don't you? And the distraction gives us a nice opportunity to get into the warehouse. Did you get the key from Mary Chris?"

"Like I'd give it to him," Mary Chris says.

I ignore Drew's question. "Who stands to gain from Mr. Moss going to prison?"

Drew's smile falters. "You're too smart for you own good, you know that?"

I look past Drew's face to a pile of clothes in the corner. A shirt is draped across a familiar black box. My desktop. "You've got to be kidding."

He looks over his shoulder at the small black box that brands him a thief. "Berry, I can explain."

I stand up, backing up to the wall. "You broke into my house."

"I had to see the pictures you got of Moss."

"I thought you were my friend. You were helping me. You could have asked to see the pictures. Instead, you made me go to a dance by myself so you could break into my house and steal my computer?"

The words are out of my mouth before I realize that Mary Chris could have given me the exact same speech. She may have, actually.

Is this what I've become? Am I no better than a guy who would hold a gun to a dog in order to get what he wants? How did this happen?

"You're not listening." Drew stands up, grabbing my wrist. Hard.

"Let go of me."

"Berry," Tanner says in my head. "I'm coming in."

"No," I say, "Not yet."

"Not yet?" Drew repeats. He pushes me against the wall, trapping me with his weight. "Who are you talking to?"

"Berry, you need to get out of there." Mare is panicking in my ear.

"Keep away from the glass door, I'll blow it open in twenty seconds," Tanner says.

Drew keeps me pinned to the wall. He brushes a strand of hair behind my ear and fishes out the earpiece with his finger. "What kind of game do you think we're playing here?"

I force myself to look at Drew. "I can't let you sell that formula to the highest bidder."

Drew shakes his head. "Why can't you admit you might be wrong? I'll give you the files you want. Can you say the same thing about him?"

He's right about Tanner. There's nothing I can say. But suddenly getting the files doesn't seem nearly as important as stopping Drew. He's right in a way. I need to finish what she started. She can't have died for nothing.

"I didn't think so." Drew steps back, freeing me from his makeshift prison.

There's a loud crash behind us as glass shatters and rains onto the carpet. I move toward the sound as Tanner bursts into the room, but when I turn back to look for Drew the front door is closing and he's nowhere to be seen.

Chapter 42

L ittle pieces of safety glass coat the room like a layer of snow. Tanner reaches for my hand. "We need to get out of here."

I ignore him and run over to the pile of clothes covering my computer. I tuck the computer under my arm and walk through the hole in the wall on my own. I don't start running until I'm covered in the darkness of the parking lot.

"Are you okay?" Mary Chris holds open the van door.

"I'm fine." I turn on Tanner. "I thought the plan was to take Drew in after he gets the files."

"Too risky."

"For future reference, you might want to clue in the rest of the team on the real plan, instead of sending me in there at a complete disadvantage."

"It's not like that. A plan is a fluid thing. Once Drew admitted he planned to steal the documents, we had enough to bring him in." Tanner turns to look at me. "What Drew said. About me not helping you."

"Doesn't matter. I'm not relying on you to get me anything. What matters is thanks to your stunt, Drew is going to go after the files on his own. We have to stop him the hard way." It's the truth. Getting the files for myself is not nearly as important as keeping them from Drew.

Ryan looks over his shoulder at us from the driver's seat. "I've got him. He's headed to the west parking lot."

I fold my arms across my chest. "Where have I heard that before? Oh, I know, right before I walked into an ambush."

Mary Chris looks back. "I'm the one who thought I saw Drew leave the hotel. Yell at me if you want to take it out on someone."

I close my mouth. "Sorry." Nothing is going the way it's supposed to. All that matters now is stopping Drew. There's no way I can take the chance that he's going to give the formula to the wrong people.

As we drive, Tanner keeps trying to talk to me, but I stop him every time. I don't need to hear an explanation. I know the answer. He jumped the gun again. Because of me. If there was any doubt that we don't belong together, it's clear now. I am pure poison.

Tanner hands me his earpiece. "Ryan will need to talk to you."

"Not interested."

"Don't take this out on him, Berry. He's trying to help."

"Help with what? Making sure I don't get anywhere near the files about my own mother?" I lash out at Tanner as a means to put some much needed distance between us. The only way we get Drew tonight is if he focuses on the job at hand. It will be easier if Tanner's not trying to save me from invisible threats.

"So you're willing to take Drew's word for it without even listening to my side of the story?"

"I'm not talking about Drew. I heard you say it, okay? I heard you talking to your mom."

Tanner doesn't deny it. He just looks at the ceiling and shakes his head. "I'm not the only one who was trained to do this."

We pull into the parking lot for Moss Enterprises.

Mary Chris brings up a blueprint of the warehouse on a monitor. "Drew thinks the second file is in the warehouse computer. There's only one. It's downstairs near the main loading bays. The bays are sealed with metal doors, the best way in is through the door on the east side."

Tanner flips through the screen in front of him. "What about vents?"

"None large enough to fit through. Ryan and I will go into the main offices to access the real file from Preston's desktop, but I'll be monitoring the grounds remotely." Mary Chris sounds like a pro. I should take her on more jobs.

Tanner holds out his earpiece to me.

"No thanks."

"Mary Chris will keep an eye out for Drew on the laptop and let us know what direction he's coming from," Tanner says. "Trust me, it's information you'll want to know."

"Did you seriously just ask me to trust you?" But I'm not a fool, and I take the earpiece from his hand. I put my messenger bag over my shoulder and follow Tanner to the warehouse, while Mary Chris and Ryan head in the opposite direction.

"Berry, I can explain."

"Don't. We've only got a few minutes head start. We need to find a spot to wait for Drew, then we'll grab him when the time is right. No sooner. Got it?"

"I'll grab him. You are not going anywhere near—"

"Stop. Get over this knight complex or jealousy or macho man stuff or whatever it is that makes you want to keep me out of Drew's path. I'm in this, okay? Toughen up and act like a professional."

"I'm not going to let him hurt you."

"I'm not going to let him get near that formula. That's our priority. You're not my guardian, Tanner. You're not my—" I hesitate. "Anything."

Even in the dark, I can see the cloud that crosses Tanner's eyes and turns them stormy gray. "Fine." The single word is clipped.

Good. It's better if he hates me. He needs to focus on the mission. Logically, this makes sense. It hurts, but it makes sense.

It shouldn't be a surprise that the back door is locked when we get there. Still, Tanner looks at a loss.

"No plan?"

"Not anymore. I used my explosive pack to get into the hotel room."

"Oh. I've got one." I take the tennis bracelet off my wrist and wrap it around the door handle. "You have a light?"

Tanner pulls a small lighter from the pocket of his jeans and lights the fuse. He grabs my arm and pulls me back about fifteen feet. The explosion is loud, but since the door is wood, it's more muffled than at the hotel.

Mary Chris talks in my head. "Assume the blast triggered an alarm. We have twelve minutes tops to get in and get out. Drew better get here soon."

We move quickly through a dark lobby and into a large one-room warehouse. There are pallets stacked with cardboard boxes in long rows along the concrete floor. It's like an indoor corn maze, minus the apple cider, hay rides, and any actual corn.

It's eerily quiet. We run up and down the rows for about three minutes before Tanner stops.

"Do you see the stairs anywhere?"

I point out a door in the back left corner. It looks like an exit door, but the only exit is the one we came in. The door must lead somewhere. It does. Right into a set of stairs that head down. "Let's go."

The stairs twist in a circle as they go down, then go down some more. Finally, they end at another door. Tanner gives it a try, but it's locked. "I don't suppose you have more explosive powder?"

"We won't need it." This door is standard issue. The lock is old and unprotected. I take a bobby pin from my messenger bag and slide it into the lock, jiggling it until it catches.

"There's a car pulling into the lot," Mary Chris says in my ear.

"Let me guess, red hatchback?"

"It's Drew," Mare confirms. "He's headed straight for the warehouse." She can't hide the pride in her voice. Drew believed her lie about the second file being in the warehouse.

The door clicks open, and we slip inside. The basement is dark except for a light high on the ceiling, at least three stories up. It casts just enough light to see the stacks of boxes piled nearly two-thirds of the way up, casting long shadows on each other.

"Any idea where the computer is?" I hesitate at the threshold, reluctant to go in. The air is stale and heavy.

"Nope." Tanner moves past me. "Only one way to find out."

I follow him as he runs along one shadowed corridor to another. He starts to turn right when we get to a wall, but I grab his arm and stop him. "Look." I point up. There's a lower ceiling, about ten feet above our heads, about the size of a small room. "How do we get up there?"

Tanner looks around and points behind us to a row of iron rungs in the wall. We change course and climb up. As our hands and feet make contact with the iron, the clunking sound echoes in the large room.

We come up on a small landing, just wide enough for us to walk to a tiny office with just enough room for a single desk and file cabinet. The computer monitor flashes a screen saver involving women in bikinis. I start skimming some of the purchase orders on the desk.

"We don't have time to look around." Tanner picks up a piece of paper and reads it anyway. "They're just delivery receipts. And Drew is here. There's only one way in. We're better off waiting for him on the ground."

I pick up one of the purchase orders anyway. It's huge. From a retail chain for all of its stores across the country. Fifty thousand cases. Cases of what?

"He's here."

"Come out, come out, wherever you are!" Drew's voice echoes.

"Fine." I drop the paper and follow Tanner out of the small office and back to the iron rungs. Tanner goes first. The noise sounds even louder now that I know that Drew is in here with us.

Tanner stops to wait for me on the bottom, and then we run down a corridor, turning left and hiding behind a row of cartons that ends at the wall. There's nowhere else to go from here.

TALIA VANCE

•

The room vibrates with the sound of an engine turning over and the smell of diesel fuel fills the air.

"What's he doing?" I ask.

"There was a forklift near the entrance."

"Why is he driving a forklift?" The sound gets closer and we hear the smack of it hitting something solid. A stack behind us starts to totter and sway. We look at each other and both turn to run the way we came, but it's too late. Gravity sends the stack tumbling forward.

Tanner pushes me back, shoving me off balance and throwing himself across me. We land hard on the concrete. It's a few seconds before I can breathe.

Tanner lies across me. "You okay?"

I nod. Considering I was almost buried alive under a pile of boxes, I feel pretty good. Tanner grins at me and for a second I think he might stay right where he is, and I might even want him to. My heart beats faster while the rest of the world slows down.

"What is going on down there?" It's Mary Chris, right there in our ears. Tanner leaps up and puts a hand out to me, just as the beep, beep, beep of the forklift backing up chimes.

"We don't have much time." Tanner looks around, but the corridor is blocked where the boxes fell, and we have more stacks on either side of us. There's a wall at the end of the corridor that's finished with drywall.

"We'll have to go up." I run over to the wall, and rummage through my messenger bag for my climbing picks. I start strapping them on my feet. "I'll go first, then I'll drop them down to you."

Tanner shakes his head. "Where did you get those things?"

"Have you never heard of the Internet?" I grasp the picks and climb up far enough to reach the top of a stack of boxes. I kick the stack with my foot and it doesn't move. A good sign. The beeping of the forklift has stopped and there's a sharp scratching sound as Drew tries to get the thing in gear. The good news is I have a little time, the bad news is that he's aiming at the stack right behind Tanner.

I have to kick myself off the wall and try to land on the middle of the stack. I just hope it holds. I take out one toehold and aim my heel against the wall to get a good push off. As I kick the wall, I pull out my hand picks, sending myself flying backward into what I hope is the middle of the stack. I land hard on my back. The stack shakes a little but doesn't give way.

I unstrap my climbing gear and throw it down to Tanner just as the forklift lurches forward.

"Drew! Stop!" I wave my hands to get his attention.

Drew stops moving forward and waves at me. He angles the forklift at the stack to my right.

Tanner has the climbing gear on and works his way up the wall. The drywall starts to give under his weight about halfway up.

"Keep climbing! You can't stop or it won't hold you."

Tanner looks up at me. "What?" But it's too late, the drywall gives under his weight and he falls to the ground. He rolls to his side, holding his shoulder.

"Don't tell me you brought your boyfriend?" Drew moves the forklift forward again toward the stack directly in front of Tanner.

The forklift charges the stack.

"Do that thing from laser tag!"

"What?" Tanner asks again.

"Laser tag!" I yell, making a twisting movement with my hands to try to get my message across.

Tanner nods and jumps to the side, diving into the fallen boxes and rolling against the wall just before the tractor hits. I leap into the air, throwing my body at the stack to my left. The stack wobbles and sways under my weight as the cartons I was just standing on tumble to the ground.

"Keep going!" Tanner is against the wall, pinned in by the fallen boxes. "Get back to the van."

The beep, beep, beep of the forklift chirps out a warning. There are crushed stacks to either side of me, but a straight line of boxes up ahead. I look at Tanner one more time, reluctant to leave him trapped there. Then the beeping stops, and I've run out of options.

"What are you doing?" I yell at Drew, just before I run and leap for the next stack of boxes.

"I'm stopping them!" Drew hollers over the sound of the forklift. He points to a fallen stack of boxes on the floor. "See for yourself."

One of the cartons is open and green plastic bottles roll along the floor.

"The door is at the end of your row," Ryan says in my ear. "The water pipe next to the frame should hold your weight." The forklift rails against the stack behind me, and I run faster. The sound of the engine behind me gets louder as I run. The wall is just up ahead, and the pipe is there. I lunge at it, just as the forklift hits the stack beneath me. I wrap my legs around the pipe, sliding to the ground.

I run through the door as a pile of boxes crashes behind me. I look back, but all I see are boxes blocking the doorway. There's no sign of Tanner.

"Keep going." Ryan's voice is eerily calm. "He'll kill me if I don't get you out."

Chapter 43

I can't leave Tanner in there. "Drew has seriously lost it," I speak into the comm watch. "I'm going back in."

"No," Ryan says. "Mary Chris is nearly into the hard drive. We'll be there in a few minutes. Wait for us."

The forklift engine cuts. Someone shouts.

"Forget that." I slip back inside the basement, pushing aside crushed boxes and stepping through plastic bottles. It takes a while to clear a path through the wreckage. Drew has knocked over nearly every stack of boxes in the room. I hear a scuffle and several grunts and groans, but they echo across the large room, so I can't get a sense of direction.

Finally, I see the forklift tucked under a mountain of boxes.

Drew's voice carries through the air. "You think you've got her fooled? By the time the night is over she'll know which one of us is really on her side." Drew has a warped sense of loyalty if he thinks we're on the same side of anything. Whatever his intentions with the formula, the fact remains that he's here to steal it.

I pull the knife from its sheath beneath my shirt, moving along a wall toward the spot where I last saw Tanner.

A flash of Drew's hair peeks from behind a pile of boxes. I move closer, staying against the wall until my path is blocked by more boxes. I pick my way behind the pile until I can see Drew, pacing back and forth in front of something on the ground. At first I can't tell what it is. I stifle a gasp when I realize it's Tanner. He's on his stomach with his feet duct-taped to his wrists. A line of tape circles his head around his mouth. A second section of tape covers his eyes. Adrenaline surges through me, and I have to hold myself back from leaping at Drew from behind. I can't get a good angle from here, and I won't be able to help Tanner if I'm a victim too. Logic battles with something deeper, an instinct that won't allow Tanner to be hurt.

Drew's hands are clenched into fists the size of large rocks. He stops pacing and hits Tanner in the ear, knocking Tanner's head back. "Not so tough now, are you? Don't worry, it will get a whole lot worse before it gets better." He raises a fist again.

"Stop!" I blow any cover I had by yelling, but I can't bear to watch him hit Tanner again. "You made your point."

Drew whips his head around, but I duck out of sight before we make eye contact. "Berry! I knew you wouldn't be able to stay away. The truth is more important to you than safety. That's the part dimwit here never understood. He doesn't get you. Never has."

I crouch behind a pile of boxes, clutching the knife with both hands. I need to get Drew away from Tanner before he hits him again.

"We're on our way," Ryan says in my ear. "Don't do anything stupid." He's right. I should wait a few more minutes. But I can't. I have to do something.

Drew's footsteps are soft, but getting closer. I press my back against the debris pile, not daring to look around it. At least I've gotten him away from Tanner.

Drew walks right past the pile, but he doesn't look behind it. I hold my breath, waiting for him to get another few yards away. I run to where Tanner still lays on the ground. I slash at the tape that binds Tanner's feet and wrists.

"Berry!" Mary Chris yells in my ear. "What are you doing?"

I manage to cut through the thick layer of tape binding Tanner's legs when Drew runs up behind me. Tanner rolls to his side and gets up to his knees, but he still can't see, and his arms are taped behind his back.

Drew grabs me by the shoulder and lifts me off my feet in one painful movement that sends a sharp shock down my arm. I hang onto the knife, but just barely.

"He's not your friend, Berry."

"Neither are you."

Drew puts an arm around my waist, keeping my feet off the ground so I can't get a good stance. I bring the knife down hard on his forearm.

"Ahhh!" He drops me.

I fall to the ground hard, barely keeping the blade away from my own skin. I roll toward Tanner and cut the tape at his wrists. He immediately pulls at the tape around his eyes.

Drew comes at both of us, his fists swinging. I jump to my feet and slash the knife in the air. "Stay back!"

He lunges at me, with no regard for the knife between us. He grabs my wrist so hard, I let go of the knife. It lands on the ground with a clang. Drew drags me to him, pulling me off my feet in a bear hug that cuts off my breath. The blood from his arm is still warm as it soaks into my shirt.

"Let go of me." I kick at his legs, but don't make contact.

"I'm trying to help you!" He yells in my ear. "Calm down and listen. Those bottles that are all over the floor, what do you think they are?"

I can't breathe. Everything's fuzzy. There's movement behind us. I wrench my neck to look back. Tanner has the tape off his eyes and he crawls toward the knife. I need to distract Drew a little longer. My elbows are pinned, and I can't get leverage to kick him. The room seems to get narrower as I struggle to breathe.

Drew kicks one of the bottles. "It's the energy drink, Berry. The same one your mother tried to stop. Repackaged and rebranded. It's set to go out to market in a month."

Drew doesn't see Tanner reach the knife. I barely see it. Everything's going black. By the time Drew catches the movement, it's too late, Tanner is on his feet and throwing the knife at Drew's shoulder.

Drew lets go of me all at once. I fall to the ground with a thud, sucking in air. Drew slumps on top of me.

"This is not helping!" I push at Drew, but he doesn't budge.

"What's happening?" Mary Chris asks. "Are you okay?"

"We're fine," I say, even though I'm not at all sure it's true.

Tanner pulls Drew to the side enough for me to scoot out from underneath him.

Drew yells out a curse. He tries to lift his arm, but he can't.

Tanner removes the last bit of tape from his mouth. Finally free, he glares down at me. "I said no knives."

Chapter 44

I reach for one of the green plastic bottles on the floor next to me. It says "FRANTIC" in big yellow letters with a lightning bolt for the letter "I." "Did you know about this?"

"No." Tanner holds his watch to his mouth. "Send for an ambulance."

Drew groans from the floor as Tanner pulls the knife from his shoulder. Tanner rips off a big hunk of his shirt and presses it to the wound on Drew's shoulder. He grabs a roll of duct tape from the ground and uses it to secure the makeshift bandage.

"Is he okay?"

"I got the muscle. And if the way he was fighting is any indication, you just broke the skin. It will just hurt like crazy for a while." Tanner looks at the blood covering my shirt. "Did you get cut?"

"The blood's not mine."

I'm relatively unscathed, which is more than I can say about Tanner. His cheek is red and already turning purple. There's a cut at the corner of his lip. I touch it with the pad of my finger. "Does it hurt?"

"Not even close." He takes my finger in his hand and brings it to his lips, kissing it lightly.

"Oh."

"Just shoot me now," Drew mumbles.

"The ambulance is on the way." Mary Chris is in our ears. "We're almost there."

Tanner pulls his watch off and lobs it over a stack of fallen boxes. He looks at me expectantly. He takes the button-cam off his shirt and does the same.

"What was that?" Ryan's voice gets louder. "Tanner? Do not go offline. Tanner . . . "

Tanner tries to smile, but winces instead.

I pull the earpiece out of my ear and toss it after Tanner's, along with my watch and button-cam. Tanner takes my hand, leading me around some fallen boxes to a corner that's relatively closed off from where Drew still lies.

"We only have a few minutes before they get here." He pauses anyway, searching for words.

"It's okay. I already know that you're not allowed to let me see the file. I get it." I can't ask Tanner to put me ahead of his family, but I want to anyway. I stare down at the ground. At the bottles of Frantic strewn around the floor. Problem is, I don't understand anything. Is Moss really planning to release the same dangerous product my mom stopped eight years ago? What if Drew was telling the truth? I kick a bottle. "Did you really not know about Frantic?"

Tanner picks a bottle off the floor and turns it around in his hand. "This isn't about a stupid energy drink."

"Of course it is. That's all anyone cares about, isn't it? You aren't here to help me find out what happened to my mom. You're here to protect the formula." The truth tastes sour on my tongue. "No one was there to protect my mom. She was killed for what?" I glance around at the mess of boxes and bottles. "For this?"

"No." He looks stricken. "It's not what you think."

My heart freezes. Tanner knows. He knows what happened to my mother. He knows everything. I hold my breath, terrified that he is going to tell me. More terrified that he won't. The seconds stretch as we stand there. Not touching. Not moving.

"Are you sure you want to do this?" he finally asks. "There's no going back."

"For who?"

"For you. Me." He opens his mouth and closes it again, holding back whatever he wanted to say.

But it doesn't matter. I need to know what happened to her. I don't want to go back to being the scared little girl who thought her mother left on purpose. I can only move forward. And I'm not foolish enough to believe that Tanner Halston will ever be part of my future. I need this. "When did you find out?"

"This afternoon. After you mentioned my dad could be involved."

"And when were you planning on telling me? Never?"

"It's not that easy."

"You know this is important to me."

He throws the bottle of Frantic at a pile of boxes. His silence hangs in the air between us, an invisible chasm that gets wider with every second that passes.

Tanner doesn't owe me anything. I'm just a distraction. A damaged girl who keeps getting in the way of keeping the formula, and his father, safe. I turn away from him and start walking back toward where we left Drew. "Forget I asked."

Tanner runs to catch up. "You deserve to know the truth." He reaches for my hand, lacing his fingers with mine, as if the physical connection will bridge the distance. As if his acknowledgment of my deserving to know is the same as telling me.

It's nowhere near, but I don't blame Tanner. The ending of my mom's story will always be the same, no matter how it happened. No matter how important learning about the past might be to me, Tanner would be gambling with his present. His future. Maybe I don't want him to be the instrument that destroys his own family. If it came down to protecting my own dad, I would hold tight to my secrets.

I squeeze his hand. "It's okay."

He watches me closely, like he's not quite sure he believes me.

"Don't think I'm giving up or anything." I don't know if I'll ever be this close to the truth again. Maybe I won't. Tanner tries to smile again, but it's a sad smile. I can almost feel the past, our parents' past, between us.

A door opens with a bang, and Mary Chris's voice carries across the warehouse. "Berry! Tanner!"

Tanner doesn't move away from me. He kisses me lightly on the forehead. "I'm sorry," he says.

I stare up at Tanner. His mouth is so close that all I have to do is lift my chin and I could kiss him. "Me too," I whisper.

Tanner steps away from me and shoves his hands in his pockets. He looks at something past me, avoiding eye contact. I keep my eyes trained on his face, daring him to look at me.

He doesn't. He's already as good as gone.

All at once there is a rush of voices and the sound of boxes and bottles being cleared as paramedics make a path to Drew from somewhere on the other side of the boxes.

Ryan and Mary Chris run up behind me. Mare takes one look at my blood-soaked shirt and her eyes widen.

"I'm okay," I say. "How did it go?"

"Ryan is amazing. He disarmed the firewall in under five minutes." She smiles up at Ryan with total admiration. "Turns out Dave taught Ryan everything he knows."

"Mary Chris is too modest." Ryan puts a proprietary arm around her. "This girl knows her way around a file encryption." He holds up a thumb drive in his other hand. "Mission accomplished."

"We'll take it," Tanner says, reaching for the drive. "Someone needs to go to the hospital and keep an eye on Drew so we can take him into custody as soon as he's released." He looks down at the blood splatters on his ripped shirt. "There'll be less questions if you go."

Ryan nods. "On it."

"Wait," I say. "Aren't you going to call the police? You have the evidence Drew was trying to steal the formula."

Tanner shakes his head. "Michael likes to keep things private."

"But Drew?"

"Is handled," Ryan says. He looks at Mare. "Later?"

"I was hoping I could come along." She grins, and it's obvious that they are back on in a big way. Good for Mary Chris. I always liked Ryan. Except Mare needs the file to get her dad out of jail.

"What about your dad?" I ask. "We need those files to clear his name." Dave Preston is the one who should be behind bars.

"Mom called a few minutes ago. Dad's out. Dave Preston found evidence that Heather Marrone was paid to say she lied about witnessing the accident. The police can't believe a word she says. My dad's been cleared."

And so has Dave Preston. Somehow I'm guessing that Dave didn't tell the police the whole story. I stare at the hard drive as it passes from Ryan to Tanner. The answers are there. Doesn't Mare want to see the proof of her father's innocence? "Don't you want to know?"

Mare blinks. "I know my father. He wouldn't hurt anyone. I don't need to fact-check it."

I don't know if it's love or faith or naivete that makes Mare so sure about her dad, but it occurs to me that whatever it is, I don't have it. Whether it's something that was sucked out of me on the day my mother died, or something that was never there to begin with, there is no question that it's not there now.

Mare's blind faith puts her right in the path of a proverbial semi-truck that she'll never even see coming, but at least she's happy now. The problem with living your life with eyes wide open is that those happy moments are harder to come by and far more fleeting.

Tanner closes his fingers around the hard drive.

The problem with knowing the semi's coming is that it doesn't hurt any less when it hits.

"Dude," Ryan says, and takes Mare's hand.

Tanner waits for Ryan and Mary Chris to leave, watching them disappear around the corner. He tilts his head to the side, finally making eye contact. He flips the drive around in his fingers.

"What?"

He holds the hard drive out to me. "Take it."

I stare at the little black box. It's nondescript, but it takes a concerted effort not to flinch away from it. I want to know until I'm confronted with the proof.

Tanner pushes it at me. "You need to see this. Even if you hate me."

"I don't hate you, Tanner, remember?" Not by a long shot. And now he is going to give me the evidence that will put his father away. Evidence I won't be able to ignore.

"You might." He takes my hand and places the drive there, closing my fingers around it. He lets go and steps back quickly, like he's afraid I'll bite.

I tighten my fist around the drive, torn. The truth is here, in the palm of my hand. But at what price?

Tanner takes another step away from me. "I swear I didn't know."

A box crashes to the floor behind us. We both turn toward the sound.

Michael Moss steps over some plastic bottles and strides toward us.

I slip the hard drive in my back pocket, relegating its secrets to the dark for just a little while longer.

Chapter 45

M r. Moss looks like he just came from the golf course. It's hard to believe he's spent the day in the police station. "I understand you've caught the infiltrator." Mr. Moss's gaze is hard, making me feel more like the captured than the captor.

"We did," Tanner says.

Mr. Moss looks at Tanner. "And the formula?"

"He never got near it." Tanner's eyes dart to my hand, just as Dave Preston comes around the corner.

"The file's been compromised. We'll have to move—" Dave stops talking abruptly when he sees me standing next to Tanner.

Seeing Dave and Tanner together makes it impossible to deny that they're related. Impossible to separate the father from the son. The murderer from the, what? What is Tanner to me now?

"It's fine," Tanner says. "Ryan got the file out. Drew never saw it."

Dave looks from Tanner to me, a question in his eyes. He wants to know if I've seen it. If I know the truth.

"No one saw it." Tanner answers the unspoken question.

"Good work." Dave winks at Tanner, and I want to slap him. Good job keeping Berry from seeing the files is what he means. Good job making sure my crime stays buried.

It's strange standing face-to-face with the man responsible for Mom's murder. Without a gun pointed at my chest, he looks almost normal. Like someone's father. Like Tanner's father.

"Where is the file?" Moss asks.

Tanner shakes his head. "We destroyed—"

"I have it."

Everyone turns to stare at me. Dave Preston holds out his hand.

I put my hands in my pockets. I'm not getting out of here with this thing, but I'm in no hurry to give it up yet either. Tanner looks shocked, but I'm not going to let him do this for me. I'm done hurting my friends.

And there's no question now that Tanner is a friend.

"Well?" Dave says.

I kick at a green bottle on the floor, rolling it toward him. "Explain this."

Dave's forehead crinkles. His knees bend slightly as he picks up the bottle.

Mr. Moss smiles. "Try it."

I reach down and pick up a bottle. "I think I'll pass."

"It's perfectly safe, Berry, the result of ten years of research and development."

He might as well be asking me to drink a bottle filled with my mother's blood. "No. My mom was going to stop you, and now that she's out of the way, you think you can just sneak this drink out into the marketplace without anyone knowing. Well, you can't. I know. Drew knows."

"Berry." Tanner steps beside me and grabs my wrist.

He may as well be putting a leash on a tiger. I have no intention of letting Mr. Moss get away with drugging half the population. "My mother died for this." I glare at Dave. "And it won't be for nothing."

Mr. Moss shakes his head. "Your mother saved this company from a potential disaster. It was through her work that we were able to discover the dangers associated with Juiced. We were able to pull the product before its national launch. It took us eight years to fix the problems, but we did."

The gray stripe in Moss's hair seems whiter than normal. "You fixed it?"

"Of course. The FDA has already tested it and cleared it."

I step toward Dave Preston. "But you killed my mother anyway?"

Tanner tries to pull me back, but ends up moving with me.

"You think I killed your mother?"

"I know it. You paid Heather Marrone to go to the police before the accident happened. The only way you could know it was going to happen in the first place is if you planned to kill her."

"I didn't kill anyone." Dave stares at Tanner's hand around my wrist.

Tanner lets me go. He can't help me anymore. If he ever really could. Tanner, the one person I let get too close. We are tied together. His father is responsible for my mother's death. That's not something I can pretend didn't happen. Dave can deny it all he wants, but there's only one explanation.

SPIES *and* PREJUDICE

•

285

"Had her killed. Semantics."

"No one killed your mother." Michael Moss picks up one of the green plastic bottles and turns it over in his hands. "Dave saved her life."

"Funny how she ended up dead then, isn't it?"

Tanner rests his hand on my shoulder. He says my name so quietly that I might imagine it.

I look from Mr. Moss to Dave to Tanner. They all have the same expression on their face. The same, pitying, sorry-for-me expression that I've seen a million times. My fingers shake as I push Tanner's hand away. There is no reason for them to feel sorry for me now. I'm where I want to be. Confronting my mother's killer. Finally, finally, I have someone to blame. But instead of anger, all I feel is fear. The hole in my heart is still here. Right where it's always been. There is no solace in having an enemy. No closure.

I will always be broken.

"What?" I finally ask, panic making the word come out too high and too loud.

Tanner looks at the floor. "She deserves to know."

I stare at him, but he doesn't look up, he won't make eye contact.

"What?" I say again, pleading this time.

Mr. Moss nods his head toward Dave. "Go ahead."

Dave blinks. He looks around the mess of crumpled boxes and plastic bottles before his eyes settle back on me. "What I'm about to tell you can't leave this room. Ever."

"If it's about how you killed my mom, I'm pretty sure I can't keep that to myself." I cling to the last shred of anger I find. It's the only thing that keeps me upright, the only thing that keeps me from collapsing along with the stacks of boxes.

He shakes his head. "I didn't kill your mother. No one did."

The seed of anger takes root and expands. I don't buy the suicide story. Not anymore. Dave Preston can parade a thousand witnesses in front of me and I will never believe that my mother left me that way. "She didn't kill herself," I say with a certainty I feel in my bones.

Dave nods. "Correct."

He's agreeing with me? "It wasn't an accident either." The accident was staged. By Dave Preston.

"Also true." Dave rubs his hand through his hair. It's the same gesture I've seen Tanner do when he's uncomfortable. When he's about to say something he doesn't want to say.

"Then how did she die?" I picture the gun in Dave's hand, held to my mother's face. I can see her clearly, her gray eyes flickering with fear, her brown hair curling where it sticks to her neck.

Dave sighs. "She didn't."

My mouth goes instantly dry. The large room seems smaller somehow, like the walls are closing in around us. The lights flicker until all I see are white spots. My legs shake, but my brain is still trying to process what Dave Preston says.

My mother didn't die.

My mother didn't die.

It's impossible and completely insane and so, so, so freaking *wrong*.

Dave starts to say something, but I hold up my hand. "Don't." I can't hear any more of this. I can't.

Tanner finally looks at me, his eyes full of sadness.

I shouldn't have felt anything more than sorry for you.

At least now Tanner gets his wish.

I sit down on the cold concrete of the warehouse floor while Dave Preston tells his story. I get enough to understand the gist of it, but it's all a hazy blur.

My mother found the problem with Juiced. Someone threatened her life. She asked Dave and Mr. Moss to help her. She was afraid they were going to hurt me and Dad. They arranged for her to disappear into a witness protection program. The accident was faked. My mother changed her name and her identity.

I was wrong about her.

She did leave.

She erased her life. Erased me.

All I can think is how much I hate them. Mr. Moss for putting her in danger to begin with. Dave Preston for making it possible for my mother to disappear. My mother for not standing up for herself. Not fighting for us.

But it's not until I'm in the back of Dave Preston's car on the way back to Pemberley, staring out the window, that it occurs to me that Dad was right all along. It was his letter. His threat. He was the reason Mom left. Mom was running away from invisible dangers, ghosts that didn't even exist. Dad was afraid that Moss would make her disappear. And Moss did. Just not in the way Dad thought.

Tanner glances back at me from the front seat every now and then, but I keep my eyes firmly focused outside the car.

She's out there somewhere.

It's no comfort.

Chapter 46

W hen I get home, Dad is sitting on the couch with Shauna Waterson, even though it's two in the morning. Shauna straightens her shirt and blushes up at me. Eew.

Dad smiles at her, and I have to admit I might never get tired of seeing him smile like that.

"Berry!" Shauna's voice is all sweetness and embarrassment. "We've been waiting for you."

"I know it's late," I say. "I was helping Mare with something for her father." An understatement.

Dad finally looks at me, a tentative smile on his face, waiting for my reaction. He's more worried about how I'll react to Shauna being here than the fact that I've been out half the night.

I need to talk to him, and this isn't the kind of conversation that I want to have with his new girlfriend hanging on his arm. On the outside, I manufacture what I hope is an almost-smile. "How was your night?"

"Fabulous," Shauna says, even though I was addressing my dad when I asked the question. She grabs my dad's knee and smiles at him.

Dad sits up straighter, and clears his throat. "So," he starts. "We wanted to talk to you about something."

A new surge of panic fills me. Dad and Shauna want to talk to me about something? Already? This can't be happening. Dad has never even been on a date in the past eight years. Now he spends a few weeks with Shauna Waterson and he wants to marry her? I sit down on the ottoman across from them, trying not to cry out.

I like Shauna. I like my dad with Shauna. But he needs to know the truth. Painful as it is, it's not something I can let go.

Mom is alive.

I could find her. I could explain that the threat was never real. We could have her back.

Dad looks at Shauna, and he smiles that smile, the big one that actually reaches his eyes.

I could break my father's heart.

Shauna's smile is aimed at me. It's genuine and hopeful. "We just wanted to make sure that you're okay with everything. I know it all seems kind of sudden."

Dad watches me warily. He doesn't trust me not to bark. He has no idea that the news I have is far more dangerous than a snarky comment. I have the truth.

The man who lost himself in depression would want me to tell him the truth, no matter what it cost him now.

But what about the man who smiles at Shauna Waterson so easily? What does he want?

TALIA VANCE

•

The price of uncovering secrets is steep. Knowing is no better than not knowing. It's so much worse. There's no safety net. I can't even lie to myself anymore.

She left us.

She's alive.

She left us and she never looked back.

Dad's smile falters, and I realize he's still waiting for me to say something. It takes every bit of willpower I possess to force my lips to curve up. A voice comes out of my mouth that sounds like someone else's. "It's great."

Dad jumps in. "We're going to take it slow." He squeezes her leg again. "We just wanted to make sure that you were okay."

"Slow is good," I say.

And it is. I can deal with Dad dating. As long as I don't have to see him kiss her or anything. During the year after Mom died, or left, I thought my dad might never smile again. Watching him now with Shauna, I won't be the one to take this from him.

For what? So Dad can chase after a woman who, however alive, hasn't bothered to inform us of that fact for eight years?

Whatever ends up happening with Shauna, it won't be me who breaks Dad's heart.

"Okay." It's as much of an affirmation as I can manage. Shauna grins. She starts rambling about another shopping trip with me and Jason.

It's almost enough for me to take it back, but for Dad, I make the sacrifice.

For Dad, I begin to say good-bye. To give my mother the burial she never really had.

Chapter 47

A month goes by in a haze of classes and stakeouts and Cherry Garcia ice cream.

Mare and I settle in to watch the opening performance of *Hamlet, the Musical.* It's every bit as horrific as I expected, but also campy and fun. It takes me a second to realize that the laughter I hear is my own. It's been a while since I've heard it.

No one's seen or heard from Drew since he bolted from the ambulence the night of the warehouse debacle. Not that anyone misses him. Still, it would be nice to know who he worked for. For now, I have to believe that Tanner was right.

I want to.

Tanner sent a few e-mails, but I didn't respond and he eventually gave up. Smart boy, that one. I try not to think about him. And for the most part it works. I've got plenty to think about.

Like her. My mother is an itch deep inside that I can never reach. A secret pain that I have no choice but to keep buried.

For now, I just want to sit back and watch my friend sing his way through his death scene while the crowd cheers him on. I don't miss the fact that Collin Waterson is sitting in the second row, clapping and cheering louder than any of them. I'm pretty sure Jason doesn't miss it either.

When the show is over, Mare and I walk out together, crossing the quad to our little wall. It's strange to be here at night, like the world has turned upside down and inside out. She sits down and looks up at the stars.

"Jason was good, right?"

"If by good you mean, bizarre and off-key but somehow perfect, than yeah, he was good."

Mare grins. "Something like that."

"I thought I might find you here." Ryan walks toward us, his blond hair shining in the moonlight.

I resist the urge to look for Tanner. Ryan's been coming down to see Mary Chris for weeks now. Always alone.

"You came!" Mare runs up and throws her arms around his neck.

Ryan hugs her back easily. "Like I was going to miss the world premiere?"

"Yeah, but you've heard Jason sing." Mare kisses him lightly.

I look away.

"Have you seen Jason yet?" Mare asks.

Ryan shakes his head. "Not yet. I'm a little intimidated by the throng of fans waiting backstage."

"I'll take you." Mare looks back at me, a question in her eyes.

"Go ahead. I'll wait for you here." It's not that I don't like Ryan.

I do. It's just impossible to be around him and not think about Tanner.

Mare walks over to me. "We won't be long."

"Take your time."

Mare reaches into her purse and hands me a folded piece of paper. "Don't read this yet, okay?"

A note? Mare hasn't given me a note since we both got cell phones in fifth grade. I put the note in my pocket. "When?"

"You'll know." She smiles again, then runs over to Ryan.

I watch as they disappear into the darkness. I'm tempted to read the note now, but Mare has me wondering what exactly it is that I'm waiting for.

I'm distracted by a movement to my left. I'm not even sure I see it, more like I sense that someone is there. I'm on my feet and walking toward the shadows, determined to find out who is lurking.

I duck around a tree and almost crash headlong into a dark figure. Only his hands on my shoulders keep me from running into him.

I don't have to raise my eyes to his face to know that it's Tanner. I smell cinnamon and fabric softener and something else that is uniquely him. Warmth spreads from his hands at my shoulder to my chest, my toes, and all points in between.

"Were you spying on me?" I ask, more breathless than I should be.

"I was just trying to get up the courage to talk to you." Tanner's hands are still on my shoulders, but I don't do anything to pull away. It takes a conscious effort to keep from pulling him into a hug.

"And?"

"And, I was afraid you wouldn't talk to me."

TALIA VANCE

•

"I can't talk to you if you're hiding in the bushes. So you might as well come out and give it a shot." My hands are restless at my side. He's here and all I want is to be closer. To touch him.

"Really?"

"What's the worst that can happen? I tell you I never want to see you again and then you're off the hook, right?"

He drops his hands. "You don't want to see me again. I knew this was a bad idea."

The truth is I don't know exactly what I want where Tanner is concerned. But I do know that the idea of not seeing him again is not it. "It wouldn't be the first bad idea you've ever had. Probably not the last either. I think that's one of the things I like about you."

"That I have bad ideas?" Tanner runs a hand through his hair.

"I hated you when you were too perfect."

"You thought I was perfect?"

"You thought you were perfect. There's a difference."

He finally smiles. "I know better now."

"Me too."

"About what?"

I choke on the words. There's a part of me that still wants to lock them up tight. But I'm not that girl anymore. I'm not the girl with the dead mother. I'm not the girl with the dead heart. "About me. You were right."

Tanner's eyes widen. "Excuse me?"

"I know it's hard to believe, given all your flaws."

"What was I right about?" Tanner's eyes search mine.

I bite my lower lip. "I might be capable of loving someone."

"Might be?"

I give in to the temptation to touch him, letting my fingers push a strand of his hair away from his face and linger there. "Maybe."

He covers my hand with his, holding it against his cheek. His smile is every bit as dangerous as it ever was, but this time I don't fight against the little flip my stomach does. I go with it. I lean forward and brush my lips against his.

He laughs against my lips, sending rumbles of heat to every part of me. And something lighter too. Something that confirms that I might not be broken after all.

"Berry Fields," he whispers, "you are amazing."

When he kisses me, I don't hold anything back.

Neither does he.

It's not until I'm home in bed that I remember Mare's note. I have to wake up Lulu to find my rumpled jeans on the floor. She yawns as I pull out the carefully folded piece of notebook paper, then flops back over on her side.

"U. O. Me," the note says. "I convinced Tanner that you might not hate him."

I take the note and set it on my dresser.

How am I ever going to top this?

Acknowledgments

This book owes everything to my publisher, Elizabeth Law, part editor, part writing coach, part ninja-sensei, who helped me find my way from idea to draft to the heart and soul of the story, with unflagging enthusiasm and support. This story could not have been in better hands, and we (Berry, Tanner, and I) owe you a debt of gratitude. Thank you for taking a chance on fifteen pages and a concept and then giving me the time and tools I needed to bring it to life. Any writer would be lucky to work with you, and I am blessed to be one of them.

To Sarah Davies, who has a few ninja moves of her own. You made this book happen by sheer force of will. I'm glad you are on my side, because you are a force of nature. In the best possible way.

To Carolyn Hanson, thank you for helping find my way to Tanner and teaching me about romantic tension. To the YA Muses, Bret Ballou, Donna Cooner, Katherine Longshore, and Veronica Rossi, thank you for reading an early draft of *Spies* and then reading it again. And again. But mostly thank you for being wonderful friends and amazing writers who inspire me. Every. Single. Day.

Thank you to Lisa and Laura Roecker and Megan Miranda for reading and supporting this book. The feeling is entirely mutual.

To the team at Egmont USA, Alison Weiss, who always responds to my shameless begging for books, to Katie and Robert, who made me feel so welcome at ALA, and my lovely copy editor, Veronica Ambrose, who made sure we had the proper spelling for Disneyfied.

Thanks to my real-life love interest, Jeff Vance, who encouraged me to keep going with this story, even when it meant starting over. To Sammy, who actually, maybe, sort of, kind of liked this one. To Crystina, who may recognize a few of Berry's lines. And to Hunter, who never once rolls his eyes when Mom talks plot points (at least not when I'm looking).

To Huckleberry, who snored in the background through the writing of this book. Someday I'll get you one those T-bones like Lulu had.

Lastly, to all the amazing book bloggers who have supported me and welcomed me into the YA community. You know who you are, and you rock.